# In Your Place

## a novel

## Rachel Ann Nunes

ISBN: 1-55517- 797-2
e.1

Published by Cedar Fort Inc.
www.cedarfort.com

Distributed by:

Typeset by Janet Bernice
Cover design by Nicole Shaffer
Cover design © 2003 by Lyle Mortimer

Printed in the United States of America
10 9 8 7 6 5 4 3 2 1

Printed on acid-free paper

Library of Congress Cataloging-in-Publication Data


Nunes, Rachel Ann, 1966-
In Your Place : a novel / Rachel Ann Nunes.

ISBN: 1-5551-7-797-2

Library of congress Control Number: 2004110364

# In Your Place

a novel

Rachel Ann Nunes

CFI
Springville, UT

# Other Novels by Rachel Ann Nunes

# Author's Note

Many of my readers ask me if *Ariana: The Making of a Queen,* was my first novel, and I have to admit that it wasn't. Like most writers I have several unpublished manuscripts gathering dust in a closet where I won't stumble over the training wheels. Though the plot was strong, I never got around to rewriting it because it just wasn't what the publishers were looking for at the time. Like many first efforts, I had been inspired by *Saturday Warriors,* and publishers were saturated with pre-earth life drama and what some call the "Saturday Warrior doctrine" or SWD. It didn't matter that mine was different, exciting, and romantic. They were taking a break from such stories.

Before I go further, I must add that I don't adhere to the SWD, or that there is a "one and only" out there for everyone. In fact, I believe that ANY two people who are attracted to each other and who put the Lord first and then their partner before their own needs, can create an eternal relationship that is glorious and satisfying to both of them. They can stay in love forever and work out their eternal salvation as partners.

Love is the most powerful emotion in the world. Stories of love between two people have ruled novels and movies for, well, just about since the beginning of time. Think *Romeo and Juliet, The Scarlet Letter, Pride and Prejudice, Stars Wars Episode 2.* The list could go on and on—for non-fiction, literary books, and popular fiction. Those of us who love to read about love, recognize the power in relationships. And I think we're intelligent enough to realize that fiction isn't real life, but an echo of our fondest hopes, dreams, fears, and desires. Just because a novel tells about two people being "meant" for each other, it doesn't mean that *we* need to search for a "one and only". It doesn't mean if the relationship we're in isn't working as well as we want, that we should abandon ship. No. Instead, it should inspire us to put all our efforts into making the relationship we're in be the relationship we crave. It should inspire us to become better people who can participate in a celestial relationship.

So, for the sake of fiction and to inspire true and lasting love everywhere, let's ponder a little. What if there was a couple—maybe just one—who fell in love in the pre-existence? In all the multitudes of phenomena that exist throughout the universe, stranger things could happen. But would the couple actually end up together? Who knows?

Not me. But I have a good imagination. So I imagined, and the result was my first attempt at an LDS novel. It sat for ten years gathering dust. Readers continued to ask about it, and finally, when I had baby number six and was taking a break from my usual writing, I dug in the back of my closet (well, actually in the back of my hard drive) and found the file containing the book called *In Your Place*. Yes, you are holding it in your hands as we speak (or as you read).

It was a little awkward (those training wheels were screwed on tight!) but I cut, chopped, and pasted, and now it's in a state I feel happy sharing with you. In fact, I could have written a whole new novel in the time it took! In the end, it remains one good story.

So read on, and enjoy!

# Part One

# Chapter One
## Pre-Earth Life

*T*he family life lesson was over, and Rae breathed a sigh of relief. Though she loved the spirits the Father had given to her and Tiago to prepare for earth life, she was nervous about her impending journey to earth and it was difficult to focus on anything else.

To finally go to earth! To receive her body! She had never been so excited.

"We'll see you next time," Rae said, standing. She wasn't surprised when all seven spirits made no move to leave. She slid once more to her comfortable seat in the grass.

"I'm going to miss you now that you're going," Michael said. Brown eyes that reminded Rae so much of Tiago's looked earnestly at her from a handsome face framed in straight black hair.

Rae smiled. "You'll be too busy to miss us long. Soon the Father will assign you some spirits to teach."

"That'll be fun." Kira sat beside Rae, pushing curly brown hair out of her dark eyes with a delicate hand. "But I'm a little scared."

"There's nothing to be scared about," said Jenny. She also had dark brown hair, but her eyes were a curious mixture of brown and green. "But I still don't see why I have to take physics if I'm just going to forget it all when I go through the veil!"

Tiago's eyes met Rae's, unable to hide his amusement. "You know very well, Jenny, that the more we learn here, the faster we'll learn on earth and—"

"And the more we'll be able to learn after earth life," Jenny recited. "How many times have we heard that, Kira?"

But Kira didn't answer. Her expression was distant as she dreamed aloud. "Rae and Tiago will go down and meet and fall in love, and you'll have us. Then we'll all be a family there! That's what I hope happens."

"We'd all like that, Kira," Rae said into the abrupt silence that followed. "But we don't know *what* will happen. As much as we would like to be a family, nothing is certain." Despite her resolve to be positive, Rae frowned.

"Oh, don't say that!" Michael said. "We can always hope that we'll really be a family someday."

"You and Tiago were meant to be together," Jenny insisted.

"Rae's right." Tiago's dark eyes were troubled. "If it were up to us right now, we would become a family on earth. But we're going to lose our memories when we pass through the veil and we may not even go to the same country. And even if Rae and I do meet, who's to say we'll get married? We'll both have our agency, you know."

Rae nodded, though her heart rebelled at the words. She leaned forward to hide the emotion, and her blonde hair fell over her shoulders, so different from the dark tresses of the spirits surrounding her. "I know we always joke about becoming a real family on earth, but the Father has told us that many different combinations of couples can be happy together if they put Him first. Why, I found out only last week two of the spirits who taught me—two I was sure were meant for each other—have married other people, even after meeting at BYU. Now one lives somewhere in North Carolina and the other in Texas. They seem very happy." Rae felt an overwhelming sadness as she spoke.

"What about your teachers, Tiago?" Michael asked.

"As far as I know they're both still single, living in Utah. At least they're both members of the Church. That's something to be happy about." Tiago glanced at Rae and gave her a smile that tore at her heart. She loved him so much! The thought of not being with him for eternity was unthinkable. But she would trust in the Lord. He knew her heart and He would do what was best for her. She smiled back and put her hand in Tiago's.

"Well, I'm going to ask Father to please make us a family," Kira said softly, her eyes riveted on their hands.

"We had all better get to our next class," Tiago said.

"Aw, do we have to?" Jenny asked. "It's not like I'm going to be creating worlds any time in the near future—like say tomorrow. Why do we have to learn it now?"

"Goodbye," Rae said. "You don't want to be late."

As the others left, Rae gazed at Tiago's familiar face with his huge brown eyes that always seem to look at her so intensely. She felt happiness spread through her being. Just being with him right now was enough.

She and Tiago had been assigned to teach this family life class shortly after graduating from their own classes. They looked the same as they did when they were first given spirit bodies, but inside they had grown and progressed. Soon, they would be ready for earth. They were sad at leaving the spirits they had grown to love, especially those they had helped teach, but the excitement of going to earth overcame the fear and uncertainty.

"What is it?" Tiago asked, slightly tightening his grip on her hand. As spirits they had a similar mass and consistency and could feel each other as they would not be able to feel a person with an earthly body.

"I'm not sure," Rae said, smiling. "I guess it's all coming to an end so fast."

"No, things are beginning. Earth life is only the beginning."

"Yeah, I know. I guess it's just that things are changing so fast. I mean, it'll never be the same again."

Tiago nodded, a new light coming into his eyes. "But we're

going to earth, Rae! That's a good thing. We've waited so long for our turn."

"I know. I can't wait!" Despite her worry about being separated from Tiago, Rae was excited to be born. She had looked forward to this day with anticipation ever since the Father had made the announcement so long ago. "You're right. I can't believe we're actually going. There'll be so many new things to see."

"So much to learn and do."

"So many programs to write." They laughed at that. Rae was always saying how she was going to become a computer programmer on earth and create programs that would change the world. "It could happen," she always said.

After a while, Tiago's face grew serious. "I hope I know you there, Rae."

"There's a chance, Tiago. We just have to hope."

"And pray," he added.

"And pray."

They sat silently together until they saw three of their friends—Lisa, Dave and Selena—approaching in the distance. Abruptly, their hands dropped to their sides. They rose to meet the others.

Lisa, with her hair a thick dark-brown, was in the lead. Her big, earnest eyes were also brown, framed with dark eye lashes. "How'd class go?" she asked.

Rae shrugged. "Good. The usual."

"Well our class," Lisa waved a small hand at Dave's thin frame, "was pretty wild. The students can't get it out of their minds that we're going to earth soon. Sometimes, I think they're more excited about it than I am!"

Green-eyed Selena snorted. "Impossible! It's all you ever talk about!"

"She's got a point," Dave said. "But then it's all any of us ever talk about."

Lisa smiled. "Okay, I admit it. I can't help but be excited. Now remember, we're all going to meet to find out our destinations together. They'll be posted on the board in the Destinations Building in two days, earth time." Lately, Lisa had taken to referring to earth time instead of the system they used in the Spirit World. The differences could be confusing, but as Lisa's close friends, they were used to the references by now. "Don't forget," Lisa added.

They all rolled their eyes. How could they possibly forget something so important?

\* \* \* \* \*

"Many of you will soon begin to train new spirits," Selena was saying the next day in new spirit training class. Her short form was positioned in front of the large group where she could be seen by all. "And believe me. If you think you've learned a lot from your teachers, wait until you begin teaching. Then you'll really learn!"

"But what if I know someone I'd like to partner with," asked a girl seated in front. She looked meaningfully at Michael who was seated next to her with his legs crossed.

"Then submit your request now. But be careful. I know many of you would like the people you are assigned to work with here to be the same ones you meet and marry on earth, but when you pick your own partner, many times you won't even go down in the same decade. That's what happened to me. My partner went to earth before me, and by the time I get there, he'll more likely be my grandfather than my husband!"

She laughed merrily, her striking green eyes twinkling, and the class laughed with her. Everyone knew that there would be many worthy candidates to choose from on earth. Not many harbored the hope that on earth they'd find and meet someone they had cared for in the Spirit World and fall wildly and passionately in love.

When the laughter died, Kira asked quietly, "But aren't there some couples that are just meant to be together?"

A vision of Tiago and Rae flashed before Selena's eyes. *If ever there was a couple*, she thought, *it should be them.*

But aloud she said, "I don't know, Kira. But I do know that the Father knows and loves each one of us. There will be someone prepared for each of us to marry—in His own time. We have to trust in Him."

The class went on and Selena taught it efficiently, but try as she might, she couldn't get Kira's question out of her mind. Weren't there some couples who really *were* meant to be together?

\* \* \* \* \*

The next day, somewhat after the appointed time, Rae saw her friends crowded together in front of the Destination Building talking excitedly. She and Tiago were late meeting them as planned because the earth life class they were taking got carried away discussing the many possibilities awaiting them on earth. Usually time wasn't much of a concern, but today all the friends had wanted to be together when they found out their earth destinations. Rae knew that by now her friends would have already learned their destinations.

"They're here!" Selena shouted as they approached. Lisa and Dave had been watching for Rae and Tiago in the other direction. Their heads turned with one accord.

"Well, are we all going together?" Rae asked, biting her lip. "Is it good news?" Her friends' smiles faded.

"Oh, Rae, I'm so sorry." Dave was the first to speak, his somber eyes echoing his words.

"What is it? Tell us," Tiago said. His voice was compelling, but Dave studied the ground and said nothing.

"It isn't you, Tiago. You're going with us—or at least in the same general area," Selena said. "It's Rae. She's . . . well . . ."

"Just tell me!" Rae could feel her throat closing, making it difficult to speak.

"You're going to Portugal, the oldest child of nonmember parents." Lisa spoke for the first time, shaking her dark head back and forth in sympathy. "It won't be so bad, really, it won't."

"Yeah, it'll be okay, Rae." Everyone was suddenly crowding around her, offering condolences. Only Tiago said nothing, but stared down at the group. He was at least a head taller than everyone, even Dave. Rae's chest constricted so tightly she could hardly breathe.

"Okay? How can it be okay?" Rae exploded. "I'm going to be born to nonmember parents in a country that barely has running water and certainly no branch of the True Church—they don't even have missionaries!"

"Yes they do. They got them years and years ago. I checked," Dave said, refusing to meet her gaze. "Besides, we're promised that everybody will hear the gospel, everybody. We all get a chance. Whether it's on earth or after, you'll hear the gospel."

"Portugal may be an underdeveloped country now," Lisa added, "but it's certainly not backward. They have running water, same as in the States. Plus, there've been huge leaps in technology in Portugal in the past years, and there will be even more in the years after you're born. As for the Church, the whole world is really opening up to the gospel." She reached for Rae's hand, but Rae pulled away.

"And if I don't accept the gospel when I hear it? You all know how stubborn and bull-headed I am! You're always teasing me about it. Really and truly, do you think I'll accept some young teenagers telling *me* about religion? It's so much more certain if we're born to faithful parents. Oh, what am I going to do?" She was crying now, unable to hold back.

"You will accept the gospel, Rae! Don't underestimate yourself or the Spirit!" Tiago looked directly into her eyes, wiping the tears away with his fingers as they fell from her eyes.

"Being born to member parents isn't always a guarantee," Selena put in. "Sometimes people take the gospel for granted and let sin get the best of them. Or maybe they never were truly converted and, when trouble strikes, they fall. There are really no guarantees."

Tiago nodded. "That's why it's called a test. And I do have faith in you. You'll make it."

"Oh, Tiago," Rae moaned. "Don't you see? That's just it. *I* don't have much faith in me. I'm not like you. They could send you down alone to a deserted island and you'd still find a way to be baptized! Oh, what am I going to do? I want so much to come back here and live with Father and all of you." She took a deep breath before tumbling on. "And what about my dream of being a computer programmer? What if there's not the potential in Portugal that there is in the States? What if I don't get an education? I feel as if I'm lost already."

"She's got a point there," Dave said. "There is more emphasis on technology and education in the States."

Tiago frowned at Dave. "A lot can change in a few years. Rae can do it—I know she can!" He set his hand on Rae's shoulder. "And most importantly, she'll be getting a body!"

The disappointment and fight seeped from Rae, as though released by Tiago's touch. She glanced at the beloved faces of her friends guiltily. "Oh, you're right. Of course, you're right! I'm sorry. So sorry! What can I be thinking?" She shook her head in disgust. "I'll be getting a body and my chance on earth! That's what's really important." She was embarrassed that her lack of faith was showing so clearly. She had no right to complain. None at all. For so long, she had waited for a body, and here was her chance—and she was wasting time complaining. If the Father was sending her to Portugal, there was a good reason, even if she didn't know what it was. Her job was to exercise faith.

"What about all of you?" Rae asked. "Are you going to the United States? To member families?"

"Yes, all of us," Selena said. "And Tiago and Lisa are even going to Utah just a few miles from each other! Can you believe it?"

"Wow! To be born in the state where the Prophet lives! How wonderful! I'm so happy for you!" Rae found she was telling the true. She *was* happy for her friends.

Dave touched Rae's arm. "I'm going to be born in California. Believe it or not, Lisa and I are going to be cousins, isn't that right, teaching partner?" He made a face at Lisa. "Now we're stuck with each other for real. And it seems that I'm going to have a twin sister as well." He turned to Tiago. "It says you're going to be the second son born to your parents. What was his brother-to-be's name—Jon, wasn't it?" The others nodded.

"Where are you going?" Tiago asked Selena.

"To Washington," she said, trying to flip her brown hair back in a careless gesture. Instead, the lock of hair landed in her face.

"So when do we go?" Rae asked, hiding her smile.

"One day for you and me. Earth time, that is," Dave answered. "It's a few more words of advice from Father and Mother and then, bang, we're out of here! The others will come later."

"Well, come on guys, we've got to get to our last earth life class." Selena motioned to Dave and Lisa. "For once I'm glad we have the late class. We really have something to tell them!" She touched Rae's hand briefly and walked off, leading the others.

Rae and Tiago watched their friends leave with large smiles of anticipation on their faces. Only Dave looked back over his shoulder with a farewell smile. Rae waited until they were out of sight and then sighed.

"It's not too late to turn back, you know," Tiago said softly. "We have to agree to where we are sent down—we have our agency."

Rae shook her head. "Have you ever heard of anyone who didn't go? Or asked to be changed? I haven't heard of anyone. After all, this is our big chance to show what we're made of. And who am I to question Father? He's omniscient. Not like me, I only pretend to know everything." She let her gaze drop to the ground. "The one thing I do know is that He loves me, and so this must be for the best. I'll go where I've been called."

"But you don't seem very happy about it."

Rae met his stare. "Oh, yes, I am. I'm so happy to be getting a body. Very happy! And it's not that the idea of Portugal that's so bad. I just . . . well, mostly, I think I'm afraid." She looked away from him again and started off down the garden path to their right. Tiago went with her, taking hold of her hand. They walked silently for a while, completely caught up in their thoughts.

Tiago stopped abruptly, pulling Rae also to a standstill. "It's going to be okay. Really."

"I know," she replied softly. "But thanks for reminding me. You are such a dear, good friend. You know, the very saddest thing about this is . . . well, I hoped that maybe we'd go down together. I know nothing is for certain, but deep down inside I always figured that we'd meet and . . . oh, you know." As she said the words, Rae knew that more than anything, this was what was bothering her. She didn't want to think of life—any kind of life—without Tiago beside her.

"I know. I hoped the same thing." He hugged her tightly, and she returned the hug with equal feeling.

Moments later they drew apart, and Tiago pulled Rae down to sit with him on the grass along the deserted path. Once more they were silent as they sat closely together. Rae tugged at the strands of brilliant green grass, while Tiago reached over to caress her long, golden hair.

"I should have known that we wouldn't become a family with Kira and the other students from our family life class," she said, reminded by his touch. "They all have dark hair like you, instead of a mixture."

"I don't know, Kira's is kind of lighter."

"Not by much. And all seven of them have dark eyes." A single tear slid out of the corner of her eye, and though she turned her face away, she knew Tiago could still see it rolling down her cheek. He reached over to turn her face gently toward him.

"I don't think that matters much, Rae," he said. His eyes were also full of tears. "You never know what will happen."

Seeing the love in his eyes, and wanting to make him happy, Rae nodded. "I guess we don't have to give up exactly—"

"That's it. Miracles do happen, you know."

"So we'll let the future take care of itself." Her hand clasped his. "I'll try to remember to be grateful—there is much to be grateful for. No matter what happens we'll be friends forever."

"You got that right!" Tiago gave her another hug.

*  *  *  *  *

The next day began bright and early. When Rae said goodbye to their class for the last time, everyone had tears in their eyes, but the excitement could also be seen shining through. So many new experiences were in store for them! They hugged and hugged again, and finally it was time to go.

"We'll see you soon, Rae," Kira said in her quiet way as she left with the others. "You wait and see." Then they were gone.

"You'll spend time with them before you go down to earth, won't you, Tiago?" Rae asked worriedly, looking after them long after they had disappeared.

"So much that they'll get sick of me." Tiago was trying to make her laugh, but failed.

She gave him a weak smile. "Well, let's go."

"Uh—I'm going to have to go separately, Rae." Tiago said, slowly, as if choosing his words carefully. He suddenly appeared nervous. "I've got something I have to do first."

"Okay." Rae was slightly puzzled but not upset. Tiago was always trying to surprise her with something. "I'll meet you there."

"I love you, Rae." Tiago walked away quickly.

"I love you too, Tiago," she whispered after him.

Their friends were already waiting for her at the Birth Building where the last interviews were held. They waited outside as long as possible for Tiago, but he didn't appear.

"Where can Tiago be?" Rae asked for the millionth time, looking around frantically. "How could he not be here?"

"Oh, I'm sure he'll be here to see you before you actually go. Maybe he got held up a little," Selena said calmly.

"Well, come on. I don't want to be late for my interview with Father. He has so many to do." Rae and her friends entered the building, and, despite Tiago's absence, Rae felt excitement well up within her. Too much time had passed since she had been with her Father. She wanted especially to apologize for her reaction to her assignment.

The feeling inside the building was one of reverence, an amazing feat considering the many spirits who were there preparing for their births. They walked slowly up the long hallway to the wide see-through desk where several people waited for them. Rae moved up to the table slowly, feeling nervous and excited all at once. Dave stood next to her since he needed his departing interview, too. Selena and Lisa stood slightly behind them, clearly showing that they were here only to see them off.

"May I help you?" A black-haired woman asked. Rae glanced quickly over at Dave who was already being helped by another woman at the desk. "Uh . . . yeah . . . I think my interview is right now." She cast a backwards glance over her shoulder, still hoping to catch sight of Tiago. She didn't know for sure if she'd have time after the interview to say goodbye.

"How exciting!" the woman said, smiling at her. "Your name, please?" Rae told her and watched as she pushed some symbols on the otherwise transparent table, a huge Urim and Thummim.

"I'm sorry, but I think there's been a change." The woman raised her eyebrows in puzzlement. "Hmmm, that's strange. Yes, there has definitely been a change. Come, follow me, please." The woman motioned to the group in a sweeping motion, excluding Dave who watched them with an arched brow.

Rae, Selena, and Lisa followed the woman down a large side corridor. Once more Rae cast a backwards glance over her shoulder. *Where is Tiago?* she wondered. *And where is this lady taking us?*

# Chapter Two
## Orem, Utah

The pains had started when she went to bed the night before, but Holly Love had figured it was more false labor like she'd been having for the last two weeks. The contractions weren't bad and she had slept, only to be woken early in the morning as the pains worsened. The digital clock on the small nightstand by her bed read 4:00 A.M.

The early May morning was still, not a sound disturbed the silence except the gentle snoring of her husband who lay in the bed next to her. She felt cozy and safe in the two-bedroom Provo apartment where they had lived for over a year now. She was more than ready for the baby to come. Lying on her back, she reached out with both hands to massage the skin that had stretched unbelievably, almost grotesquely, as the baby had grown inside her.

Richard had made a great joke out of telling the baby to wait until the exams for his Independent Study classes at BYU were over. Obligingly, the baby was already eight days over due. Holly hadn't found the wait too upsetting; she wanted Richard to be able to spend time with her and the baby. Besides, taking care of a baby inside her stomach was a lot easier than caring for it on the outside. This, she had already learned.

She lay in bed a bit longer, enjoying the quiet of the early morning and debating if this was finally the real thing. A sudden onslaught of pain convinced her that it was. The luminous numbers on the clock showed that it was now 4:07 A.M.

"Honey." Holly nudged her husband gently, and then less gently as another contraction came, closer this time, probably brought on by her movement.

"Huh? What?" Rich murmured, bringing a long-fingered hand to rub his closed eyes. Then the hand went up and out, followed by the other, as he stretched slowly.

Another contraction came again, and for the first time Holly grimaced, shutting her deep-set eyes as if to ward off the pain.

"Are you, okay?" Rich had opened his blue eyes with her sudden intake of breath, and when he saw her face, his sleepy look vanished. "Is it time?" he asked. Holly only nodded and Rich touched her arm with one hand, running the other back and forth in his tousled blonde hair as he decided what to do first.

Holly was ahead of him. She slid out of bed as the contraction eased, picked up the phone, and handed it to Rich. Then she began to dress in the slow, deliberate movements of a full-term pregnant woman. Rich quickly dialed the hospital, whose number was taped to the phone, to let them know they were coming. Next, he called their doctor, Lorraine Trapper, who was a personal friend of Holly's mother. He also dressed, and afterwards tied Holly's shoes while she brushed her short, light brown hair with quick, decisive strokes. Another contraction came, but she was becoming accustomed to the pain and tried to let it flow through her, dulling the hurt—for now. Her labor, while real, was not yet at the overwhelming stage. Her family had a history of long, mild labors, followed by an excruciating but short delivery.

Between contractions, Holly called her mother, Jill. It was 4:25 A.M. Jill picked up after four rings.

"Hello?"

"Hi, Mom. It's me. We're going to the hospital now."

"Have you called them yet?"

"Yes, and Lorraine, too."

"I'll meet you there."

"Thanks. Bye Mom."

"Goodbye, honey."

While she was talking, Rich had gone into the other bedroom in their apartment and emerged carrying the sleeping form of their twenty-two month old son, Jon Richard. In his sleep and with his white hair forming a halo, the child looked like a little angel. His cheeks were rosy with sleep, but the rest of his face and his hands were white, contrasting sharply with the bright red of his sleeper pajamas. Over his shoulder, Rich carried her pre-packed hospital bag which also had a change of clothes for little Jon. They were ready to go.

Another contraction came, less than five minutes after the previous one. Holly took deep breaths to relax and tried to picture her body preparing for the birth, while Rich looked on somewhat helplessly. After the contraction was over, she went to use the toilet, thinking gratefully that soon her body would be her own again; no longer would she have to make hourly trips to the bathroom.

The contractions were only four minutes apart when they reached the fourth floor of the hospital in Provo. Holly had planned it that way, not wanting to be there for twenty hours like she had been when giving birth to Jon. She tried to relax between contractions in the delivery room. Lorraine was already there, bursting with her usual energy, even at five o'clock in the morning. Grandma Jill had also arrived and was nearby, holding little Jon on her lap. (Oh, how Holly longed to hold him close to her once more as she had before her big tummy had come between them!) He had awaken and cried, but Holly calmed him down between contractions, and he was now giggling happily as his grandmother tickled his tummy.

Holly asked for an epidural. She hadn't had an epidural with Jon, but she found she couldn't go on this time without one. She sighed with relief as the pain faded, and watched the monitor to check on the contractions. The doctor turned up the speaker so she could hear the steady thump of her baby's heartbeat. Before long, the contractions were all running together, making the short breaks in between seem almost nonexistent. She felt the urge to push, and told Lorraine.

"You're fully dilated," Lorraine confirmed with a smile. "Let's get this baby here."

During the next contraction, Holly pushed, glancing quickly over at little Jon, who was sitting with Jill near the head of the bed. He seemed interested in what was happening, and not at all stressed.

Holly pushed again, and was amazed that she felt no pain. With Jon she remembered that her body had felt ripped apart, as if it would never be the same.

With another push, the baby slipped out, guided by nature and the doctor's experienced hands. A rush of amniotic fluid followed, soaking her and the pads that covered the bed.

"A girl. It's a girl," Rich exclaimed.

A rush of emotion brought tears to Holly's eyes.

Lorraine finished cleaning the crying baby's mouth and nose, and gently lifted the bundle onto her chest, making sure the cord was long enough to reach. It was now 7:47 A.M.

"A baby girl!" Jill said happily, coming closer so the fascinated Jon could see his little sister more clearly.

"Hi there, little one," Rich cooed, touching the baby's cheek lightly with his finger. "It's okay. It's all over now."

"Shhh—don't cry, precious." Holly rocked the baby softly. The baby stopped crying and began to nurse. Jill let Jon onto the bed to snuggle up to his mother's shoulder.

"Would you like to cut the cord?" Lorraine asked Rich.

Through the parted curtain of the fourth floor window, rays of light from the rising sun shone onto Holly and the new baby. Holly wore no make-up and her hair was plastered with perspiration from her labor, but holding that precious, tiny baby, she felt heavenly, if not beautiful.

"She's our own little ray of light," she whispered. "Straight from Heaven."

"Let's name her Rae—no, Raelyn," Rich suggested, stroking the oh-so-soft little cheek.

"Yes," Holly answered. "But we'll call her Rae."

# Chapter Three
## Almada, Portugal

*T*iago Carvalho knew that his father had been in pain for a long time. He had used a cane now for many years, and when he walked up the cobblestone sidewalk on his way home from the small family bookstore, a quarter of a mile away, he had to pause often to rest. People who knew him would stop and talk to him, for the old man was beloved by many.

"Hi, Mr. Silva they would say (or Daniel, if they were one of his peers)!" "Thanks for helping me out with that problem I had with my boss." Or, "Here's the money I owe you. Thanks for the loan." The old man would look down—at six foot three, he was a good head taller than most of the other Portuguese men—and smile, his green eyes shining.

He wasn't really that old—only fifty-five—but he looked much older because of the halting way he walked. He had a severe circulation problem and in the past few months every step he took had become excruciating, though he rarely complained. Now, he often took as long as forty minutes to walk the short distance to the three-bedroom apartment he had bought for his family sixteen years ago. He had also smoked for many years, causing him to wrinkle and age before his time.

Not that Tiago's mother would let Daniel smoke in the apartment. Maria had never appreciated the "dirty habit" as she called it, though Tiago knew she loved his father deeply. And because Daniel was a good man, and because he really did believe that smoking was a dirty habit, he indulged only on the balcony at home, where he could also watch the busy people scurrying around below, each intent on their own lives. Tiago often spent time on the balcony to be close to his father.

When Daniel wasn't smoking on the balcony, working in the bookstore, or at his job selling pharmaceuticals, he was with his wife, Maria, and their children, Tiago and Marcela. They spent much more time together than the average Portuguese family. As the children had grown, Daniel and Maria had taken them camping and fishing, or just out walking around the neighborhood. They also spent long hours reading together or talking about the world and its mysteries.

Tiago and his younger sister, Marcela, especially loved to go down to the corner diner with their parents to eat. For five hundred escudos each, they could all have a *bitoque*—a meal that included a steak, eggs, fried potatoes, rice, and a roll with butter. It was as much as any full grown man could eat, or growing children, for that matter. As petite as her husband was tall, Maria alone could never finish all her meal, though she had gained a bit of weight with the two pregnancies that produced Tiago and Marcela.

Daniel was a religious man. He never went to church, but he could see the hand of an omniscient Being in all of nature and in the people around him. He knew that God lived and believed that people should live their lives in the best way possible. And so Daniel did.

Tiago knew his dad was special. One had only to listen to his mother's friends talk—and talk was one thing at which they excelled.

"Maria, I don't know where you found that man," one would say. "I wish my husband would stay at home with me and the children instead of going off to drink in the bars with those other slobs."

"Daniel's such a good provider!" another would exclaim.

"He's always working so hard. And who ever heard of a man washing the dishes?"

"And those eyes!" the first would squeal, not to be outdone. "There's not many with eyes that color here in Portugal. Marcela is really lucky to have inherited them. Why, with her curly brown hair and green eyes, I swear Marcela looks exactly like a movie star in one of those American movies they always have on the TV!"

This last statement was an exaggeration because while Tiago's younger sister certainly had Daniel's large, striking, green eyes, her other features were quite ordinary; a fact no one ever seemed to notice after looking into her eyes. On the other hand, Tiago took after his dark-eyed, black-haired mother—in everything but his tall height.

"But your Tiago is definitely going to be a heartbreaker," the women would always add as an afterthought. "Too bad he's so shy . . ."

Tiago didn't mind that he looked like his mother and that his sister took after his father. While he loved his father intensely, he loved his mother even more. For all the nearly twenty years of his life, they had been very close.

Then came the fateful night that changed all their lives forever. Tiago had spent the day in school, as usual, studying to become a computer programmer. He had discovered an ingrained talent and love for just about anything related to computers, and as technology blossomed in Portugal, he had jumped into his studies knowing that he would never want for a good job.

After classes, some of Tiago's buddies convinced him to go for a *bica*, a strong black coffee that he relished. Occasionally, he did drink a beer as well to keep his friends company, but it wasn't often. The outings were rare and always planned by Tiago's friends. Not that he was anti-social, but lately his friends talked about things he didn't appreciate, especially when it came to women. He considered relationships special, and like his parents had always taught him by example, if not in words, he believed that the intimate part of his life should be saved for someone special, not bragged about in a bar. In this he was unusual, and occasionally, teased by his friends.

"Got a girlfriend yet?" they'd ask.

"Been too busy," he'd always reply. The fact was that he'd never had a girlfriend, had never met anyone he cared enough about to overcome his shyness. When the time came, he knew he would do it. Until then he'd study, spend time with his family, and read the science fiction and mystery books he adored.

That night at the bar he said goodbye to his friends and left for home. As usual, he took the bus, getting off at the stop nearest their apartment. There he saw his mother hurrying up the sidewalk. She had apparently closed the store and was on her way home. Lately, she was working there full-time, as his father had been busy with his main job, selling pharmaceuticals. He would be quitting the drug business soon, though, because the new store had finally built up enough customers to support the family.

"Hi, Mom!" Tiago called, waving to catch her attention.

"Hi, Tiago." Giving him a tired smile, she closed the few steps between them and proffered her face to be kissed once on each cheek.

"Is Papa home?" Tiago asked, reaching for the plastic sack which held the store's proceeds for the day. He would carry it to the house for her and then tomorrow she would probably ask him to take the money to the bank on his way to school.

"Yes. He seemed a little tired today, more so than usual. That last selling trip took a lot out of him. He wanted to stay with me at the store but I made him leave an hour ago."

They walked the rest of the way in comfortable silence, nodding to people as they passed, or waving as people occasionally greeted them from the windows and balconies of the high apartment buildings that flanked both sides of the narrow road. The fall evening was still warm and the luscious smell of cooking meats filled the air, wafting from various small shops and restaurants along the street—baked cod fish, sizzling barbeque chicken, grilled steak. The intriguing smells blended together so that it was difficult to tell them apart, though the aroma of olive oil and garlic was prevalent. Tiago was tempted to stop and buy a barbecued chicken, slathered with sauce, and a bag of greasy home-style potato chips, but knew that his mother would have already prepared the evening's meal during her two-hour lunch break.

Marcela and Papa were watching TV when Tiago and his mother arrived. It occurred to Tiago that Marcela should have at least set the table for their mother, and the fact that their father hadn't was a sign of how tired he was.

"Good evening," Maria said cheerfully as she walked into the family room.

Marcela bounded up to kiss her cheeks, and nodded to Tiago who was kissing his father (oh, how old he looked today!) in a similar fashion.

"How was school?" Maria asked Marcela. She had started college this fall in banking.

"Lots of work."

Tiago didn't believe it. Everything was a lot of work to Marcela. She was eighteen now, but Tiago thought she acted more like eight.

After a few moments of idle small talk, Maria kissed her husband, patted his arm gently, and went to the kitchen. "Tiago, set the table, please," she said. But Tiago was already on his way to the kitchen.

Everything seemed normal—the broiled pork chops with rice and fried potatoes, the fresh fruit for dessert, the conversation, the jokes, watching TV as a family, Father excusing himself to smoke on the balcony. There was nothing to warn them of the coming disaster.

It came late that night when Tiago was in bed. He was jolted awake by his mother shaking him.

"Tiago! Come quickly! It's your father—he can't breathe!"

He leapt from bed and stumbled to the door, shaking his head quickly to clear the sleep from his brain. He ran into his parents' room where he found his father slumped forward on the bed, struggling for each breath.

Time slowed as he dove to his father's side. It shouldn't take so long to get there. From the corner of his eye, he saw his sister emerge from her room, muddied-eyed, her face frozen in an expression of fear—the same fear Tiago could feel on his own face. A fear that came from deep in his heart. At last he reached his father. Gently, he laid him on his back and checked his pulse. It was weak.

"I'm going to call an ambulance," his mother sobbed. Tiago heard her running down the hall, into the family room where they kept the phone.

She returned shortly. They sat together, watching Daniel gasp for air. The waiting was horrible. There was nothing they could do except to smooth his forehead and hold his hand.

Then, all at once, he lay still. Tiago quickly felt for a pulse. Nothing.

"Breathe, Papa! Breathe!" he cried, his face wet with tears. He pushed on his father's chest once, twice, and then again and again, while his mother breathed air into his lungs. Marcela stood by the bed, staring down at them in frozen horror.

"Go wait for the ambulance!" Tiago yelled, trying to jolt his sister from her shock. She nodded and ran to the door and down the stairs.

"Breathe Papa!" Tiago pushed again and again on his father's unmoving chest. Abruptly, his father took a hacking breath and his heart started beating again, faintly.

They waited. Why was the ambulance taking so long? His father struggled to breathe, each breath more torturous than the last.

Still no one came. Tiago suddenly knew that his father would die. He felt the truth spread throughout his body in one agonizing rush.

*Don't leave us, Papa!* his heart cried with fear and anguish.

The ambulance workers came then, and Daniel was still breathing, but he died on the way to the hospital in Lisbon. Maria, disheveled and carelessly dressed, was with him in the ambulance. She wept in low, heart-wrenching sobs.

\* \* \* \* \*

Tiago wanted to die. His father was gone forever, and so was the happy life he had known. For Daniel to have been taken away from his family at such a young age was too cruel for any God. That was how Tiago knew there was no God, that there never had been, despite his father's belief. If a God existed, his wonderful father would not have been so mercilessly taken from them.

It meant nothing to him that Daniel had died of heart failure from a lung-related disease caused by his smoking. Millions of people smoked and lived, why should his good father be punished? The agony Tiago felt was unbearable. Never to see his father again, to hear his laughter, or listen to his wisdom! What kind of life was that?

He seriously considered suicide. Only his love for his mother and sister prevented him from acting rashly in the aftermath of his father's death. But a part of him stopped living even so. While he had once been carefree and full of plans for the future, now he simply existed.

But without hope or God, that existence was meaningless.

# Part Two

# Chapter Four
## Ladders-
## Provo, Utah

*T*he whistling came from the window of a slowly approaching car. Raelyn Love and Lisa Peterson both stiffened in exasperation, expecting the worse. Couldn't they even walk home from church on Sunday without having a problem? Too many times they had been accosted by less-desirables as they made their way from the BYU campus to their apartment five blocks away. Rae had learned that the men she enjoyed dating usually didn't whistle at women from cars.

"Wanna ride?" drawled a male voice from the car that had stopped behind them.

Rae turned quickly, her long blonde hair spreading out in a fan at the motion. "Oh," she said, suddenly biting her tongue to still the sharp words that were ready to come bolting out. "It's only you."

"What do ya mean 'It's only you?'" Their friend Andrew replied with false indignation. "I've come to pick you up. I'd think a thank you should be in order." He jumped from the car and motioned to its newly-painted red exterior with a flourish. "Madame Love, your chariot awaits."

"You're nuts," Rae said, laughing.

"About you," Andrew countered, his eyes meeting hers only briefly. He pushed his metal-rimmed glasses up his nose with a practiced gesture and opened the car door to let Lisa slide into the back, her dark, short-cropped hair moving slightly in the cool spring breeze. Rae settled quickly into the front, rolling up the window as Andrew entered the car.

"Why do women always do that?" he asked.

"Do what?"

"Roll up the window even on beautiful, sunny April day like today."

"You've really got a lot to learn about women, Andrew."

"Well, tell me, so I'll know."

"It has something to do with curling irons, time, and the fireside tonight," Rae hinted, pushing her hair back from her cheeks.

"Oh," Andrew said, though she knew he really didn't understand. "So what time am I picking you up for the fireside?"

"It starts at seven. So just before that will be good. Are you coming, Lisa?"

Lisa shook her head. "No, I'll meet you there. My cousins are moving here from California—the twins I told you about. Their family's going to stay at my parents' for a few days while my aunt and uncle search for a house. I want to go home to see them. Maybe I'll even bring them with me tonight. The guy, Dave, got back from a mission to Ecuador last year. He's studying to be a lawyer now. Boy, is he good-looking!" She whistled and winked at Rae.

Rae noticed how Andrew's mouth tightened. "I'm sure they're both nice," she said lightly.

When they arrived at the apartment complex, Andrew opened his door and jumped out, sliding his seat forward so that Lisa could squeeze through.

"See ya tonight," she yelled as she went for her own car.

Andrew walked with Rae to the apartment she shared with Lisa and two other girls. "How long have we known each other, Rae?" he asked as they climbed the three flights of outside stairs that lead to her door.

"Nearly eight years," Rae answered. Even though they lived in different cities when growing up—her in Orem and him in Provo—they had been in the same stake since they both lived on the borders of their respective cities. They had met at a stake youth conference held up Sundance Canyon.

"I was so embarrassed," Rae remembered with a smile. "I had gotten up late and didn't have time to put on my make-up or even curl my hair. I didn't think we'd be meeting any interesting *older* men."

"Yeah, you were almost fourteen, and I was the ripe old age of fifteen." He shook his head. "Eight years. That's a lot of history."

"Yeah, but if you recall, you were hung up on Lisa." She and Lisa had been inseparable in those days, and Lisa had come along to the conference even though she didn't live in the stake boundaries.

"Don't remind me," Andrew groaned. "Still, that was only for the first hour or so. I soon learned that Lisa is beautiful but her intelligence—"

"Don't say it, Andrew. Lisa's a wonderful person, and she's been my best friend since we were five." Rae understood what Andrew had against Lisa—he considered her a vain, shallow, boy-chasing busy body. Though many of those accusations were true, Rae loved her childhood friend—and had since the moment they'd met in kindergarten. She most certainly didn't want to discuss her faults. She and Lisa were connected, as though they had know each other forever. Rae hadn't felt that even with Andrew.

She unlocked her door with a key, but before she could open it, Andrew put a hand on her arm. "Rae, I need to talk to you."

Rae looked at the oh-so-familiar face of her dear friend—the short blonde hair, the ordinary blue eyes behind the thin glasses, the narrow face and small ears—and heard his words as if from a loud speaker. She knew what he wanted to say: he wanted to make their relationship permanent. He had been hinting around for months now, and she had waited, not sure what to do when the time came. She had no idea what she wanted.

"Tonight then," she said, her heart pounding loudly in her ears. "After the fireside. Right now I have to go. It's my night to make dinner."

"Okay. Pick you up at fifteen to."

"Okay. See ya." She entered her apartment, her mind racing.

Since that day at youth conference, Andrew had always been there for her. He had come often to see her on his bike, riding the two and half miles that separated their houses in record time. They talked for hours on the phone at night, discussing nearly every subject under the sun. They were young and happy, and shortly became close friends. Then school started, and Rae became so involved in her classes at Mountain View in Orem that she drifted away from Andrew, who was attending Provo High School.

Rae enjoyed school and meeting new people—many more exciting and handsome than Andrew. Later, when she became an adult, she discovered that most of those "exciting" guys didn't have his quick wit or firm testimony of the gospel. But that hadn't mattered back then. Soon they were both of dating age, but though they kept in touch, they never dated. Rae knew it was her fault. Andrew would have been more than willing had she given him the chance.

Andrew went on with his life. After graduating, he went on a mission to Texas, and once again they became close through the many letters they wrote. When he returned a year ago, they began dating for the first time. Much to Lisa's chagrin, Andrew quickly became Rae's other best friend, and they spent most of their free time together.

Andrew worked full time with a drafting firm his uncle owned and went to the Utah Valley State College, while Rae worked part-time at Mervyn's, a local department store, and attended BYU full time, working toward a marketing degree. Between schooling and work, Andrew and Rae didn't have time to pursue other relationships, and their friendship had grown to a point where it might be actually be more than simple friendship. He had even moved to the same apartment complex, where once again they were in the same stake.

These thoughts flashed quickly through Rae's head as she opened the oven and slid in the spaghetti casserole she had prepared the day before for her roommates. Was she ready for a permanent commitment with Andrew? Eight years they'd known each other. Shouldn't she know how she felt by now?

\* \* \* \* \*

After dinner, Rae stood alone in the room she and Lisa shared. She looked down at her hands which were white from clutching her Book of Mormon so tightly. Deliberately, she loosened her hold on the book and fell to her knees in a gesture that was so familiar it felt comfortable. Her parents had always taught her to pray, and now, as her emotions were churning inside her, with no hope of resolution, she turned to the One she knew was always there for her.

"Oh, Father, what should I do?" she whispered into the silence, her head raised heavenward in supplication. "I know Andrew wants to marry me, but I—I don't know that I feel the same way about him. I love him so much—but more as a friend. Is that enough? I know I'm supposed to make a decision, but I don't know what to do. I don't want to lose him. Please help me know what to do!"

There was much more left to say, but she heard the faint ringing of the doorbell. Andrew had arrived, a few minutes early, as usual.

He liked to talk to her roommates and tease them about their boyfriends or their lack thereof.

Rae blinked away the tears quickly and took a moment to compose herself before leaving her room. Thankfully, her roommates didn't notice anything different when she emerged. Nor did Andrew.

Lisa came up to them as soon as they arrived at the church. "I've saved us seats in the middle of the chapel." Then she grabbed Rae's arm and whispered close in her ear, "He's gorgeous! You're going to *love* my cousin!"

She pulled Rae along and was soon introducing her cousins, Dave and Michelle Channing. Dave had dark brown hair, bright blue eyes, and a laugh that made Rae want to join in. His twin sister Michelle was his opposite, being very fair, her eyes so colorless that it was almost impossible to tell they were blue.

"Hi," Dave said, flashing his contagious grin when Lisa introduced her and Andrew. "I've heard so much about you."

"Yeah, I know how Lisa talks." Rae turned to look at Lisa, but she was already deep in conversation with some people at the other end of the row. "She's told us a little about you, too." She looked at Andrew and smiled. "Hasn't she, Andrew?" He nodded glumly.

The fireside began and the room grew quiet. They had the usual song, prayer, and introductions and then the speaker, Merrill Edwards, a long time bishop and now their new stake president, came to the pulpit. For a long moment after his introduction, the tall, peppered-haired man surveyed his audience without speaking.

"I'm so grateful to be with you tonight," President Edwards began finally. "You are such a wonderful bunch of young people. I can feel your spirits, and I know that you are trying to do what the Lord would have you do. As your new stake president, I have felt an overwhelming need to talk to you today about ladders." He paused a moment to let his audience wonder what ladders might have to do with the gospel. Every eye riveted on him as he continued. After a short while, Rae, and everyone else, realized he was talking about marriage.

"After my mission, I slowly began to understand that I had reached the end of the ladder I was climbing in my progression to become more like our Father-in-Heaven. You see, I was on a single ladder that had just ended. I had progressed as far as I could progress in my single state and I couldn't go any further alone. That's when I realized that it was time for me to marry—time to move over to a married ladder that extends all the way back to the Father."

President Edwards continued, talking about how he went about finding a partner, dwelling some time on the fact that many people waited for marriage to happen to them instead of actively working to make it happen.

"Now, sometimes actively searching for a mate might involve a little risk," he acknowledged, "but you all need to try. I have been increasingly concerned by the many single adults who continue to remain single long after they leave college. Many of you are returned missionaries and have come to me asking why you can't find someone to take to the temple. Well, I asked those young men—good looking guys, all of them—how many girls they had dated in the past month and most of them said, 'one' or 'none.' Can any of you deduce their problem?"

Laughter waved through the crowd. The president waited until it died down to continue. "I think I can. And to those same young men—who, incidentally, are here in this audience—and to all of you, I say, look around you and see all these beautiful sisters, most of whom are searching for someone just like you are. Isn't it time to take a little risk? Time to open your mouth and ask someone out?"

There was a hush over the room, but President Edwards wasn't through. "Young women also play a part in finding an eternal partner . . ."

Rae could feel Andrew's eyes on her, but she didn't meet his gaze. Nor did she look at Dave sitting on her other side. The words, "I had progressed as far as I could progress in my single state," kept playing over and over in her mind.

*Is that what I'm doing? Am I going nowhere? Do I have to get married right now? Is this the answer to my prayer?* The air in the room pressed in on her, and suddenly she couldn't breathe. She needed to get away! She stood and slipped by Andrew. As she left the chapel, she caught a glimpse of Lisa following her.

"Hey, what is it?" Lisa asked as Rae plopped herself carelessly on one of the dark brown couches in the foyer.

"Marriage, marriage, marriage. They bombard us from all sides. I'm not ready!"

"It's Andrew, isn't it?" Lisa perceptively pinpointed the problem. "I always thought you guys were just friends, but lately there's something else."

"He's going to ask me to marry him," Rae replied miserably. "Especially after that pep-talk." She gestured toward the chapel where the stake president was still going strong.

"How do you feel about that?"

"I don't know!"

Lisa's brown eyes twinkled. "Well, let me put it this way. Don't you think Dave's good-looking? Wouldn't you like to get to know him better? I know you're usually too busy with working and with school to go out much, but wouldn't you like to see Dave again without having to worry about Andrew?"

Rae thought about Lisa's question. After a few seconds she nodded. "Yes, I would—assuming he would ask." She sighed. "He seems really nice."

"He is. And I know him pretty well, what with all of my summer visits to California. So I guess that means you have your answer for

Andrew." Lisa was smiling her lopsided grin, her face radiating the self-satisfied expression she had when she knew she was right. Rae didn't mind. She had received her answer about Andrew tonight, not from the speaker at the fireside, but from her beautiful, doe-eyed friend. If she still wanted to date Dave, there was no way she should marry Andrew.

"Thanks." Rae shook her head, looking at Lisa fondly. "You know, you're a lot smarter than people give you credit for."

"I know." They both laughed.

Now Rae had to figure out what to tell Andrew.

"Oh, there you are." Andrew, with Dave and Michelle in tow, was coming from the chapel, signaling the close of the fireside. "Is everything okay?"

"Yeah, everything is fine—now. Lisa . . ." Rae's voice trailed off as she looked for her friend, but Lisa was nowhere to be found.

"Where is Lisa?" Michelle asked a little worriedly. "She said she'd take me home right after the fireside was over. I—my parents could only baby-sit until eight-thirty. They still have to go to Salt Lake City tonight, my grandmother's expecting them. They're going house hunting with her early tomorrow morning."

"Babysitting?" Andrew asked.

"Uh, yeah. Didn't Lisa tell you I have a little girl?" Michelle looked at them steadily, but Rae could see that she was afraid of what they might think.

"No, she didn't mention it," Rae said. "How old is she?"

"She's four now." Michelle looked around again for Lisa. "She could have stayed with Lisa's parents but I don't like to leave her with people she doesn't know very well."

"Why don't I run you home?" Andrew said. "I know where Lisa's parents live. It's not far. By the time I get back they'll still be eating refreshments."

"I'd appreciate it." Michelle smiled at Andrew, and suddenly her whole face was transformed. She had the same beautiful smile her brother had, only she used it less.

"I'll be right back," Andrew said to Rae. "Save me some cookies."

"No way!" Rae called after him. When Andrew and Michelle were gone, she patted the cushion beside her. "Have a seat, Dave."

"Don't mind if I do."

"You know, your sister has a beautiful smile. She should use it more."

"Yeah. It's not something she's done too much of since little Hope came along." Dave made a grimace.

"How'd that happen? I mean, if you don't mind telling. Lisa's mentioned it before, but I confess I haven't paid much attention. She has a lot of cousins to keep up with."

"Well, Michelle was pretty wild as a teenager, and we all tried to warn her about her actions, but she never paid attention. She was a genuine black sheep. When she became pregnant, no one was surprised. Some people in our ward weren't very nice about it, but most were understanding."

"I know what you mean." Rae remembered when her brother and his wife, Lenna, had been in the same position. "Jon, that's my brother, wasn't very wild but he did start dating too soon. My mom was heartbroken when he told her his girlfriend was expecting. Lenna had Shane three months after their wedding. It was a long, hard haul for a while. But, you know, they've been sealed in the temple now and had another baby, Jonny, a year ago. My brother's almost through BYU now, and they seem pretty happy."

"Are they still active?"

"Yes, very."

"That's great. My sister's boyfriend dumped her about six months after the baby was born. She had thought to get married—though he wasn't a member. In fact, that was why she didn't give the baby up for adoption. But apparently he had other plans. He didn't even say goodbye in person. He just left her a note saying that he gave up all rights to the baby and disappeared. Of course, his parents knew where he was, but they weren't saying. They still aren't saying."

"Don't they at least want contact with their grandchild?" Rae asked, saddened by his story.

"They don't even admit that Hope *is* their grandchild, and Michelle hasn't pursued it. We did go to a lawyer and get papers drawn up and Duke—that's Hope's father—signed it. She didn't want him coming back and trying to get custody or visitation years down the road. She's very protective." Dave sighed.

"With all the movies you see now-a-days, I don't blame her one bit," Rae said, shaking her head. "Poor Michelle. I bet it's been really hard for her."

"Yes, but my parents and I've stuck by her. By the time Hope was six months old and her father out of the picture, we were all completely and totally in love with her. My mom never could have anymore children due to complications when we were born, so she's really enjoyed having Hope around. And as for Michelle, well, she's completely changed—and I mean completely and absolutely. It's been a very long road and a lot of heartache, but she's stronger and more faithful in the church than I ever thought possible. Honestly, I can tell you, she's going to make somebody a great wife someday. In fact, finding someone worthy of *her* will be difficult!"

An uncomfortable silence followed his declaration. Rae suddenly realized that they didn't know each other very well and had been talking about things very close to their hearts. She smiled. "Well, I guess we've broken the proverbial ice, haven't we?"

"Yeah," Dave returned her smile with a wide grin. "Would it sound like too much of a line if I said that it seems like I've known you before?"

"Yes, it would," Rae agreed. "But I know exactly what you

mean. Maybe we were friends in the . . . Naw, that sounds too corny."

"Still—who knows?"

"Not me," Rae shrugged. "I can't remember anything. We went through a veil, remember?"

Dave snorted. "No, I don't remember. But wasn't that *your* point? I only know what they say." They both laughed, and Rae felt herself relax for the first time since she had realized that Andrew wanted to marry her.

They were still laughing when Lisa rushed up to them. "Where's Michelle? I forgot that I was supposed to take her home right after the fireside." Her hands were full of cookies, and as she spoke, she handed them each a couple. They were chocolate chip, Rae's favorite.

"Andrew took her home. Don't worry about it."

Lisa sighed and sank down on Rae's other side. "That's a relief. Good old Andrew. But to think that I missed the grand finale!" She tried to take a bite of a cookie but when she held it up to her mouth, it bent in half. She brought the cookie closer and took a big, gooey bite. "Mmmm. Now that's a good cookie— and still warm!" Even when munching cookies, Lisa was beautiful. Her dark good looks were something Rae had long envied.

Rae quickly tried to swallow her own mouthful of cookie. "What do you mean? What grand finale?"

"Didn't Dave tell you? I can't believe it!" Lisa looked at them with mock suspicion. "What have you two been talking about, if not that?"

"Tell me," Rae urged. She turned to Dave, "Or you tell me."

"I haven't got a clue what she's talking about." Dave shrugged.

"Men!" Lisa exclaimed. "They just don't know what's important." She rolled her eyes and explained. "No sooner had I followed you out when our beloved stake president began choosing people out of the audience and told them to date each other! He called four different couples—can you believe it?—and I missed the whole thing!"

"Yeah, and you could have been one of those called!" Rae teased.

"So that's what's got you excited," Dave said. "Too bad for you. But, you know, *we*," he looked at Rae meaningfully, "don't need such help. We're doing just fine on our own!"

The next half hour was wonderful. Rae, Lisa, and Dave talked and laughed with their peers. Inside, Rae felt the old familiar excitement of meeting someone new, someone she was really interested in. Andrew didn't get back until much later, shortly before time to leave the church.

"What took you so long?" Lisa asked.

He laughed and shook his head. "Well, I walked your cousin to the door, and the next thing I know I'm inside playing with her daughter. She's a hoot, that one. I couldn't stop laughing. Then the kid wouldn't let me leave."

"And I bet you loved every second." Rae could attest that Andrew had a way with children. Her own younger brothers and sister adored him. In fact, he was always giving them attention and inviting them along on their dates. His love for children was one of the reasons she cared so much about him.

Rae and Andrew said goodbye to their friends and climbed into his car, but Andrew didn't start the engine. They watched as one by one the other cars drove away until they were completely alone. In the past forty-five minutes Rae had completely forgotten that Andrew had something to tell her. Now she looked out over the empty parking lot and waited in silent apprehension.

Finally, Andrew opened the door and climbed from the car. He went around to the trunk and pulled out a blanket and a cassette player. He spread the blanket on the church lawn in front of the car, put some romantic music playing, and went to open her door. Rae smiled but she felt her heart ache.

"What's all this?" she asked. This was not the practical Andrew's style, and she suspected that he was trying to impress her. She loved romantic things, he knew, though he would probably have felt more comfortable slipping in the Big Question during normal conversation.

"Sit down," he invited, motioning her to the grass. Rae sat carefully, spreading her dress out around her. She purposely avoided Andrew's eyes. *Oh please*, she prayed silently, *help me know what to say*. Andrew knelt before her and her heart filled with sweet tenderness, although, strangely, it was not directed towards Andrew.

"We've known each other a long time," he began without pretense. "We have the same eternal goals, and we're best friends. I love you." Here his voice wobbled slightly, showing her how nervous he was. "I think we should get married." His gaze was earnest, his desire for her apparent in his eyes. He didn't have a ring, and she hadn't expected one. He would never imagine that he might be able to choose something she would adore.

"I . . . oh, Andrew." Rae reached for his hand. She felt her love for him swell in her heart, but there was nothing in that love urging her to make their relationship any more than what it was. "If I was to get married now, it would be to you. You are one of my best friends, and I do love you, but . . . well . . . I've prayed about this, and I know it may sound funny, but I'm not supposed to get married now." A warm, reassuring feeling burned in her chest as the Spirit testified to the truthfulness of her words.

"Why not? You'd make a wonderful mother."

She met his eyes, saw the hurt there. "It has nothing to do with children. It has to do with how I feel about us, and how my prayers have been answered."

"But my prayers about you have been answered. I know you'd be a perfect wife for me!" His voice was insistent but not impolite.

Still, his words annoyed her; he usually gave her feelings greater consideration.

"What about me?" Rae let go of Andrew's hand. "Did you pray to find out if *you* are the perfect husband for *me*?" She winced as the sudden widening of his eyes showed that her words had hit home.

When he answered, he didn't lash back at her. "No, I didn't." He shook his head sadly. "I—I guess I don't even have that right."

"Oh, Andrew. I didn't mean to hurt you. But too many men have used the revelations they receive to convince women to marry them. And maybe it's real revelation and things work out, or maybe he wants it so badly that he's trying to force her to believe it's right—not that I think that's what you're trying to do—but, regardless, a woman has the right to receive confirmation of whom she's supposed to marry. The General Authorities of the Church have told us that. Even you and I have talked about similar situations before. There has to be love, trust, desire, need, and then confirmation."

"Are you saying you don't feel those things for me?" His hurt had deepened. Dear, simple, down-to-earth Andrew could never hide anything from her. She looked down at the blanket, avoiding his gaze. She had always been honest with him before, but she didn't know how to tell him that though she found him nearly a perfect match for her in every other way, she wasn't attracted to him. And it wasn't his looks, it was simply how she felt.

"I—uh . . ." Rae sifted through her thoughts for the best way to explain it to him. *Please, Father, help me!* "I do love you, Andrew. I enjoy being with you. You're considerate, kind, good with children, faithful in the gospel. You're all of the things I want my husband to be . . ." She stopped.

"But . . ." Andrew urged. He wanted the whole truth.

Rae couldn't bring herself to hurt him further. How could she when he stared at her so earnestly? "But it's not right for me."

"That's not exactly a no," his voice was hopeful.

45

"For marriage, it is," Rae whispered. "But for friendship, of course not. I . . ." Andrew held up his hand to stop her from talking.

"Let it ride a bit, Rae," he pleaded, taking her hand. "We'll continue on as before. Who knows how things might change?"

"Okay." She felt the tears in her eyes as she looked at his kind face. "Thanks for being my friend."

"I'll always be that."

"I'm glad. I need you." He smiled slightly and helped her to her feet. The stars twinkled above them and he leaned over and kissed her once, very softly, on the cheek. Rae felt even sadder when he did because, though she wished to comfort him, she felt absolutely no desire to return his kiss.

For no reason she could define, thoughts of Dave Channing filled her mind.

# Chapter Five
## Rae and Dave

*E*arly Wednesday morning before school, Rae sat at the computer in her bedroom, her fingers deftly pouring out her feelings as she wrote in her journal. Her computer stood on a desk in the corner next to the big window. It really didn't look good stuffed into that corner when she and Lisa still had one wall completely bare, but it was in a perfect spot for looking out the window to dream, or look for inspiration while she wrote.

She hadn't seen Andrew over the last three days though he had called her twice. They had talked like old friends, carefully avoiding any mention of his proposal. Rae was immensely relieved, though she felt sadness at the strain she sensed in his voice.

Luckily, she didn't have much time to think about Andrew. She was deeply involved in studying for school finals and also busy with her work at Mervyn's in the University Mall. She worked in the jewelry department and they were receiving shipments for their big Mother's Day sale. It was her responsibility to log everything that came in and to make sure the display cases were well stocked and attractively arranged.

She enjoyed her work and was very good at it, but it wasn't the work she was trained for. As soon as she finished her degree, she planned to apply to one of the big businesses in the area who might need a marketing director.

"Raaaeee. Oh, Raaaeee!" Lisa's voice made its way into her conscious thoughts, as she finished her journal entry.

Rae pushed the keys to save the file and then went to the door. "What is it?" she called as she closed the bedroom door behind her. She knew Lisa was busy making cookies for a new guy who had moved into the ward. "Some guy is on the phone for you!"

Once in the kitchen, Rae spied the freshly baked cookies on the counter. She reached for one but Lisa appeared from nowhere and wrestled her for it. "Hey, I burnt the others!" Lisa protested. "These are from the good plate. Put it back!"

Rae dodged her for few minutes before relinquishing the cookie. Laughing, she picked up the phone. "Hello?" she said a little out of breath.

"And you're already breathless, just thinking of talking to me, eh?" Dave asked, his voice playful.

Rae made a face at Lisa and covered the phone. "You didn't tell me it was your cousin," she whispered.

Lisa grinned. "You didn't ask!"

"I was wrestling your cousin for a cookie," Rae told Dave. "You wouldn't believe how possessive she can get."

"Am not!" Lisa shoved a plate toward her. "You can have any of these."

Rae turned one over, eyed the burnt bottom, and rolled her eyes.

"Fine, be that way." Lisa wrapped tinfoil around the plate of good cookies. "I'll deliver these on the way to my first class. I'm going to see if the way to a man's heart really is through his stomach."

"Uh, Rae?" Dave said in her ear. "Is this a bad time?"

"No, I'm sorry. It was Lisa. But she's gone now . . . or almost." Rae waved as Lisa cast her a last mocking look from the doorway. "So," she said to Dave, "Lisa tells me you went to Salt Lake to help your parents find a house."

"Yeah, my parents were all set to find a place in Salt Lake until I found the perfect house here. Or practically. It's in Orem."

"That's great! That's where my parents live."

"Well, I have my heart set on going to the Y to finish school—I'm studying to be a lawyer, you know—but now it won't be such a push to find my own apartment for a while. I'll stay with my parents and work on finding a job. So what do you say we go and celebrate!"

"Tonight?"

"Unless you've got something better to do."

Rae couldn't think of anything she would rather do than go out with Dave. She had a full day ahead with work and the coming school finals, but this evening she was free. "No. I'd like to go," she said.

Later that evening, he picked her up for a movie date, with dinner planned for afterwards. "Well, which would you like to see?" he asked, as they waited in line for the tickets at the Windsong in Provo. Rae looked up at the choices. There were only two that really interested her, one was a PG and the other was a Walt Disney film. She was embarrassed to admit that she wanted to see the cartoon.

"Uh, well, I guess the first one," she said, pointing to the board.

Dave face fell. "Oh, but I really wanted to see the cartoon! Would that bore you to death?"

Rae smiled. "I guess I could stand it."

"You sure? Because I don't mind the other."

"Trust me. I'd tell you if I wasn't okay with it."

They bought tickets to the Disney movie and found seats in the middle of the theater. Since they were early, they started into an interesting discussion about the making of the film with some of the children sitting near them. Dave was a natural with the youngsters, taking time to explain what he knew in detail and on a level they could understand. The way he treated them distinctly reminded Rae of her own father—kind, thoughtful, patient, not demeaning or condescending. Rae suddenly wondered how Dave might be with his own children.

"Penny for your thoughts." Dave turned at that moment to see her expression.

"What! They're worth more than that," she stalled. How could she tell a man she had only know for such a short time that she was wondering if he'd be a good father for her children? Rae shook her head and laughed. She looked up at the big screen. "Oh, look! The movie's about to start."

"Okay," Dave said. "You get off the hook—this time." Rae smiled to herself. This was the best date she'd had in years!

Rae had a wonderful time with Dave. He was a perfect gentleman, opening doors, seating her at the restaurant, doing little things that reminded Rae of how her dad treated her mother. When he drove her home, he simply walked to the door and said good night. She felt no pressure to kiss him or to rush their relationship.

The next morning at work, Dave surprised her with a visit. Rae was busily rearranging a display case, making room for the new merchandise she had been cataloguing, when a shadow fell over her. She looked up to see him there, watching.

"How long have you been here?" She straightened from her crouched position behind the counter.

He smiled. "Long enough to see that you are very concentrated on getting everything just right. You bite your lip when you're thinking."

Rae shrugged, slightly embarrassed. "It sells better if it's displayed correctly."

"I like a woman who knows how to concentrate." He leaned forward and added in a whisper, "Especially if it's on me."

Rae laughed. "Well, maybe you should become a gold necklace."

"Then I wouldn't have arms to carry these." Dave reached down and picked up a vase of red roses hidden out of sight. Rae's mouth dropped. She had received flowers before, but never from someone she liked as much as Dave. Not even Andrew brought her flowers.

"Oh, Dave, they're beautiful!"

"Like you."

Rae blushed. She knew she was attractive, but had never considered herself beautiful. Such a word was, in her mind, reserved for people who looked like Lisa.

That was the beginning of two weeks of fun, of getting to know and love Dave. In many ways, Dave replaced Andrew in Rae's life. As with Andrew, Rae and Dave had so much in common that at times it was almost uncanny. But while her relationship with Andrew had developed slowly over many years, the bond with Dave simply existed from the beginning—as though they had known each other before in some other time or place. They played racquetball, went roller-skating, watersliding, and hiking—all Rae's favorite activities that she had often shared with Andrew. More often than not, they had Dave's sister or Lisa tagging along on these adventures.

Rae couldn't help noticing how completely different Dave was from Andrew. He was confident, bold, outspoken, and romantic. With his dark hair, deep blue eyes, and engaging grin, he was a person everyone noticed, while Andrew was often overlooked in a crowd. Dave knew exactly what he wanted in life and was not shy about going after it. At the moment it seemed that he wanted Rae, and she found she didn't mind at all.

Dave called her one Friday morning at work. "Hello, Rae . . . Love." After their second date, he had begun to include her last name when he addressed her, but the way he paused after her first name made it definitely more of an endearment that simply her last name. "What shall we do tonight? I found a job this morning and I'm in the mood to celebrate!"

"That's wonderful! Where? How?" Rae continued to clean the glass on the display cases with the phone propped between her shoulder and her ear.

"That lawyer firm I told you about called last night and asked me to come back in today. They offered me the job on the spot! It's dirt work, but at least it's in a real law office, and they'll work around my school schedule." There was no mistaking the excitement in his voice.

"That's wonderful! I'm so happy for you!" Then Rae had an idea. "I know, let's have the gang over tonight to celebrate. Lisa, Michelle, you, me. Our other two roommates if they don't have plans. Some of the others in the complex. We'll have a video and lots of food."

"Sounds like a great idea. And probably safer than being alone."

"Don't worry, I won't bite."

"Aw, that's what I was afraid of!"

"Oh brother, that joke again? I swear, Dave, you're incorrigible!"

"You're lucky I'm studying to be a lawyer and even know what that word means. Otherwise, I might think you're trying to flirt with me."

"Like I said, incorrigible!"

"So, what time do you get off?" he asked.

"Not till five."

"We'll then, I'll call Lisa and my sister to let them know. Lisa can call the others."

"Yeah, she'll know who." Rae glanced up and noticed a customer who was looking around for help. "Hey, Dave, I've got to help someone now. Tell everyone to bring something to munch on, okay?"

"Okay, Rae . . . Love. I'll see you later."

She was about to hang up but then she remembered. "Oh, and Dave?"

"Yeah?"

"Tell Michelle to bring little Hope." Rae had met Hope once before at Dave's parents' house and had been immediately taken with the cherub-faced child. She also knew Michelle would be more likely to come to the party if Hope was invited.

"Okay, I will. And thanks for thinking of her."

\* \* \* \* \*

As Lisa entered their apartment later that evening, Rae was just hanging up the phone with her little brother Chad, who was the youngest of the five Love siblings. "Oh, you just missed Chad," she told Lisa.

Lisa smiled. "What'd he call for?"

"To know when we were coming over. That boy has got a major crush on you, you know?"

"Yeah. He's cute. Too bad he's only eleven, or I'd marry him and give up this rat race." Lisa set her huge shoulder bag on the kitchen counter and began pulling packages of potato chips and Oreo cookies from it. Licorice, taffy, and a box of donuts followed. She seemed to have an endless supply.

"Are we feeding an army?"

"Naw, I just feel like eating tonight." Lisa pulled some chocolate bars out of the very bottom of the cloth bag, wadded the bag into a ball, and threw it into the corner by a stack of paper plates and cups Rae had bought.

"Bad day?" Rae asked.

Lisa sighed and jumped up to sit on the counter next to the packages of chips. "My parents are having some marital problems. I don't know exactly what's going on with them yet. And Todd and I aren't going to date anymore." Todd had been the recipient of Lisa's cookies two weeks earlier, but apparently his stomach wasn't the right way to his heart—at least not permanently.

"Wow. That's tough about your parents." Rae thought of her own parents and knew how horrible she would feel if they had serious problems. It would hurt, even as old as she was. "When did this start?"

"I don't know. They never told me anything. I just noticed in the last month that they've been acting kind of strange. Then my mom told me today that they were talking about a temporary separation." Lisa ripped open a chocolate bar with her teeth, pushed down the wrapper, and took a big bite. "I guess they'll work it out," she mumbled through her candy. She swallowed and sighed loudly, her face mournful. She took another huge bite.

"And, Lisa, about Todd—he was an airhead. You're better off without him. Anyway, you've only been dating him a few weeks and it's not as if he's the love of your life. You'll find someone else. Someone who deserves you."

"Hey, it's not like I haven't been looking." Lisa scrunched her beautiful face in a scowl. "I talk to everyone. Andrew says that I chase boys. That's not true, of course, but I do know and talk to everyone. Why can't I find Mr. Right?"

Rae motioned for Lisa to follow her to the front room. They sat down on the couch and Rae listened as Lisa talked on. Everything she was saying Rae had heard before, but she knew her friend needed to talk. They were always there for one another. It had been a promise since they were in kindergarten class together, all those years before.

"Rae," Lisa continued, "guys are always so cute when they ask me out, but then when we're on the date, they mostly turn out to be jerks. They either want to make-out or talk about themselves all night like Todd. Why can't I find someone witty and deep like Andrew?" For all that Lisa and Andrew were almost always at odds, Lisa admired many of his qualities.

Rae put her arm around her friend. "And I told you before, Lisa, there's nothing wrong with you. With the possible exception that you're a little too good-looking. That scares a lot of the good guys away because they're afraid a girl like you wouldn't give them the time of day. If your looks were more ordinary, I bet you wouldn't have so many problems."

"Oh great!" Lisa shook her head, a smile cutting through her gloom. "That's one I haven't heard before—I'm too good-looking to get a decent date! Ha! I can just see me telling that to the stake president." Lisa struck an angelic pose. "You see, President Edwards, I'm too good-looking to be marriage material." She batted her eyelashes for added effect and both girls laughed. Once started they couldn't stop and were soon rolling on the floor, in tears from laughing so hard.

"Oh, Rae, you're good for me," Lisa said, wiping a tear from her eye. She leaned her head back on the brown carpet and sighed. "Somehow you always make me feel better."

"You do the same for me. Remember that bully in kindergarten? The one who used to hit me over the head with his book bag?"

"Cootie Calvin—how could I forget?" Lisa giggled. "I fixed him good." She made a fist, just as she had beneath Calvin's nose all those years ago.

"And I'm eternally grateful." Rae fell silent as they both remembered the past. "You know," she began more seriously, "sometimes things don't happen when or the way we want them to. It's the Lord's timetable that counts in the end. Like with me for instance—"

"Yeah, what about you?" Lisa interrupted. "I've barely seen you since you began to date my cousin—my gorgeous cousin. I'll have to tell him he's monopolizing all your time. He's worse than Andrew!"

"Well . . ." Rae sighed. " Oh, Lisa, I really like him, but I have to say that I don't know if he's The One. I always felt that I'd *know* the man I was going to marry, like I'd feel something so different that I couldn't possibly make a mistake. Maybe I was wrong, or maybe I'm scared this is it or—"

"—Or scared that maybe it isn't." Lisa nodded. "With all our friends getting married, it kind of makes you want your own family, doesn't it? Well, I guess you'll find out about Dave soon enough. What about Andrew? How's he taking your relationship with Dave?"

"We haven't been out since he asked me to marry him. He's pretty much backed off. We've talked on the phone a couple times, and I saw him briefly when we had that stake activity at the skating rink. Oh, and my mom says he's come over a couple of times to horse around with my brothers at their place." Rae sighed. "I really miss him when I have time to think about it."

Lisa grinned. "I bet my cousin doesn't give you much time to think about Andrew."

"Nope. He doesn't." Rae felt herself smiling back a little too widely.

Lisa opened her mouth to say more when the door burst open letting in their two roommates, a group of friends from their apartment building, and more people from the buildings next door—including Andrew, his hands resting in the pockets of his jeans. Rae glanced up at him, her stomach churning. She wasn't sure getting Dave and Andrew together in the same apartment was a good idea, but she smiled and stood to greet him.

"Hey, glad you came," she said, feeling a genuine pleasure at seeing him as the initial shock faded.

He stood in the open doorway while the others disappeared with Lisa into the kitchen, carrying bags of chips and plates of freshly baked chocolate chip cookies. "Hi, Rae, it's good to see you." His voice was casual, but he stared intently at her.

Her heart sank. "Andrew . . ."

"I know, I know." He held up a hand as if to ward off an attack. "It's just that . . ." He hesitated, hearing voices on the stairs.

Dave, Michelle, and little Hope appeared behind Andrew, who moved over to let them inside. "Hi, guys." Rae nodded at them, relieved for the interruption, but worried about Dave's and Andrew's possible reactions. "Come in." She pretended not to see little Hope as she stepped into the front room, her fly-away blonde hair sticking out in many directions. "Hmm, I thought I told you to bring Hope. Now where could she be?" Rae looked everywhere except down in front of her where little Hope stood giggling.

"What! Who's laughing? Oh, it's you!" Rae stooped down so she was even with the little girl's round face. "Hope, I'm so glad you could come. It's good to see you again. You remember me, don't you? From the other day when I came to your house?" From the corner of her eye, she saw Andrew grimace slightly as he apparently understood that she had been there with Dave.

"Yes," Hope said shyly. "It's me."

"Andrew, you remember David and Michelle Channing, don't you? From the fireside."

He nodded, his brow drawn as his gaze rested on Dave.

"Yes, you took me home," Michelle recalled. "Thank you so much."

Andrew smiled and his forehead smoothed. "Glad to help."

Rae felt a tugging on her leg. "Where can I put these?" Hope held up a package of chips.

"In the kitchen," Andrew said before Rae could answer. "I'm going there now. Would you like to come with me?" For the first time Rae noticed that Andrew was carrying several liters of soda pop in a plastic bag. Little Hope looked back at her mom, her face pinched with worry.

"Don't worry, honey," Michelle said, smiling. "I'm coming too." They followed Andrew as he turned on his heel and started into the kitchen, where laughter came from the other partiers with Lisa.

"And what about me, Rae, Love?" Dave asked, speaking for the first time. "Where shall I put these?" He brought from behind his back a large bouquet of red roses and baby's breath, tied with a large red bow.

"Oh, Dave they're beautiful! Thank you." Rae reached for the roses a little self-consciously, noticing how Andrew's step faltered when Dave brought out the roses.

"Rae, do you know where I put the videos?" Lisa called, breaking the tension. "You guys better help me find them before I eat all the chocolate bars!"

As they set up the food in the front room and turned on the videos, Rae worried that Dave and Andrew would come to harsh words and spoil the party. But Hope wrapped them both around her little finger. Almost immediately, she found a large box of blocks Rae's nephews had left the last time she had watched them, and went right to work building a village in the short wide hallway that led to the kitchen.

"You help me build the castle," she ordered Dave. "And Andrew has to build the roads. If we don't have roads, we can't get to the castle."

Neither Dave nor Andrew could fault her logic, so they went to work. Rae never saw building with blocks as an art before, but now it took on a whole new meaning. She could hardly believe the elaborate creations that came to life underneath their hands as the men competed for the title of the best building. Books, plates, cups, and even a brownie became building materials. Each man glanced to her for approval. Rae tried to keep her eyes glue on the TV screen, glancing over only when she was sure they weren't looking.

Eventually the construction required negotiation for certain needed blocks, and that meant Dave and Andrew had to talk. In fact, they made so much noise that the others had to shush them several times in order to hear the movie.

"You any good at racquetball?" Dave asked Andrew as the construction came to an end.

Andrew's chin went up at the scarcely-concealed challenge.

"Rae and I play all the time," Andrew replied.

Rae winced. They had played a lot—before Dave came along.

"I challenge you to a game."

"Okay. How about tomorrow?"

Lisa giggled, also overhearing the exchange. "Yeah," she said. "When lacking dueling swords, I always go for racquetball."

Dave and Andrew glared at her, but she shrugged and popped the brownie topping Dave's castle into her mouth.

"Hey. That was mine!" Dave growled.

"Finders, keepers." Lisa hopped over Andrew's castle and went to get another bottle of soda from the fridge.

"Do you want to come with us, Rae?" Dave asked. "I'm going to beat Andrew in racquetball."

Rae shook her head. "I have to work." Besides, there was no way she was going to get between them. If they didn't kill each other first, they might actually become friends.

After the videos were over and the last chip inhaled, Andrew left, and Lisa gave Michelle and Hope a ride home. Dave stayed behind. Since their other roommates were inside, they went out onto the small stairway balcony for some privacy. Rae leaned against the black metal railing. The soft light of the moon and stars shone upon them.

"You look beautiful tonight, Rae." Dave's voice was soft.

"Thank you." Rae was glad the darkness hid the sudden color that had come to her cheeks. Her heart hammered inside her chest.

He reached to take her hand. "You know, Rae, Love, I didn't think I'd be ready for a long time to get married, but with a girl like you . . . I mean, it's kind of scary. You're the first girl I've dated who really has a testimony of the Church. I've had a lot of fun on dates before, but when it got time to be serious, the girls I've dated never seemed to have a strong enough testimony. I always told myself that I couldn't pursue the relationship because I didn't know if they had what it takes to be a strong member and an eternal companion. Now I can't use that excuse anymore. You *know* the Church is true."

Rae pondered his comment. The Church had been a part of her life for as long as she could remember. She had been baptized the first Saturday after her eighth birthday, becoming an official member. At first, she had relied on the firm testimonies of her parents, but gradually her own testimony had grown strong. She believed with all her heart in the Church of Jesus Christ of Latter-day Saints. She was grateful for the knowledge, and she couldn't imagine living without the guidance membership gave her.

"I do know it's true, Dave," she said softly, looking up at the beautiful night sky. "After seeing all this," she motioned at the heavens with a sweep of her arm, "how could anybody doubt that God lives and loves them no matter what? You know, sometimes I wish I could tell everybody how much He loves them, how much He wants them to be happy."

"I feel that way too. But I especially felt it on my mission."

"Tell me about it."

The conversation shifted to his mission in Ecuador until Rae noticed the time. "I have to go, Dave. It's nearly midnight already. I have to work early."

"Yeah, and I've got racquetball with that other boyfriend of yours." He kept his tone light, but Rae couldn't ignore the underlying seriousness. "You know, I was prepared to really dislike Andrew, but I have to admit, he seems like a nice guy. I can see why you like him so much."

"I knew you would. You two are a lot a like."

"I'll take that as a compliment."

"That's how it was meant." Rae felt goose bumps break out on her arms and neck as Dave's head bent closer to hers. She could smell his aftershave in the air. His lips were almost on hers when

Lisa turned the corner of the parking lot and waved up at them.

"I'm back!" she called.

The moment was lost.

Dave shook his head. "She's got to work on her timing!"

"Well, see you later," Rae said with a smile.

"Until next time, Rae, Love."

He went down the stairs and out into the night.

# Chapter Six
## Birthday

*A*week after the Friday night video party, the day before she turned twenty-two, Rae got off work at eight in the evening. She was exhausted from the long day and grateful to have Saturday as well as Sunday to rest before returning to work. School finals were over but she had worked until ten almost every night. That meant she hadn't seen much of her friends the past week and was looking forward to spending time with them, especially with Dave.

Since the attempted kiss, there was a romantic tension between them that was scary and exhilarating all at once. Rae was almost sure he was the man she would marry. She had prayed fervently about Dave and had received what she considered a mixed answer. When she asked if they could be happy together, she felt a wonderful assurance that they could. But when she asked if he was the man she was supposed to marry, she hadn't felt so positive. She wondered what that meant.

She was thinking about this as she slid from her car and climbed the seemingly long flight of stairs to the apartment. The light above the door was dark but she could see the glow of dim light from the front window—probably one of her roommates watching TV. She turned the key in the lock and opened the door.

"Surprise!" screamed a slew of voices.

She blinked in surprise as the overhead lights came on, revealing a room full of people, streamers, and balloons. "I don't believe it!" she said, looking around at her friends and family who were practically crammed into the small space. Her parents and her four siblings were there, including her older brother Jon and his wife, Lena, and their two children. Friends included Lisa, Dave, Michelle, Andrew, her roommates, two girls from work, and several other friends from the apartment complex. Her exhaustion vanished. "You guys are great! I never suspected a thing!"

"Come on birthday girl, give us a pose." Her mother held up a camera, and Rae obligingly held up her hands in exaggerated surprise as the flash brightened the room.

"And walk this way. There's more to come." Dave was at her side, putting his arm through hers. Lisa grabbed the other arm, and together they dragged her into the kitchen which was also decorated with balloons and streamers.

Refreshments lined the counter, and there was a pile of presents on the table where they seated her ceremoniously. Holly, Rae's mother, motioned for Andrew to bring the cake, a large one with strawberry icing. The group sang happy birthday to her in loud voices while Andrew lit the candles.

"Andrew made the cake," her mother said. Andrew looked a little embarrassed but pleased to be noticed.

"It looks wonderful!" Rae said.

"Make a wish! Make a wish!" her little brother Chad shouted.

"Yeah, make a wish, Aunt Rae." Shane, her four-year-old nephew adored Chad and considered it his duty to copy everything his young uncle said.

Rae shut her eyes quickly to make a wish, one very close to her heart, and blew out the candles with one long breath.

"Whew," she said. "If I get any older I won't be able to blow them all out."

Chad nodded in agreement. "Yeah, you are gettin' old. You're twenty-two already!" The adults laughed.

"Not till tomorrow," Rae said.

"Don't worry, Aunt Rae," Shane said solemnly. "I'll help you blow out the candles."

"Thanks, Shane. I'm glad to know you'll be here to help me in my old age." Rae smiled at him. Then she looked down in time to see baby Jonny, Shane's younger brother, sticking his fingers into the cake.

"Jabba baba daba," he jabbered. Everybody laughed, as Rae's sister-in-law, Lenna, picked up the baby.

Rae spent the next few minutes opening presents. Dave gave her a dainty silver necklace with a unicorn pendant, and from Lisa came the new bathing suit Rae had planned on buying. Her parents and siblings gave her mostly clothes, though Jon and Lenna gave her a backpack. Her other friends had gone in together and bought her a portable CD player. A potted plant and several CDs made up the rest of the gifts.

"Thank you all so much." Rae found herself blinking back tears. "This is a birthday I will remember for the rest of my life." She meant it . . . but why did she feel something was missing?

"Let's dig into this great-looking buffet!" Dave got up from his chair and pulled Rae to her feet.

Soon everyone was spread out in the two main rooms, eating and playing games. Gradually, the evening wound down, and most of her friends departed, leaving only her family and her closest friends in the front room. During a lull in the games, Rae slipped into the kitchen for some water. Abruptly her fatigue returned, and she rested against the counter.

"Hey, good-looking," Andrew came into the kitchen carrying an empty plate.

Rae smiled. "Hey, yourself."

"I've been waiting to get you alone all evening," he said in his blunt way. "I've got something for you in the car. The cake wasn't your only present, you know."

"Oh, Andrew, it was enough. It was good, too."

"Well, that was number one, but your real present is in the car. Come on, Rae."

On the way to the car, they talked and joked like old times. It was almost like his proposal and Dave had never come between them.

"What's this?" Rae asked when they got to his car and Andrew opened the trunk to reveal many different sized packages.

"These are your presents. One for every year we've been friends."

Rae smiled, amazed at his thoughtfulness. "You shouldn't have."

"But I did."

"It's a wonderful idea." Rae realized that this was the most romantic, spontaneous thing he had ever done for her.

"Well . . ." Now Andrew looked a little sheepish. "It was my idea, but to tell the truth, Dave pushed me in the right direction."

"Our Dave?" Rae asked.

"Yeah. Well after I killed him in our first game of racquetball, he insisted on a rematch. So we've spent a little time together this week while you've been working. He knew I wanted to do something special and he kind of got me started thinking about something I could do that would be meaningful only to the two of us." He shook his head. "I really hoped I could hate the guy, but I can see why you like him."

Rae recalled that Dave had said almost the same thing about Andrew. "Well, you certainly out-did yourself this time," she said quickly to hide her discomfort. "How does this work? Do I get to pick which one to open first?"

"Sure," said Andrew as he felt inside his pocket. "But I've got the last one right here."

Rae proceeded to open the presents, each one recalling a special memory. The black umbrella to remind her of how it rained at the youth conference the first day they met; a toy telephone that recalled the long hours they had spent on the phone before they were old enough to date; a large package of stationary to represent the time they had spent writing while Andrew had been on his mission; a key to his car to remind her of how they had shared his car when hers had been out of commission for three weeks; the black, leather-band watch in memory of the one she'd lost when they had gone hiking last month; the CD of their favorite band; and of course, the cake which showed he remembered when she had once said that men should take more responsibility in the kitchen.

"I'll remember this forever," Rae said fervently, looking over at Andrew.

"Well, there's still this." He handed her a small oblong package. Rae carefully opened the paper and gasped when she saw what was inside.

"It's the bracelet!" Rae exclaimed pulling the thin gold bracelet from its box. She looked at it for a long moment, remembering how she had told Lisa over three months ago that this was a bracelet that wouldn't twist or damage if someone wore it all the time—even to sleep in. Thought it was inexpensive as gold bracelets go, she and Lisa had agreed that it was still a bit much for their tight budgets. She had forgotten until now that Andrew had been with them at the mall.

Rae knew immediately that she couldn't keep it. Shaking her head firmly, she handed the bracelet back to him. "Thank you, Andrew, but it's just too much, especially with all these other presents. I really appreciate the thought, though, and if things were different between us—"

"Rae, don't worry about the money," Andrew interrupted her. "I work full time, remember? And it's a good job; it's not like I don't have enough money. Besides, I *was* saving up to buy an engagement ring, you know."

"That's my point, Andrew. There isn't going to be an engagement ring for us."

"Don't you think I understand that?" Rae could hear the hurt and anger in his voice and she ached inside knowing that she was the cause. In all the years she'd known Andrew, Rae had never seen him angry before.

"I know you don't want to marry me," he continued. "And maybe that's for right now or maybe it's for forever—and maybe you're even right. But that doesn't stop me from loving you. I'm not trying to buy you or make you feel guilty. I simply want to do something special for a person I care about." Andrew's voice had gone from angry to pleading and his eyes watered at the force of his emotions.

"I'm so sorry, Andrew. I . . . I don't really seem to know how to act around you these days. I miss our friendship but . . . oh, I don't know. I guess I feel that you should keep these special gifts for the woman you *are* going to marry."

"Oh, Rae, that doesn't matter now. Don't you see? You've been beside me all these years encouraging me, being my friend, and most of all, just loving me. When I was in compromising or difficult situations in my life, I chose the right because I knew that I wouldn't be worthy of you—or someone like you—if I didn't. Because of you I've become a better person. I don't think that any future wife of mine would begrudge a little bracelet to a woman who helped make me what I am today. Do you?"

"I guess not." Rae blinked hard and tears rolled down her cheeks. Holding out her arm, she allowed Andrew to fasten the bracelet onto her wrist. "It's very special to me," she said when he was finished. She brought both hands up to her face and wiped the tears away. Together they started back toward the apartment.

Hope and Shane met them at the apartment door. "Andrew, Rae, come and see what we built with the blocks!" Andrew picked up little Hope and put her on his shoulders.

"Whee! I like this!" Hope yelled as they went into the kitchen to check out the children's house.

"I want a turn too!" Shane followed them.

Rae watched from the kitchen doorway while Andrew examined the building. Michelle came up beside her. "He really loves kids," she said.

"Yeah, he does."

"How do you like your party?"

Rae tore her eyes away from Andrew and the tower. "It's great! You're all great. I have the best friends in the world!"

"You deserve us!" Dave said coming up from behind her and making her jump.

"David, you scared me!"

"Why, Rae, Love, I do believe that is the first time you ever called me David instead of Dave."

He was right and she couldn't say why it slipped out. "What's that got to do with anything?" she asked. "It is your name, isn't it?"

"I don't know, but it's got to mean something." He grinned and put his arm around her possessively. He noticed her bracelet. "I see old Andrew gave you your present. I thought he'd never finish. I kept looking out the window—"

"You didn't!"

"No, but he did send the kids out there," Michelle piped in, laughing.

"Guilty as charged." Dave didn't look as if he felt guilty.

All too soon Rae was on the front porch saying goodbye to everyone. She noticed happily that Dave didn't make any move to leave but stayed comfortably seated on the couch in the front room. Rae felt her emotions tumbling around inside of her, but hoped none of her turmoil showed on the outside.

"That was really nice of you to help Andrew with my present, Dave," she said, sitting next to him on the couch.

"Hey, so now you're back to calling me Dave."

"Everybody calls you Dave."

"Yeah, well, you're not everybody."

"Would you rather I call you David?" She knew his mother and sister called him that.

"No, no. I think I'm just nervous and I'm trying to make conversation."

"Oh, I didn't know you got nervous."

"Only where you're concerned." There was a short silence before Dave continued. "About Andrew. I didn't do anything to help, really. But the point is, have your feelings toward him changed after tonight?"

"No. I'm surprised, of course. But I don't feel romantic about him—if that's what you mean."

"That's what I wanted to know." Dave put his arms around her and pulled her close. Rae's heart jumped wildly as she hugged him back. His head bent toward hers, and this time there was no interruption as their lips met.

Rae had supposed their first kiss would be amazing—a thing that stopped time and even the very rotation of the earth. But her feelings were not at all what she anticipated she would feel when the man she was going to marry kissed her. Almost, it was like kissing a brother. She pulled away, confused.

"No, Dave. I . . . "

"What's wrong?"

She shook her head, not knowing how what to think. "I need some time—that's all."

"But I thought . . . Okay. Fine. We've got time." There was reluctance in his voice, but he smiled all the same. "I'll go now, but I'll see you tomorrow, okay?"

"Yes. That's great." Rae sighed. "Thanks, Dave."

"You're welcome, Rae, Love." Dave squeezed her hand warmly.

After he was gone, Rae fought the tears until she made it to her room. Then she collapsed onto the bed and sobbed into the pillow. What was wrong with her? Why didn't she feel anything when Dave kissed her? The dreams of family and home that she had been building in her mind over the last three intense weeks tumbled to the ground in shattered pieces. She had two wonderful men in her life who wanted to marry her, and she didn't want to marry either of them. First she had hurt Andrew, and now she would have to hurt Dave. Or should she marry him after all? Who was to say that she'd ever find anyone as good as he was? What if she was destined to be an old maid? How was she to know that what she was feeling was right and real?

* * * * *

After a restless night, Rae didn't feel any better, only more tired, and so she did the only thing she could think of doing—a thing women have done for years. She dressed, bought herself a donut, and drove to see her mother in Orem.

"Rae—hi!" Her mother looked up from the stove she was cleaning as Rae came in the back door through the garage. Her chin-length blonde hair was swept up in a kerchief and tied on the top. "I would have thought you'd be sleeping after that party last night."

"I guess I'm used to getting up early. And I felt like a drive."

Her mother set down the sponge and pulled off her gloves. "A little chocolate donut didn't hurt either," she said with a smile.

"How'd you know?" Rae sat on one of the kitchen stools, breathing in the unique scent that to her meant home.

Her mother touched the side of her mouth in response to Rae's question. Rae licked her own mouth and found chocolate in the corner. She laughed. "Caught!"

"I guess I should have brought you one, huh?" Rae said.

Her mother shook her head. "Definitely not. I don't need any more temptation. My hips are still feeling the weight of Andrew's cake. It's different when you're older."

Rae studied her mother. In the stark light coming in from the kitchen windows, her wrinkles were more prominent, and her sweats were tighter. Why hadn't she noticed this change before? In her mind her mother was an unchanging, permanent fixture. But that was ridiculous. Everything changed.

"So why are you really here?" Her mother came around the counter and sat on a stool next to her. Rae heard the blare of a TV followed by laughter and knew that her younger siblings were watching Saturday morning cartoons—all but sixteen-year-old Taylor who was likely sleeping off all the chips, cake, and ice cream he'd inhaled at her party.

Fleetingly, Rae hoped that she could be as perceptive as her mother when she had children. She took a deep breath. "I don't want to marry Dave."

"Did he ask you last night?"

"I think he was about to, or at least try to make our relationship more permanent, but I suddenly realized that I couldn't marry him—although I think we could be happy together."

"Well, do you love him?"

"Oh, Mom, it's not that simple!" Rae propped her elbows on the counter and let her head fall into her hands. "I do love him, and I love Andrew, too. But last night when Dave kissed me, it just wasn't right. It was pleasant and I enjoyed it but . . ."

"Not like you expected to feel?"

Rae nodded.

"Is this the first time you felt this way about him?"

There was a long pause as Rae thought about her mother's question. She lifted her head.

"I guess I did feel that way several times before—when he would hold my hand. It seemed awkward. Or rather like something was missing. Something really important that I just couldn't remember. But I thought it was because I was nervous because he's so good-looking."

"You don't fall into love with someone simply because he's good-looking."

"I know, Mom. It just that . . . Oh, it's hard to explain. He's such a good person—maybe I *should* marry him."

Her mother shook her head. "Rae, marriage is hard enough when everything's going smoothly. You need to be very sure about your choice. You can't ever settle because you feel this is a chance you may never have again."

"But I'm twenty-two now. I need to get started with my life and having a family."

"You *are* getting started. You're getting a good education, and you'll need that to teach your children. Remember that your time is not the Lord's time."

At her mother's words Rae froze. "That's what I told Lisa last week." She smiled thinly.

"Well, you were right. Sometimes what we want isn't right at that moment. Like how your father and I tried so long to have more children after we had you, but we didn't until six years later when we finally had Taylor. And then how after Bria and Chad we weren't able to have any more." She gave a small chuckle. "Believe it or not, we always wanted at least seven children and were only able to have five."

"But sometimes it's so hard to wait," Rae replied.

"Anything worthwhile won't be easy."

Rae turned her face toward Holly. "Well, Mom, tell me this. How did you know that Dad was the man for you? How did you feel when he kissed you?"

"Well . . ." Her mother tilted her head back in remembrance. "We had become very good friends, and I loved him madly. I wanted to be with him constantly and couldn't bear the thought that we might not end up together. And when he kissed me it was a continuation of that. I knew it was right. I'm not saying I didn't have second thoughts—I did. Sometimes I got very scared about getting married, but those thoughts were never strong enough to stop me from marrying him. The positive feelings far outweighed the negative ones."

Rae nodded. She had felt much of that with Dave—but not all of it.

"Does that help?"

"Yeah. A lot," Rae said.

"Good." Her mother slipped from the stool and retrieved her gloves. "If you need to talk, I'm always here."

Rae kissed her mother's cheek, said goodbye, and went out the door. "She couldn't bear the thought that they might not end up together," she said aloud in the confines of her car. She smiled. "Well, much as I care about both Dave and Andrew, I'm more worried about hurting their feelings than living without them. I think everything's going to be just fine."

With that last thought Rae drove back to her apartment, fell into bed without changing her clothes, and drifted off to sleep.

A dream came then. A dream of two dark, love-filled eyes that seemed to pierce to the very center of her soul.

# Chapter Seven
## Tiago

*T*iago Carvalho looked up from the computer pieces he had spread on the coffee table in the living room. He heard the door and thought it was his mother, but he soon recognized Marcela's step. Tiago bent again over the pieces he was soldering, ignoring the terrible ache in his back. His sister thumped into his room, then to the kitchen. The sound of clattering plates broke Tiago's concentration, but he tried to stifle the quick irritation that threatened to become open hostility.

Shortly, Marcela came into the living room with a plate of rice, topped by a spicy mixture of curry chicken. She nodded at Tiago, who grunted in reply. Marcela sat in a padded chair and flipped on the remote. Loud voices instantly filled the room.

Tiago let the soldering iron clatter to the plastic computer covering.

"What?" Marcela said in annoyance, taking her eyes from the images. Her fork dug into the rice and went to her mouth, the thick silver bracelet on her arm skidding over her flesh with the movement.

Tiago shook his head, the angry words inside him dying as he stared at the bracelet. Their grandmother had given them each one for Christmas many years ago, and once Tiago had worn his almost continuously, just like everyone else in Portugal. Wearing jewelry was as ingrained in their culture as eating cod fish and fried potatoes. But he had stopped wearing his bracelet on the day his father died. There was no joy in him, no reason to care what he wore. He had even quit school. Nothing mattered. Tiago lived in a world that, without the color of his father's life, was muted and gray.

Oh, so much had changed since that terrible day!

If only Daniel hadn't died.

Once, Marcela would have helped Tiago with his computer. Once, she would have sat at his side asking about each piece. Once, Tiago wouldn't have minded her questions. There would have been no irritation bolting to the surface at her very presence. No urge to be left alone, locked away in his solitary hurt—solitary because he seemed to be the only one who couldn't adjust to his father's absence.

After her tears had dried four years ago on that fateful night, Marcela had announced that like Tiago, she no longer believed in God. Yet she often blamed their father's death on the very Godshe claimed to deny. In response to this, their mother doted on her, as though her love and devotion alone could wipe away the tragedy and her unbelief. And maybe it had worked. Marcela continued her college courses, went out with friends, and wore her bracelet. To Tiago's mind, his sister had become spoiled and selfish, betraying the memory of their father.

His mother, though hit very hard by her husband's death, had also gone on with her life. As a mother and a business woman, Tiago knew she'd had no other choice. She had to forge a life for him and Marcela. She had to pay the bills, put food on the table. "Besides," she'd said several times, "if the good Lord saw fit to have things happen this way, who am I to second-guess Him?" Tiago witnessed her pain dim over the years, as she came to some sort of uneasy peace. Unlike with his sister, he did not begrudge her the feeling.

Yet now Tiago alone stood vigil, permitting neither time nor love to heal the deep wound that festered in his broken soul.

# Chapter Eight
## Lisa's Dream

*T*he ringing of the phone brought Rae to consciousness. "Somebody get that," she called from her bed where she had been trying to take a nap after visiting her mother.

No answer. Apparently Lisa and her other roommates weren't around. "A girl should be able to sleep all day on her birthday," she groaned. Pushing herself from bed, she ran for the kitchen and the phone. "Hello?"

"Rae?"

"Yes, is that you, Lisa?" Rae glanced at the clock and saw that it was nearly one. She had been asleep for three hours.

"Oh, Rae, I've got to talk to you! I'm at work but I get off in five minutes. I just want to make sure you'll be there when I get home. You weren't there when I left this morning."

"I went to my Mom's. But I've been back for a while."

"You're not leaving again?"

"No, I'll be here. Are you okay?" Rae didn't like the anxiousness in Lisa's voice.

"I'm fine." But she began to sob quietly. "It's my parents, they're getting a divorce. My mom came by just now to say that she's on her way to see some lawyer friend. She didn't want me to go with her."

"Oh, I'm so sorry. Why don't I come pick you up?"

"Don't be ridiculous." Lisa sounded almost like her old self. She sniffed twice. "I'm upset but not incapacitated! I'll be there in about twenty minutes."

"See you then."

The minutes ticked by slowly, and Rae made her way outside to the top of the stairs to wait. *What's keeping her?* She'd waited for over forty minutes when suddenly Dave rounded the corner of the building at a run.

"Dave!" she called, surprised to see him.

"Come down here!" he called, motioning with his arm. "Hurry!"

"But I'm waiting for Lisa."

"She's been in a car accident! We need to get to the hospital. I'll explain on the way."

Rae locked her door and flew down the steps, barely registering that she hadn't combed her hair since her nap and her makeup consisted only of what she'd been wearing the night before.

As Dave drove to the Utah Valley Regional Medical Center, he explained. "No one was home at Lisa's, so they somehow got a hold of my parents as next of kin. I was on the way to the BYU library when Michelle called my cell. She and my parents are already on their way. I stopped for you because I knew you'd want to be there."

"I appreciate that." Rae's stomach clenched inside with the uncertainty. *Poor Lisa. She must have been more upset than I thought.*

When they arrived at the hospital emergency room, Lisa was being rushed into surgery. Her condition was critical. "Could we please give her a blessing?" Dave's father asked Dr. Thompson, the doctor on call.

He nodded. "That would be a great idea. And say a prayer for me while you're at it. I can use all the help I can get."

Gradually, more family and friends began to arrive, Rae's parents among them. Dave had located Lisa's mother, who appeared shortly, her fear showing clearly on her face as she paced, wringing her hands with worry. Lisa's father also arrived, but the two said little to each other. The tension between them was obvious as each scrupulously avoided the other's gaze.

The group prayed for Lisa, together and separately. They also began a fast. Over the next excruciating hours, Rae and the others took turns pacing the waiting room.

Five hours later, Dr. Thompson emerged from the surgery, looking very tired, yet strangely elated. Everyone crowded around him hopefully.

"Well?" Lisa's mother stared at him with pleading eyes.

"You're her mother?"

"Yes."

"Well, your daughter has extensive internal bleeding and is still in critical condition, but I think she's going to pull through."

"Critical condition?" Lisa's mother sagged, her body shaking and her face so pale that Rae worried she might faint.

"He said she was going to be okay," Rae murmured, putting an arm around the other woman to steady her. Rae herself felt weak and frightened, but no one else seemed able to throw off their shock to comfort Sister Peterson.

"Rae's right," Rae's mother said, coming to her side and embracing her. Rae smiled gratefully at her.

"It's all my fault," moaned Sister Peterson. "I shouldn't have told her about the divorce like I did."

Seeing her misery, Dr. Thompson seemed to come suddenly to some private decision. "Your daughter's going to be all right," he said. "I really feel that. And if I didn't, I wouldn't say it. Just give her a little time. You'll see."

Rae felt peace spread through her, and knew Lisa's mother felt it, too. Her color was slowly returning to normal. "Thank you, doctor," she murmured. "Thank you so much."

"But you said she's in critical condition," Lisa's father said harshly. "Doesn't that mean it's still very serious?"

Dr. Thompson nodded. "Yes, but I really feel that she'll be

okay. I can't tell you better than that. It' just a feeling that—"

"But medically speaking?" Lisa's father interrupted. Dr. Thompson looked uncomfortable.

"Oh, Sam, can't you just take his word?" Lisa's mother asked, tearfully. "Must you always question the way God works? Don't you know that He lives—that He has performed a miracle today for our daughter?" She reached out a tentative hand to touch her husband but he glared at her with anger and disbelief.

"Mr. Peterson, your daughter will be okay," Dr. Thompson intervened. There was a sudden silence that to Rae seemed unbearable. How could Brother Peterson deny what the three of them were so obviously feeling?

"When can we see her?" Rae asked quickly.

Dr. Thompson looked at her with distinct relief. "Oh, I'll let her parents go see her for a few moments now, though she won't know they're there. She'll be sleeping at least another few hours, maybe more. I only want immediate family to visit while she's in critical condition, but I'm predicting that status will change by tomorrow or the next day at the latest. The other friends and relatives are better off going home to wait. We'll notify the Petersons of any change in her condition."

"Thank you so much!" Sister Peterson said again, looking at the doctor with gratitude, ignoring her husband's dark stare.

"Come on," the doctor replied, motioning to her. "Let's go see Lisa."

\* \* \* \* \*

Early the next morning, Rae received a call from Sister Peterson. Lisa was awake and asking for her. Though she wasn't out of critical condition, the doctor thought it best to let Rae visit because of Lisa's insistence. Happily, Rae showered and dressed. It was only seven in the morning and she knew she'd have plenty of time to visit Lisa at the hospital before going to the multi-stake regional conference at the Marriott Center with Dave at ten.

She arrived at the hospital by seven-thirty and shortly found the small room where they had moved Lisa. The smell of medicine filled the air, and Rae wrinkled her nose slightly. Sister Peterson looked up from her chair next to Lisa's bed. "Hi, Rae," she said. "Lisa, look who's here." At her words Lisa opened her eyes and smiled at Rae.

"Hey, Lisa. How ya doing?" Rae bit her bottom lip to help steady her thoughts. Lisa's appearance was absolutely horrible. Her head, one leg, and one arm were covered in bandages. What could be seen of her face was badly bruised and swollen. Only the eyes were the same, except that they weren't dancing with mischief like they normally were.

"Rae," Lisa whispered, beckoning with her unbandaged hand.

"Look, I'll leave you two alone a little while," Lisa's mother said. "I'll go get something to eat."

"Here, Sister Peterson," Rae suddenly remembered the bag she had brought. "I thought you might need this."

"Thank you. You're so thoughtful." She looked through the bag briefly. "Granola bars, fruit, magazines, even a change of clothes. Just what I needed. I think I'll go find some place to clean up a bit."

"Take your time. I've got an hour or so before I have to leave for church. I'll stay until you get back." Rae pushed the chair closer to Lisa and sat down.

"Thank you." Lisa's mother turned to leave but said over her shoulder, "Now, Lisa, don't get excited. You know what the doctor said. You have to rest." She blew a kiss with her hand and slipped out the door.

"You really look awful," Rae said the moment she was left alone with Lisa, knowing that her friend would see through anything except the truth. "For the first time in our lives I can truly say that you look quite lousy."

"Well, according to you I should be able to find a husband better this way." Lisa's voice was very soft and weak, and Rae had to lean forward to hear her.

"Is that what you brought me here to tell me? You know, Lisa, you'll probably be taken off the critical list any moment now, and I would have come to see you then. What was so important that you had to upset everyone to see me now? Not that I'm not glad to see you. You really had me scared for a while there."

"I'm sorry." Lisa frowned. "It was all my fault. I shouldn't have been driving when I was so upset."

"No, actually it wasn't your fault. The man in the other car had been drinking. The witnesses say he drove into your lane."

"But, Rae, if I had been thinking better, I probably could have avoided him." She paused and grimaced a little in pain.

"What is it! Should I go get the doctor?"

"No, the pain comes and goes. They've got me as doped up as they can without putting me out."

"Then you should rest."

"Darn it! Don't you at least want to know why I wanted to see you?"

"Oh. I thought you just wanted to make sure that I didn't blame myself for not going to get you. I did feel bad, but I know it wasn't my fault."

"It isn't that. It's about the dream I had when I was unconscious. I have to tell you before I forget completely. It was about you and, well, someone else—someone with dark eyes. You loved him so much and he left, but he kept telling me to tell you how much he loved you and that—" She shook her head. "Oh, I don't remember how it was, but you can't marry Dave!"

Rae put her hand on Lisa's. "Sh," she said softly. "It's okay.

Don't worry, I'm not going to marry him. I know he's not the one for me—at least not right now."

"Oh, good," Lisa sighed. "I didn't want you to be unhappy because of me. I introduced you."

"Oh, Lisa. You're a nut! You can tell me all about this when you're better. When we're old we'll laugh about how crazy you acted, how you defied your doctor and mother just to tell me not to marry Dave—someone you set me up with in the first place! Ah, but speaking of doctors, what about that one of yours? I don't remember ever seeing a doctor that good-looking except on TV. He's young, too."

"He is?" Lisa blinked. "I hadn't noticed."

Rae wasn't sure if she was telling the truth. "Right," she said. "That'll be the day!"

# Chapter Nine
## Pre-Earth Life

The room was utterly quiet. After the woman at the desk had told them there was a problem with her upcoming birth, Rae and her friends had been ushered to a side room in the Birth Building where they were asked to wait on the plush couches and chairs for a counselor. Only Dave stayed behind at the desk for his departing interview with the Father. Tiago, of course, was still missing. Rae wonder where he could be.

They had only waited a few minutes when a man came in to see them. He had brown hair and tanned skin. His brown eyes reminded Rae of Tiago. "Rae?" he asked, looking at her. It wasn't really a question. He knew who she was.

"Yes?"

"I'm Zoram, one of the destination counselors. I'm sorry I wasn't out there to meet you when you came to the desk. I got held up a little."

"Is something wrong?" she asked.

"Not at all. But there has been a change in your destination. You're now called to go to Utah—to Orem, to be exact. You'll be the second child. You already have an older brother named Jon."

"Wait a minute." Rae arose from the soft chair. "Tiago was supposed to have an older brother named Jon." She looked anxiously at the man. "Where is Tiago? Please, tell me, what's going on?"

Zoram's face was kind and loving, and Rae felt somewhat comforted. "Well," he said, "I can't tell you exactly why things worked out the way they did, but I can tell you that Tiago asked to be sent down in your place . . ."

Zoram continued his explanation, but Rae didn't hear anymore. *In my place! That's why he acted so strangely*, she thought. *What have I done? Oh, Tiago, you can't risk your chance of salvation for me!* The rush of emotion made her gasp aloud.

"Excuse me?" Zoram asked.

"Where is he? I have to see him!"

His eyes widened. "But, I thought you understood. He left for earth. He's already been born."

The soft words hit Rae with force, and an impossibly large ache began in her heart. *He loves me so much*, she thought. *And now I'll never see him again. Not until it's too late for us.*

"Rae?" Lisa asked, coming to her side. "Are you okay?"

"I'll never find him," she whispered.

From her seat on the couch, Selena frowned. "There's as much chance now as there ever was of you two meeting. You need to have faith."

"Uh," Zoram said, lifting a hand, "there's something else. You've also been called to be foreordained to serve a mission on earth. Now, that doesn't guarantee you'll go on a mission once you're there, it only means that you've been called. On earth you'll have your agency."

"Could I go to Portugal, Brother Zoram?" Rae was suddenly more interested in what he was saying.

"That is entirely up to the Father. But there will shortly be a Sisters Mission Conference for all of the sister missionaries who are going to earth in the next little while. There you and the others will be foreordained to serve missions. You could try to put in a good word when you attend."

A light pierced the darkness in Rae's soul. "Oh, thank you! Thank you! I'll ask. I've got to find Tiago and bring him the gospel!"

"I'll help you!" Selena jumped up from her couch. "Since I'll hopefully serve a mission too, we'll find Tiago together." Rae reached over and grasped Selena's hand tightly in thanks.

"I guess now I know why Tiago wasn't foreordained to serve a mission," Lisa said. "I thought it strange that Dave was but he wasn't. I guess now we know why."

Rae had wondered at that herself. The lack of a mission call had worried Tiago, but, overwhelmed with her own fears, she hadn't paid much attention. She sighed, regretting her self-absorption. "I just wish I could have seen him before he went."

Lisa put her arm around Rae's shoulder. "Uh, I did see Tiago yesterday," she said close to Rae's ear. "He seemed awful worried but when I asked him what was wrong he wouldn't say. He just said that if you should ever need to hear it and he wasn't around to tell you, that I should remind you how much he—"

Her cheerful voice broke.

"How much he loves you. And I promised him that no matter where I was, even hovering on the brink of death itself, if you needed to hear it I would tell you immediately."

# Chapter Ten
## A Strange Sensation

The Marriott Center parking lot was full when Rae and Dave arrived half an hour before the meeting began. People were now using the stadium parking lot down the road and walking up to the Marriott Center. Inside, the lower seats were nearly all filled. They quickly found seats and began the game of trying to find others they knew. Since it was an eleven-stake conference, there were many people they had never seen before.

The last time Rae had been to the Marriott Center was for a BYU basketball game. Then, everyone had been dressed casually and the spirit was one of competition rather than reverence. But just as she had been at that game, Rae found herself once more fascinated by watching the antics of the people around her. One pretty young woman had removed her tall high heels so as not to lose her balance while going down the steep steps. The girl didn't seem to care about how dirty her stockings were getting or how incongruous she looked in no shoes and her Sunday best. Another girl, five rows in front of them, was with friends, but instead of sitting in her seat, she was turned around standing in front of them, occasionally looking at the people above her as if searching anxiously for a another friend. Many people near Rae and Dave were watching the girl, and she appeared to enjoy the attention.

Around her, Rae could hear bits of conversations—people remembering when there were fewer stakes, someone asking about how so-and-so was doing on his mission, mothers from the family wards telling their young sons to tuck in their shirts, babies and small children crying. The many different movements and sounds made by the growing crowd reminded Rae of the ripples and waves of the ocean. She realized that she felt comfortable here among her brothers and sisters in the gospel. They were one big happy family.

"Here come the General Authorities," Dave said.

Rae looked down at the stage and wondered how he could tell that the little people entering below were the General Authorities. The figures sat down, and the opening song began. People were still filing in and taking their seats.

"That's why we have an opening song," Dave said, motioning to the late comers. "So everyone has a chance to get seated."

But people were still coming in when a man stood up to offer the prayer. When he started to speak, the people on the stairs stopped moving and bowed their heads. A hush fell over the cavernous room.

The conference was soon in full swing. Rae noticed that the people around her would often nod in agreement with something said or have the expression on their faces as if they suddenly understood something important, something that they hadn't really been sure about before. She wished that could happen to her. But while she felt the compassion and love in the leaders' voices and was grateful for what was said, she didn't feel much of it was directed at her. Her mind began to wander as she thought about Lisa and what had happened in the hospital.

*Someone with dark eyes*, she mused. She vaguely remembered a pair of dark eyes in her own dreams. She shook her head to erase the memory. *You're looking for something that doesn't exist*, she told herself firmly. *And Lisa was simply dreaming—and in a drugged state at that. It means nothing.*

Rae tried to refocus on the conference with little success. *Oh please, Father,* she prayed silently. *Help me to listen and to be attuned to Thy will.* At once her mind cleared, and she was able to pay attention to the speaker.

"We need many more missionaries," the General Authority was saying. "You young parents here today must raise up your children to plan for a mission. Help them to understand what it is to be worthy. Talk about missionary work, pray for the missionaries at home and abroad, and help your children start saving money towards their missions today.

"The call for missionaries isn't only for our worthy young men. We also need you faithful sisters who are not yet married or planning to be married. Sisters play a vital part in missionary work. Usually in the eighteen months they are out in the mission field they baptize more than the young elders who serve for the whole two years. This testifies to the wonderful and sweet spirit that our young women have. We should all be proud of their work.

"Older couples are also encouraged to . . ."

Rae felt a strange sensation overcome her. *A mission? A vital part in missionary work? Sisters who do not plan on getting married? Could that mean me?* These thoughts rushed through her mind again and again as if on a continuous reel.

"There are many more people who are waiting to hear the gospel," the man continued. "These are our brothers and sisters whom we knew in the pre-existence. They need our help. Please, look inside yourselves today and see if you could possibly accept a call to find our choice brothers and sisters. It is my testimony that we . . ."

"What's wrong, Rae?" Dave had his arm around her and was whispering in her ear.

"Huh, what?" She didn't take her eyes off the speaker.

"You look . . . well, kind of scared. Is everything okay?"

"Yeah." Rae glanced over at him and smiled weakly.

"Something he said just hit me kind of hard. I'll tell you about it afterwards, okay?"

"Sure, Rae, Love."

\* \* \* \* \*

"I think I'm going on a mission," Rae blurted when they were sitting in his car outside her apartment building.

Dave stared at her, but there was no real surprise in his eyes. "I was afraid you'd say that. Your face at the conference—well, you looked like you had seen a ghost or something."

Rae gulped and tried to explain. "It was really strange. When he talked about our brothers and sisters in the pre-existence, I felt something I've never felt before—like a fear and an urgency." Rae paused and gazed down at her lap trying to recall her exact feelings. Then she looked up again at Dave. "It was so weird, Dave. It wasn't that I was afraid of going—it was more like I was afraid of what would happen if I didn't go. Oh, I can't explain exactly what it was!"

"What about us?" Dave asked quietly.

"Oh, Dave, I'm sorry." Rae knew she had to be completely honest with him. "I really thought that . . . you know . . . that you were the one for me. That we'd end up getting married and live happily ever after. But—" She paused and shook her head. "The way I feel, it wouldn't be fair to either of us."

There was silence in the car as Dave looked away from Rae and out of the window, his jaw clenched. Rae felt terrible.

After a while, Dave turned and reached out to touch her face briefly with his hand. "Are you sure?"

When she nodded, he sighed. His eyes grew teary, but in them Rae could see the compassion and understanding that had attracted her to him in the first place.

"I can't say that I'm not hurt, even a little angry at you," he said. "But I also can't say that I'm not prepared. I think I knew it the minute that you started called me David like my mother. That's why I made such a big thing out of it."

Rae opened her mouth to speak, but he put a warm finger on her lips.

"And that's not all. This morning before I came to get you, I stopped first at the hospital and snuck in to see Lisa. She was raving about some dream she'd had and about how you couldn't marry me. I thought she'd lost it, but who knows?" His words were mild, denying the pain that was clearly etched on his face.

Tenderness filled Rae's heart. She could hardly believe how good he was being about her decision. "Well, we've had a great time, haven't we, Dave?" She somehow managed to squeeze the words past the lump in her throat.

"The best, Rae, Love."

They both smiled.

Dave walked her up to her apartment door and said goodbye. Rae watched from the balcony as he went down the stairs and out of sight, feeling both sad and relieved. She went in to her bedroom to ask for confirmation of her feelings.

As she knelt and prayed aloud about her decision to serve a mission, a tingling sensation started at her toes and spread slowly up her body, undeniably confirming her decision to go on a mission.

"I never expected that I would go," she said to herself, amazed at the strength of her answer. Before this day, her answers had been quiet assurances. Perhaps her Father knew she needed something more this time. She arose and stood before the mirror on her dresser. "Well, mission life, here I come!"

Needing to tell someone, she left her apartment and drove to her parents' house, knowing they would just be arriving home from Church themselves.

The whole family was home by the time Rae arrived. The kitchen was overflowing with activity as everyone helped make the customary Sunday lunch. Unlike many families who brought out their best roasts or casseroles, the Love family had a peculiar tradition. They always ate tuna fish sandwiches with pickles and onions, canned corn, canned olives, freshly sliced oranges, apples, or other fruit, and juice—all served on paper plates for easy clean up. Since they ate lunch late, the only dinner they would have was a snack of fruit or vegetables as they played games together before bed.

"Hey, Rae!" Chad ran to the door when she entered.

Her mother came to hug her, while her father looked up from the plate of fruit he was slicing and winked. Bria smiled, showing a mouth full of braces, and even Taylor looked up from the cans he was opening to nod.

"Hi." Rae returned her mother's hug. "Room for one more?"

"Of course." Her mother gave her a tight squeeze before going to the cupboard for another can of tuna.

Rae helped prepare lunch by mixing up grape juice from frozen concentrate. It was only when all the family was seated at the table and the prayer on the food had been offered that she told them of her decision. "I wanted to come and tell you all something kind of important." The room fell silent as everyone looked at her expectantly. Rae wondered if they were hoping she was going to announce an engagement. "Well," she began again, "I'm going on a mission!" There was a short surprised silence before her siblings started talking all at once.

"Where are you going?" asked Chad.

"What about Dave?" Bria wanted to know. At fourteen, boys were already important in her mind.

Taylor gulped the rest of his juice. "When did you decide to do that?"

Only her parents hadn't said a word. Rae looked at them. "Well, what do you think?" She bit her lower lip as she waited for their reply. Were they disappointed? Their support meant everything to her.

Her father smiled. "Well, that's wonderful!"

"Yes, it is," her mother added with tears in her eyes.

"Our first missionary." Her father was also looking a little misty-eyed, and Rae felt a moment of gratitude that she could make them happy. Her older brother, Jon, hadn't gone on a mission, but after some time of rebelliousness had married early. Rae knew his decision had been tough on her parents. "We're very proud that you want to serve a mission," her father continued. "I think you'll be a wonderful missionary."

"I'll certainly try." Rae felt the Spirit strongly in the room and was near tears herself. "I was a little worried that I might be letting you down by not getting married to Dave . . . or Andrew."

Her parents shook their heads. "We want what's best for you," Holly said.

"But what about Dave?" Bria asked again, poking out her bottom lip in a pout. "What's *he* going to do?"

Her question brought an ache to Rae's stomach. "The same thing he did before he met me, Bria. He knows—we talked about it before I came over here."

"Where will you be going?" Chad had repeated the question several times now, and his high, thin voice showed his frustration at the lack of a reply.

"She just decided today, silly," Taylor explained. "She has to talk to the bishop, fill out her papers, talk to the stake president, and then wait for a call from the prophet."

"Wow. All that?" Chad looked amazed. "Will it take long then? I'd like to know so I can go the second I turn nineteen."

"I hope it doesn't take long," Rae picked up a black olive from her plate and bit into it. "Now I've made this decision, I'm kind of anxious to go."

"Well I'm sure your bishop could get you the papers today if you call him," her mother said. "And schedule an appointment for your interview." A thoughtful look stole over her face. "There's a lot to get ready. We'll have to make an appointment with the doctor and the dentist. And we'll need to buy some . . ."

Rae's thoughts raced through her mind so loudly that it was hard to pay attention to her mother's list. *I'm actually going to do it*, she thought. *Maybe I really can do some good and bring the gospel to some of my brothers and sisters that I knew in the pre-existence.* A remnant of the feeling she had while praying in her apartment rippled through her body.

"You know," she said. "I suddenly don't feel so hungry after all." She put her half-eaten sandwich down on the paper plate and stood up. "I think I'll go back to my place and make that phone call right now."

She bid farewell to her family. In her car on the way back to her apartment, she thought, *Here I come brothers and sisters! I'm going to fulfill my promises—if I made any. I hope you're ready for me.*

Another thought came quickly after. *I wonder where they'll send me?*

# Chapter Eleven
## The Call

*L*isa stared up at Rae from the hospital bed. "You're going to do *what?*"

It had been a week since her accident and some of the bandages had been removed from her face and head. She still looked far from her normal self but it was clear, at least from her tone, that she was well on her way to being mended.

"I already did it." Rae sat down on the chair next to Lisa's bed. "Last Sunday after the conference I went to see the bishop and he was so excited about my decision that he came over to our apartment and gave me the papers right then. Earlier this week I got a check-up and did all the other things I was supposed to do, and Wednesday I had my interview with the bishop. Tomorrow I'm going to see the stake president, and Monday he'll send in the papers. My parents have agreed to help me pay for it."

"Getting it done quick so you don't change your mind, eh?" Lisa scowled. "What about school? And what am I supposed to do while you're gone? Who's going to cheer me up? Why didn't you tell me earlier?"

Rae smiled, though Lisa's questions caused a jumble of nervousness in her stomach. "My last year of school will still be waiting for me when I get back. And I didn't tell you sooner because I didn't want you to get all riled up until you were a little stronger. Doctor Thompson advised us to keep things calm."

At the mention of her doctor's name, Lisa's face immediately softened into a beautiful smile. "He did, did he?"

"Yes, he did." Rae sat back in the chair and propped her sandaled foot up on Lisa's bed. "And I don't think you have to worry about who's going to take care of you while I'm gone. Aren't you lucky your own doctor retired last year and Dr. Thompson just happened to be willing to continue your care? I can see it even if you can't. You've got a thing for Dr. Thompson, and what's more the feeling's mutual."

"Oh, really? You think so?" Lisa blushed a bright red. That surprised Rae. In all the many years she had known Lisa, she had never seen her blush. She was about to mention it when footsteps behind her made her turn.

"And how's my favorite patient today?" said Dr. Thompson, who was coming through the door.

Lisa's bruised face lit up. "I'm doing great. Thank you very much. Now when do I get out of here?"

He smiled, cocking his blonde head and looking down at Lisa with amusement in his brown eyes. "That's what I'm coming to tell you. I'm going to sign your release papers today. But only if you promise to go to your mother's instead of your apartment. You need to stay down for at least another week and then take things gradually until you're fully recovered. Of course, I'll need to see you every week for a while and you have to call me if you have any strange symptoms at all. Promise?" He said this last a little anxiously, as if it were really important to him.

Lisa glanced quickly at Rae as if gathering courage and then back to Dr. Thompson. On her face was the mischievous, lopsided grin Rae knew so well.

"Well, Doctor," Lisa drawled in a half-teasing, half-serious voice. "Do you make house calls?" He looked briefly taken aback, but then a smile stole over his face.

"You know, Lisa," he said gravely. "Maybe I could arrange

that." There was an awkward silence while both Lisa and Dr. Thompson looked at each other obviously wondering whether or not the other was serious.

"Hey, Dr. Thompson." Rae looked in her purse and pulled out her planner. "Have you seen these pictures of Lisa before the accident? These pictures were taken the day before the accident—at my birthday party. That's Lisa there." She pointed to the first one. "You can recognize her just barely, I think."

"You make it sound as if I'm never going to be the same again," Lisa growled.

Rae laughed. "I'm teasing you, my dear. I'm teasing you. I'm sure you'll be your normal gorgeous self in no time, right Dr. Thompson?"

He nodded, his eyes lingering on the picture for a while before sliding back to his patient. "Yes, I can tell from these photos that this is definitely the same girl," he said. "Barely."

"Don't you have some papers to sign or something?" Lisa's voice was grouchy but her expression was playful.

"Yes, ma'am, right away." He tossed Rae the pictures and gave Lisa a salute. "I'll be back in a few." He turned almost reluctantly toward the door.

"Uh, Doctor?" Rae asked. "Do you have a first name? I have a feeling that I am going to be using it—a lot."

"Mark," he said, flashing her a warm smile. "And I think you will." With that he left the room.

\* \* \* \* \*

For the next few weeks Rae kept busy at work and each day passed quickly. When she wasn't working at Mervyn's, she was packing her things to take to her parents and finishing up other loose ends. She also visited Lisa a great deal, pleased that she was recovering quickly. Rae didn't see Dave at all alone and she missed him, but she saw both him and Andrew often when she went to Lisa's mother's house to visit Lisa. Once together, they strictly avoided talking about anything serious. It was almost like old times, before things had become so complicated, except that now Mark Thompson had become part of their circle.

When Saturday morning dawned—a beautiful sun-filled day in late May—she had almost given up hope of receiving her mission call for the week. But once more, she passed up eating cereal with her two roommates in the kitchen, and waited expectantly on the bench near the communal mail boxes instead.

"Hi," Rae greeted the gray-haired postman as he arrived, wearing sturdy shoes and blue uniform shorts.

"You waiting for a special letter?" he asked.

Rae laughed. "You know I am. I've been out here waiting the past two days."

"Well, I think it's here." He handed her an envelope.

Rae stared at the official Church logo. "It's finally here!" she whispered.

The postman gave a knowing smile. "Let me know, huh?"

"Thank you. I will." As he turned and began putting mail in the small metal boxes, she wandered away, fingering the thick envelope.

*My life for the next eighteen months is in this letter*, she thought. Slowly, she returned to her building, but instead of climbing the stairs, she sat down on them. She'd rather retreat to the privacy of her room to open the letter, but she knew she'd never get past her roommates without them noticing that she'd been out to get the mail.

A woman came from one of the bottom apartments. She smiled and nodded at Rae as she passed. Rae smiled back.

When the woman was gone, she broke the seal and pulled out the letter, her hands trembling. First, her eyes rushed down the page, lingering on the signature of the president of the

Church—the prophet. Then she began reading again at the top.

*The Portugal Lisbon South Mission*, Rae read. *I'm going to Portugal—a foreign country! What will it be like?* Excitement welled up in her chest. *Oh, thank you so much, Father*, she prayed silently. *Thank you for trusting me with this. I promise to do my best.* A feeling of calm and peace came over her. Fingering the keys in her pockets, she went toward her car.

The drive to Orem was torturously long. In the driveway of her parents' house sat both their cars and Taylor's. Everyone was home.

Rae burst into the kitchen door. "It's here! It's here! Gather around! I know where I'm going! Hurry!" There was a babble of excited voices as the family gathered around Rae.

"Wait for me!" yelled her father from somewhere upstairs. "I'm coming right this minute!"

"Oh, I'm so nervous," Chad said. "Tell me, tell me, Rae! Dad, hurry!" Rae laughed, but waited with her lips pressed together until her dad had joined them.

"Well, I've been called to the Portugal Lisbon South Mission! Can you believe it? I'm going to Europe! I go into the Missionary Training Center in one month."

"Portugal, where's that?" Bria asked.

Rae's smile faltered. "Well, actually, I'm not sure. I thought it was by Spain, though."

"No, I think it's South America," Taylor said.

"Well, let's all go look in the encyclopedia," suggested their father.

Everyone rushed into the family room. Rich found Portugal in the book and pointed the country out on the map. "Rae's right. It's that small country next to Spain, the furthermost western country in Europe." He read aloud details of the country, but Rae's mind wandered as she reread her letter from the prophet.

Her mother put her arms around Rae. "I can't believe it," she said.

"I know," whispered Rae. "It seems so unreal. But I'm ready."

"Of course you are." Her mother smiled. "So, you still moving home today?"

Rae nodded. She wanted to save as much money as possible before she left for her mission. "Yeah, I'll need help with the rest of my things."

"I'll send Dad and Taylor with you after lunch."

"Thanks." They hugged again.

Later, as she and her mother began making lunch for the family, Rae was excited to see a letter from her grandmother, her mother's mom, lying atop a stack of bills and letters on the counter. Grandma Jill was her only living grandmother and up until a few years ago had lived in Utah near them. But after Grandpa had died, Grandma Jill had packed up house to go and live near her son in Arizona where there wasn't any snow. Rae's family now eagerly awaited her letters, phone calls, and visits.

"A letter from Grandma! Can I read it?"

Her mother looked up from the biscuits she was cutting. "Sure."

The letter was full of news from Rae's Aunt and Uncle and their nine children, and it also recounted the adventures of the people in Grandma's ward. She particularly mentioned a young widow whom she visit-taught and who had recently been diagnosed with leukemia. The ward and community had all pulled together to help the young mother raise money for a bone marrow transplant. It was obvious that Grandmother was deeply involved in organizing the different fundraisers and had become emotional and physically drained. At the end of the letter, Grandma expressed her love and how anxious she was to see them all at Christmas.

Rae set aside the letter. "Wow," she said. "Grandma's so busy. I feel tired just reading her letter. And I sure feel bad for that mother. Poor lady."

Her mother nodded. "Why don't we go call Grandma and tell her some good news for a change?"

"Mom, do you think we could buy her a plane ticket to come and see me off to the MTC? She sounds like she needs a break."

Her mother paused, phone in hand. "What a wonderful idea. I've been worried about her overdoing things. This'll be the perfect excuse for a mini-vacation for her."

Rae slipped her mother's biscuits into the baking pan, feeling content. She wanted more than anything to see her grandmother before she left. After all, she wouldn't be home for Christmas. She would be working for the Lord.

\* \* \* \* \*

The week after she received her mission call, Rae sat with her family watching a video. Even her older brother, Jon, his wife, Lenna, and their kids were there. Usually Rae spent Friday nights with her friends, but tonight going out didn't hold much interest.

Silently, Rae left the family and went to the room that she had grown up in and that was now hers again—if temporarily. She settled in her big chair, pulling her feet comfortably under her. Her computer's blank screen stared at her invitingly, but she didn't turn it on. Through the open curtain the west sky glowed a deep red as the last rays of the sun faded away. She became absorbed in the masterpiece, as temporary as it was beautiful. Somehow, it reminded her of her family and how much she would miss them.

There was a knock at the door and Rae reached up quickly to wipe away the single tear that had fallen onto her cheek.

"Come in," she called, glancing at the mirror on the wall to make sure she didn't look as though she'd been crying.

"It's me, honey." Her dad peered around the door, as if afraid to intrude.

"Come in. I was just watching the sky and thinking how much I'm going to miss you all."

"Of course, you'll miss us—when you're not too busy. The first few months will be the most difficult." Her father sat down on the edge of her bed and Rae rotated her chair to face him.

"I really appreciate that you and Mom can pay for most of my mission," she said. "I feel kind of guilty that I haven't saved enough for it. I guess I never dreamed I would be going on a mission. I thought I was doing great having money saved for my next semester of school."

"We're glad to do it. We've been saving since we were first married to be able to help our children pay for missions." Her father paused and he looked down at the tan carpet. "When Jon didn't go, it just about broke your mother's heart—because of the situation with him and Lenna having to get married so quickly. After that we didn't think that we would need the money until Taylor went. But we're pleased it's there for you. We feel privileged to support you on a mission. That's what we've consecrated that money for."

"I'm glad."

"There something else." Her father leaned toward her. "I want you to know that I have a testimony of the Church. I *know* it's true! And I know it's not going to be easy serving a mission, but you will learn so much—knowledge that will help you throughout your entire life. It'll be well worth the sacrifice of leaving us for a little while. I promise you."

"Thanks, Dad, I think I needed to hear that." Rae went to hug her father. "I love you."

"I love you too, honey. And I'm so proud of you."

"I'm glad." Rae returned to her chair and watched her father leave the room. She faced her chair to the window again but the reddish lights in the sky had given way to darkness. Another knock sounded at her door.

"Come in," she called out, expecting to see her father's face. She was surprised when Jon entered.

"*Olá*, Rae," he said with a big smile. *Olá*—hello—was the only Portuguese word either of them knew.

Rae grinned back. "Hi, Jon. What's up? Is my presence so notably missed?"

"Uh, well," Jon shifted his feet nervously. "I've been waiting to talk to you alone since you got your mission call." He walked across the room and sat on the bed, choosing the same place her father had sat a few moments before. "We used to be so close, but we never get to talk anymore."

Rae smiled wistfully. "We're grown up now, Jon. We don't have time to ride bikes or go frog-hunting anymore. Besides, those kids keep you and Lenna busy."

"Yeah, I guess they do." He sighed. "You know, sometimes I miss the good old days. I never knew it was so much work to grow up."

"Yeah," Rae agreed. "Me, either." She didn't say more, waiting to hear the real reason her brother had sought her out.

Jon looked down at the carpet for a moment and then finally into Rae's face. "I just wanted to tell you how proud I am that you're going on a mission." He bit his lower lip and blinked his eyes quickly. "You know, people are always asking me where I went on my mission, and I have to tell them that I didn't go. It really hurts—especially when I know I could have been a good missionary. But what's even worse is when I look at my little boys and feel so hopeful for them and their lives, and I know how badly I must have hurt Mom and Dad by the choices I made. I love my children so much, and I guess that's how Mom and Dad felt about me. I feel I let them down." Jon's voice broke and a few tears escaped from the corners of his eyes. He wiped them away with the back of his hand.

Rae opened her mouth to speak, but he rushed on. "I didn't know that it would matter so much to me later," he said. "You don't think about those things when you're young. Two years seemed so long back then. And now I can't go back and change things. I'm just doing my darndest to live the best life I can from here on out. I want to give my children a good example."

"You are, Jon!" Rae went over to the bed and sat by her brother, reaching to place her hand over his. "You've turned everything around. You've been sealed in the temple, you're active in the Church. I'm very proud that you're my brother."

"That means a lot to me." He smiled at her. "And guess what? Now when people ask me where I served my mission, I tell them my sister's going to Portugal. Somehow, it makes up for me not going, you know?"

"I'm glad, Jon. And believe me, I'll do my best to testify for both of us."

That night Rae dreamed again of a pair of dark eyes that dripped tears void of hope. She awoke in the night and fell to her knees. "Dear Father," she whispered. "Please help me to find this person. Please."

# Chapter Twelve
## Preparing to Go

$S$ ummer was beautiful. Though often the weather was hot and sweltering, Rae barely noticed. The days went by quickly, filled with mission preparations and work. More often than not, her thoughts drifted to her mission and what kind of service she would give to the Lord, what kind of trials she would face.

Shortly after receiving her call, Rae went through the temple to receive her own endowments. She was glad to be worthy, if a little apprehensive, to enter the Provo Temple. All her family who could attend were there—Mom, Dad, Jon and Lenna, as well as many of her friends and ward members. Inside that sacred building, her mind was filled with knowledge and her heart filled with the Spirit of the Lord. The experience was different and more wonderful than she had expected. Her testimony was strengthened as she understood completely that the temple was indeed the House of the Lord. Rae left the temple spiritually full. She vowed to return often to worship. There was no place on earth quite like the temple.

Rae rarely saw any of her friends during the week, but often on Friday evenings, the night her parents usually went out together, the friends gathered at Rae's house to watch videos and play games. The group now consisted of Lisa, Mark, Andrew, Dave, Michelle, and little Hope, though often there others were included. Rae found Mark a great addition to the group. Not only was he full of new ideas, but he was also very devoted to Lisa, who was almost as well as she had been before the accident. The scars on her body were still there—as they would always be—but the mental scars had faded with the joy of being in love.

The weekend before Rae went into the MTC, the group of friends were once more gathered at Rae's. It was kind of an unofficial going away party as Rae had thought it best to only have her family see her off at the MTC.

"Gather 'round, gather 'round," Lisa called loudly when they had all arrived. "I want to say something." Rae and the others stopped what they were doing and looked at her curiously.

"First of all, I want you to know that because of my miraculous recovery, my father has changed his ways. He's different now." Lisa's smile covered her whole face. "Mark's been a big help, of course. But the great thing is that my dad's going to counseling and he and my mother are going to give their marriage another try! It may not work, but at least they're trying."

Lisa normally used her hands expressively as she talked, but today she kept her left hand hidden deep within the pocket of her jeans. Rae barely had time to wonder at the reason when Lisa went on. "But that's not all." She pulled her hand from the pocket and held it up to reveal a diamond ring. Her face glowed. "Mark and I are getting married!"

Everyone studied Mark for a brief second as they digested the information, then the room exploded into a burst of congratulations and approval. "When, when?" several voices clamored.

"Well, we know it's rather quick," Mark said, "but we've both been searching a long time, especially me, and we know what we want." Everyone nodded, knowing that he was eight years older than Lisa.

"So we thought we'd have the wedding in about six weeks, before Rae leaves the MTC for Portugal." Lisa looked at her best friend with pleading eyes. "They will let you come to the wedding, won't they?"

"I think they'd let me come to the temple ceremony—if you have it on my preparation day—but I doubt I could go to the reception." Rae put her arm around Lisa. "But I am so happy for you both." She whispered in her ear, "Now I won't have to worry about who's going to take care of you, will I?"

Though very happy for Lisa, Rae felt a momentary twinge of envy. Lisa was getting what Rae had been searching for—what she once thought she had found with Dave. She wondered if she would ever find someone who would cause her to have the look in her eyes that Lisa had when she looked at Mark. Rae glanced at Dave and saw that he was watching her carefully, silently. When he caught her gaze, he smiled—that marvelous, infectious smile that made him so adorable. Her heart lurched.

He came to stand close to her. "Having seconds thoughts?"

"And thirds and fourths and fifths," she agreed. "But I'm going on that mission next Tuesday, Dave. I do know it's what I'm supposed to do."

"I know," he said quietly. "And you're going to be a wonderful missionary." They stood together without speaking for a long while, looking around at the others—Mark and Lisa on the sofa watching the TV and Andrew and Michelle playing blocks with Hope and Chad on the floor.

"I'll probably still be here when you get back," Dave said, his voice husky.

"I'm not holding you to that." Rae met his eyes again. "I don't want you to miss out because of me." For a moment she had the strongest urge to throw herself in his arms.

"But we'll keep in touch?"

"Of course, Dave."

"Look, I want to give you this," Dave pulled off the silver CTR ring he wore on the small finger of his right hand.

"No, Dave, I—"

"It's nothing to do with our relationship. I mean, it's not like a promise ring or anything, and I don't even want it back someday when you get home. You could maybe pass it on to another missionary or something. You see, my sister gave this ring to me before I left on my mission. She said it was so I would remember, no matter how down and discouraged I got, that she loved me and she was praying for me. It helped me countless times on my mission." Dave turned the ring over and over in his fingers. "We talked it over last night and we want you to wear this on your mission so you will always know we're praying for you and believe in you. Will you do that for us?"

Rae nodded silently. She let Dave push the ring into her palm, and she slipped it onto the second finger of her right hand. The color contrasted with the gold bracelet Andrew had given to her, but it gave her a warm feeling to wear them together. And the ring, at least, she would feel comfortable taking to Portugal with her. "Thanks," she said. "I'll probably need it. I don't know what I'd do without friends like you."

After Rae's friends had gone home, Grandma Jill called to say that she wouldn't be flying in the next day as planned. The young mother in her ward had been hospitalized and she didn't feel she could leave her or her small children.

"I'm sorry, Rae," she said. "I feel terrible. But this woman doesn't have anyone who can help her every day. Everyone else is so busy with their own families—and she hasn't any family of her own, besides the children. You understand, don't you? I will try to be there at the airport for you."

"That's okay, Grandma. I'm disappointed, of course, but I do understand." Rae felt saddened by her grandmother's decision, but she trusted that her grandmother would do her best to see her before she left for Portugal.

All too soon Rae's last few days were over and she was on her way to the MTC. She felt as if time were stuck in fast forward, leaving her dizzy and disoriented. Once at the MTC, she hugged her family for the last time. There were tears in everyone's eyes, but no one let them fall.

Rae bit back her own tears as she walked away.

\* \* \* \* \*

The two months Rae spent in the MTC were different from anything she had ever experienced. It was wonderful to be in the company of young people who all shared the same strong desire to serve the Lord. She felt immersed in the gospel as she had never been before. Morning, noon, and night, she studied the gospel or her Portuguese verbs.

Her companion, Sister Rowan Sharp, was an energetic young woman and Rae loved her immediately. They shared many fun times together, and eagerly learned all their teachers offered them. The teachers obviously loved Portugal and her people, and Rae's excitement about the country grew daily.

The week before she left for Portugal, Lisa was married in the Provo Temple. Rae and her companion were allowed to attend the ceremony, and Rae was grateful for the opportunity to see her parents and friends. To her joy and surprise, Grandma Jill was also there and Rae hugged her with enthusiasm. Rae was also happy to see that while Lisa's father wasn't at the wedding ceremony inside the temple, he waited for Lisa and her mother in the lobby.

During the wedding ceremony, Rae felt a longing in her heart that she hadn't felt since she entered into the MTC. As she stood there, she felt she could almost hear a voice that whispered, "I believe in you. I believe in us. We will make it." Rae shook her head quickly and looked around to see who was talking, but everyone was intent on the ceremony, even Dave who sat in the row of seats behind her.

Afterwards, Rae, still slightly disturbed by her experience, went to congratulate Mark and to hug Lisa. She knew this would be the last time she would see her friend until after her mission. "Good luck, Lisa," she whispered. "You finally have what you've been searching for."

"It's worth every minute of the time it took to find him," Lisa whispered back. "And every lousy date I ever had. Don't ever forget that, Rae. Someone's out there for you, too."

"Well, I can hardly think about that right now. I'm a missionary now. Besides, I've spent the last month praying *not* to meet Mr. Right until I go on my mission." This was because she knew a few cases where girls had met the "perfect guy" a few weeks before going into the MTC and were miserable about leaving them.

"That's not what I meant, Rae, and you know it! I meant in the Lord's due time, like you always told me."

"I know." Rae hugged her friend again. "Be happy. And don't forget to write me."

"I will, I promise. Now let's get outside so the photographer can take some pictures of us together before you have to get back to the MTC."

Later, as she prepared to walk back to the MTC, everyone gathered around to say goodbye.

"Take care Rae, Love," Dave said. "You are going to be great. We're rooting for you."

"I know." Rae held up her right hand to show the CTR ring. "Thanks, Dave." She wished she could hug him goodbye, but shook his hand warmly instead.

"Yeah," Andrew added. "Just work hard and be obedient and the Lord will do the rest."

"There's one very important piece of advice I want you to remember, Rae." Her father put his arm around her and held her close. "Never under estimate the power of a pure testimony. I remember when I was in the mission field and teaching a man in a hospital bed. As a veteran missionary, I used every scripture and logical thing I could think of to prove to him that what I was saying was true, but the man wouldn't believe. When I had given up hope, my companion, a greeny missionary who didn't even know the discussions, bore his testimony to the man and the Spirit touched him. He was baptized shortly after and is now a bishop in his ward. Remember, it is the Spirit that truly converts people, not the missionaries."

"Thanks, Dad." Rae felt his words etch themselves into her memory and knew that somehow they were probably the most important words her father had ever said to her.

"Remember to take care of yourself," her mother hugged her from the other side.

"And write us," Grandma Jill added, pushing aside the others for her turn at a hug.

"I will." Rae turned to her brothers and sister to hug and kiss them for the last time. "I love you all so much," she said. "Don't grow up too much while I'm gone." Her nephew, Shane, pulled on her leg.

"I want to go, too, Aunt Rae. Can I, please?"

"Not this time, Shane. Someday. Give me a kiss goodbye." The little boy obliged, but looked sad. With a little smile she waved goodbye to the group and began to walk down the sidewalk with her companion. She felt brave and thought she could handle leaving her family behind without tears. Then she heard a little voice behind her and her heart jerked.

"Wait for me, Aunt Rae. I want to go to Portugal too. Don't leave me!" Rae turned to see Shane running after her. Jon hurried after his little son, who burst into tears when his daddy caught him up in his arms. Jon waved and Rae nodded, turning her face quickly as the tears gathered in her eyes and fell rapidly down her face. She loved them all so much! What on earth was she doing? Why *was* she going on a mission anyway?

# Part Three

# Chapter Thirteen
## Mission Life

Rae had been in Portugal five months. She was long used to the routine and deeply immersed in the work. She still missed her family—Christmas had been particularly rough—but the feeling was not as strong as when she had first arrived in the mission field. She had grown to love her native companion, Sister Almeida, and the people she worked with meant more to her than she had ever thought possible.

She adored being in Portugal. It was a beautiful country, full of rich culture, and a friendly, Christian people. She and her companion worked hard and were blessed weekly by baptisms. The Spirit of God had been preparing the Portuguese people and many were searching for the gospel.

On preparations days, Rae and her companion went to visit castles, ruins, and monuments. Everything had been so strange at first, but now Rae had grown accustomed to the sights and felt at home. The cobblestone sidewalks and narrow streets of her area were now more familiar to her than her own neighborhood in Provo. She had walked nearly every foot of Almada and knew it well.

She got along well with Sister Almeida, a hard-working girl from Braga, a northern city in Portugal. Sister Almeida had been Rae's trainer, friend, mother, sister, and confidante, all rolled into one. Over the months they had become attuned to each other, and their discussions flowed well. The month before they had been the top baptizing companionship in the whole mission.

Rae knew it couldn't last forever—not in the mission field where everything changed without notice. And one Sunday night they got a call from the Mission President himself.

"It's for you," Sister Almeida said in Portuguese, handing her the phone. "It's the President."

"Thanks." Rae took the phone. "Hello?"

"Sister Love," the President's voice was warm. "I'm calling because I want to know if you feel prepared to train a new missionary who is coming in from the States this week. I feel impressed to put her in your area with you, even though you've only been in the country five months."

"Uh," Rae gulped audibly. "I don't know," she said honestly. "I didn't think this would happen for a few more months." Though not unheard of, it wasn't common for an American to train a fellow American after so short a time in the country.

"That's why I'm calling you personally, though you will be getting the official call in the mail tomorrow." The President paused as if giving her a chance to absorb his words. "I want you to know that I feel you are the person to train this new missionary."

"Then I can do it," Rae said, feeling a rush of pleasure at his confidence. "I'll do my best."

"I knew that," said the President. "We'll see you next Wednesday for orientation."

Wednesday morning Rae kissed her companion twice, once on each cheek in the Portuguese way, before going to the mission home. Both shed a few tears. Sister Almeida would be long gone to her new area when Rae returned with her new companion. As Rae walked alone to the bus stop, she looked around at all the many people that passed her. Suddenly, she felt a heavy burden fall onto her shoulders. *I am the senior now. These people are my responsibility.* She shivered. Suddenly the tall, crowded apartment buildings that flanked both sides of the street seemed even taller and fuller with people who needed her—roughly about twelve thousand people!

"You can do it, Rae," a firm voice said in her heart. Rae frowned until she spied the silver CTR ring on her hand and lifted her chin slightly in determination. "I will," she whispered.

When she arrived at the mission home, she was introduced to her new companion. Rae immediately liked her. Sister Selena Jorgeson was a short, rather chubby-looking girl who had a hesitant smile and large, beautiful green eyes. Her short, light-brown hair and stylish dress were arranged perfectly down to her high-heeled shoes. She appeared more as if she were going on a date to a very nice restaurant, or to a play, than tracting in the mission field. Only her eyes showed the strain caused by the long flight and two months of intensive studying.

Looking at Sister Jorgeson, Rae suddenly felt dowdy in the skirt and sweater she had bought in the Portuguese flea market the previous month. And her knee-length boots which she had found in one of the many little Portuguese shoe stores she had purchased for protection from the cold, not for beauty. Still, the clothes were practical, and very durable, unlike many of the clothes she had brought from home.

Rae shrugged inwardly and put her face forward to kiss and be kissed in the Portuguese fashion. Sister Jorgeson looked somewhat hesitant and unsure, reminding Rae how she had felt when she had first arrived in Portugal.

"You get used to it very quickly," she said with a big smile. She pushed back the long hair that was always falling forward when she stooped slightly to kiss the shorter Portuguese, or in this case a short American. "We give and receive a great many *beijinhos*," Rae continued, using the Portuguese word meaning "little kisses." She hastened to add. "To the women, and children only, of course."

Selena smiled back. "Of course. But it feels awkward."

"Soon it will feel awkward *not* kissing people when you meet them." Rae hooked her arm into her new companion's and went to stand by the window where they watched the rain fall onto the streets outside the mission home.

"Uh, you do have some other shoes, don't you," Rae asked casually. "Maybe some flat ones?"

"Yes, but I think I'll need some boots like yours." Selena looked at the rain and shook her head. "Do you know where I can buy some?"

"Sure, I know just the place." Rae smiled. Everything was going to work out perfectly.

The next day they attended to the first order of business— buying some practical shoes for Selena, as well as some sweaters. Though she had brought a heavy coat with her, all her dresses and blouses were short-sleeved.

"You see," Selena explained later that evening. "I was originally called to serve in Rio De Janeiro in Brazil. It's summer there now, and I was told it never gets very cold. But then they changed my mission call to Portugal. I was upset at first, but have finally come to the decision that this is where the Lord needs me. So, here I am."

Rae picked up their appointment book to plan the next day's activities. "Well, I for one am glad you're here, Sister. Who knows, maybe we were foreordained to be companions."

Selena laughed. "Yeah, right. Why not?"

Rae and Selena worked very hard in the next two weeks. Selena studied her Portuguese and tried to testify during the discussions whenever she could, but the bulk of the missionary work fell upon Rae. She would often lie awake at night thinking of the people in the area that were her responsibility. *Oh, help us to find those who need us*, she constantly prayed, *those who are ready or searching*.

Rae and Selena had been together three weeks when one of the members of their small ward, a rather large woman named Catarina, stopped the girls in the street.

"I have someone you have to meet," she said after presenting her face for *beijinhos*. They had all stopped on the cobblestone sidewalk and people were jostling them as they pushed passed. The situation was made worse because they were standing outside of a small bookstore where people were coming in and going out. Many of the people called greetings to Catarina and she answered loudly, presenting the missionaries to anyone who had time to stop. As the Portuguese are basically an unhurried people, it took some time before Rae was finally able to ask about the reference.

"About this person, Sister Catarina." In this area the members of the Church often called each other by their first names, preceded by Sister or Brother. "When can we go and meet them? We have a few minutes now."

"Yes," Catarina said with a wide smile, "right now would be good, although she can't hear a discussion at the moment. She owns this bookstore here, and she works until about seven or eight. She's a wonderful woman and she's got two children—twenty-four and twenty-two years old. Really good kids, but they need to hear the gospel. Their father died four years ago and they took his death very hard, especially her oldest." With that Catarina turned quickly and entered the bookstore. Rae and Selena followed.

While they waited for the few customers to leave, Rae had a chance to study the potential investigator. That she had once been a great beauty was obvious, though the woman's face was now drawn tight with anxiety and overwork. She wore glasses that slipped down her nose occasionally and, as she peered through them, gave the impression that she was looking down on people. Rae was taken aback. *Could this woman be open to hearing the gospel?* she wondered.

Her thoughts were interrupted as the last customer left and Catarina began introducing the missionaries. To her relief, the woman behind the glass counter leaned forward and exchanged *beijinhos* readily. At least she was polite.

"Maria, here are those girls I told you about, Sister Love and Sister Jorgeson. They're missionaries from my church. They want to come and talk to you and your children later on." She turned to Rae and continued. "Sister Love, this is Maria Marcela de Carvalho de Castro Santos da Silva." At the long name Rae didn't even blink. So many Portuguese had not only their parents' last names, but also their grandparents' as part of their official names. Catarina turned back to Maria. "So can they come tonight to give you a discussion?"

"What's a discussion?" Maria leaned over on top of the counter and peered through her glasses at the missionaries.

"Well, we have a set of messages that we share with people to teach them about Jesus Christ and His gospel," Rae said quickly before Catarina could answer. "Do you believe in Jesus Christ, Mrs. Silva?"

"Yes, I do." An emotion played on Maria's face—one Rae couldn't identify.

"We could come tonight," Rae said.

"I'm willing, but I can't answer for my children. They're old enough to decide for themselves. It's better you ask them than me though. They claim they don't believe in God." Maria looked at them intently as she spoke. "But tonight it would have to be short because I think one or the other may have school."

"Okay." Rae's stomach churned at the mention of her children not believing in God. She had taught atheists before and each time her heart had been broken. She took a determined breath. "We'll come by and meet them and set up an appointment for later. Will that be all right with you?"

Maria agreed and gave her address to the missionaries. Smiling, they bid farewell and left at a hurried pace to their next appointment . . . on foot as usual.

\* \* \* \* \*

Maria watched them leave, her heart full of unspoken emotion. *Can these pretty girls help my Tiago?* It had been so long since her elder son had shown interest in life. He helped out around the house and at the store when needed, and after much urging on her part, he had even returned to college part-time. But mostly he watched TV in the living room or stayed in his room to read books. Occasionally Marcela, convinced him to go to the beach, but even his friends had somewhat given up on him. On reflection, it seemed to Maria that their lives, which had once been rich and full of meaning, were now empty. Daniel's death had exacted a grave toll. There was no music, no laughter, no hope for the future. But she believed in Jesus Christ as she had told the young missionaries, and maybe, just maybe, He could help her son. And it certainly didn't hurt that the missionaries were pretty young girls about her own children's ages.

"I hope they can help my Tiago," Maria said softly, forgetting that Catarina was still in the store.

"If anybody can, the sisters can," replied Catarina. "I know the Church completely changed my life and my husband's. He hasn't taken a drink for years."

Maria didn't say anything. She didn't want her children to convert to this religion. She simply wanted them to believe in God and to have some hope in life. As for herself, she would never change religions. *Once a Catholic, always a Catholic,* she thought. She shrugged and turned back to her work.

\* \* \* \* \*

Rae and Selena were slightly late to their appointment with the Silvas that night. Another appointment had run overtime, and when they arrived they were out of breath.

"Come in, come in," Maria invited them into the apartment. After offering her face to give and receive *beijinhos*, she led them to the family room where her two grown children were sitting on the couch watching TV.

At first Rae had been surprised to learn that in Portugal most children lived with their families until well into their mid to late twenties—the age when many would marry. But she soon understood that expensive housing and low-paying jobs made this a logical and economical choice, and it no longer seemed strange to her.

"This is my son, Tiago." Maria motioned to the dark, slender young man who stood up to greet them. Rae quickly held out her hand to him so that he would understand that sister missionaries did not kiss young men in greeting—not even on the cheeks.

"And this is my daughter, Marcela. These are Catarina's friends—they are from her church." Maria finished the introductions and stood back watching.

"Hello, Marcela," Rae said. The sister leaned forward to offer her face for *beijinhos*, and Rae exchanged them with her. "I'm Sister Love, and this is my companion, Sister Jorgeson."

"How come you didn't kiss my brother?" Marcela asked, her brow furrowing.

"Well, we're missionaries from The Church of Jesus Christ of Latter Day Saints, and while we are serving missions, we aren't allowed to kiss boys over the age of twelve."

Marcela blinked. "That's strange. What about after?"

"After our missions, we become regular members again and can kiss anyone we please." When Marcela and Tiago nodded, Rae continued, "While on our missions we go around meeting everyone we can and presenting an important message. We'd like to share our message with you and your mother."

"I have school tonight," Marcela protested.

"Your mother mentioned that. So what would be best for you, tomorrow night or the next night?" Rae was careful to give them a choice between nights, making sure the question could not be answered with a simple no. That lesson was one she had learned well in the past few months.

"Tomorrow's fine with me," Marcela answered. She looked at her brother.

He shrugged. "I'm not doing anything."

"Then tomorrow night it is," Rae said. "About eight-thirty?" Everyone nodded in agreement.

"If you'll excuse me." Marcela thumbed toward the door. "I've got to run or I'll miss the bus. That'll mean a fifteen-minute wait until the next one comes." She gave them *beijinhos* again. "See you, tomorrow."

After Marcela left, Maria showed the missionaries around the apartment, another Portuguese custom. The Silva apartment was medium-sized with three bedrooms, a family room, a small kitchen, and a balcony. It was small by American standards, but was definitely middle class for Portugal. Afterwards, the Sisters said goodbye and left. They had one more hour before mission curfew, time enough to leave missionary tracts in an apartment building or two.

* * * * *

Tiago watched the young girls leave and a curiosity he hadn't felt in years grew inside him. There was something about them, though he couldn't decide exactly what. He only knew that he was glad they would be returning. His dark eyes wandered back to the television set, but he couldn't focus on the program. Finally, he arose and went into the kitchen to help his mother with dinner.

# Chapter Fourteen
## Teaching the Silvas

*T*he words in Rae's dream kept repeating, "Help me. Find me. I need you." She awoke with a start shortly before the alarm sounded. She watched the hands of the clock as she huddled in the warmth of her bed. At last the alarm clock shrilled in the quiet of the room, and Selena jumped at the sound.

"Nothing like that horrible noise to begin our day," Selena muttered. She looked over at Rae. "You know, I had the strangest dream. Someone was calling out to me."

Rae looked at her in surprise. "Me too. I guess someone's searching for the truth, right?"

Selena shrugged. "Why not? Probably."

That morning they knocked on doors in several apartment buildings and also contacted people in the streets. Then they went to check on the young girl they were preparing for baptism. Everything was on schedule and they felt happy as they walked back to their apartment for lunch.

There, they found several letters for each of them and they read avidly as they ate. Rae's letters were from her mother and from Lisa. She knew Lisa's letters were generally much shorter, so she opened that one first.

*Dear Rae,*

*Lots of news this time, but it's got to be short. I never claimed to be a writer, you know. I've got the best news ever—I'm going to have a baby! It will be coming early*

*September. I'm sad you won't be back yet, but at least we'll spend Christmas together. I'm so excited I could die, but I won't, of course. Mark's in seventh heaven, so to speak, about the baby.*

*Other important news is that Andrew and Michelle are getting married! They barely told us about two minutes ago so I know this letter will reach you first. Don't mention that I already told you when Andrew finally does write, but I felt you should know. The way they look all goo-goo at each other, it might be April before they remember to write to you. Incidentally, the first week in April is when they're planning to get married. Little Hope is so happy. She's finally going to have a daddy. Isn't this just perfect, Rae? I know you'll be so excited.*

*That's all now. I'll write more next time. Preach a little for me and remember your dark-eyed man in my dreams. Funny that your man should be in my dreams, even though it was only that once in the hospital. I've got to go. Mark's got the day off and we're going to pick out baby stuff. Love you lots, Lisa.*

Reading Lisa's letter was like being in the same room with her, and Rae wished she could see her friend. She was happy that Andrew was getting married. He was ready for marriage, and Michelle certainly needed a husband. Yet inside, she couldn't help wondering how much she was missing out on, so far away from home.

"What's wrong?" Selena asked, noticing Rae's expression.

"Nothing; it's great news. I . . ." Rae handed the letter to Selena who read it quickly.

"It's just, how dare they go on with their lives without you!" she exclaimed. They both laughed until the tears came.

"Sad to say," Rae said, wiping her eyes, "but that's exactly how I feel!"

"I know, I know," Selena agreed. "My mom wrote me that she's getting remarried after ten years of being divorced from my father. It's actually a relief, but why couldn't this have happened before or after my mission?" They regarded each other soberly for a moment.

"Right. And until we get home, they should put off all Christmases, elections, and brownie-making!" Rae finally said. That started them laughing again.

The letter from her mother was also surprisingly short. After writing a bit of news about each family member she said that she was going to visit Grandma Jill for a few weeks and to write to her there. Rae wondered briefly if her grandmother was sick. Her mother didn't usually go to Arizona alone, but waited until the children got out of school for the summer so they could all visit together. Surely it wasn't serious, though, or her mother would say so.

Soon it was time to work again, and Rae and her companion knelt together in their room to pray for a successful evening.

At eight-thirty sharp they arrived at the Silvas. This time they were only slightly out of breath, having used the bus to arrive close to the apartment. They were greeted politely, and, after kissing Maria and Marcela, and shaking Tiago's hand, they sat on the sofa and began explaining about prayer.

"Would you mind if we offered a prayer to ask the Lord to help us as we speak to you tonight?"

"Sure," Maria said, almost eagerly.

Marcela shrugged. "If you want."

"Go ahead, but I don't believe in God." Tiago looked directly into Rae's eyes as he spoke.

*Oh no*, she thought, *he's going to give us problems.*

In the end it wasn't Tiago who gave them any vocal problems during the discussion; he listened attentively to what they were saying and asked the occasional question. It was Marcela who challenged everything they said, especially when they began talking about the Book of Mormon.

"They didn't even know how to build boats back then," she interrupted, when Rae explained about how Lehi and his family crossed the ocean.

"Don't you think the Lord knew how to build a boat?" asked Rae.

"Show me people building a boat in the Bible," Marcela insisted. Rae was a little flustered because she had never expected the question; no one had ever questioned the Nephites' ability to build a boat before. She quickly searched her mind for a reference popular enough to be well-known to the family. Although the mother was a practicing Catholic, that didn't mean she would recognize a story from the Bible. Most people Rae had met in Portugal, Catholic or not, had little knowledge of the Bible. Still, there had to be some story they would recognize. But her mind went utterly blank.

"Well, there's always Noah's ark," Selena said softly in her still uncertain Portuguese. Relief flooded Rae's body. Thank heaven her companion could think clearly. Most people had certainly heard of Noah.

"Of course, Noah," Rae said. "Under instruction from the Lord, he built a boat big enough to hold two of every animal. Do you remember that?"

"Oh, yeah. That's right." Marcela was obviously embarrassed. "I guess I wasn't understanding the time frame." Indeed, she had been so intent on questioning their statements, she hadn't realized Lehi came long after Noah. Rae explained the time difference thoroughly and went on to review briefly the first part of the discussion, trying to bring the Spirit back to the lesson. They finished by reading the promise in the tenth chapter of Moroni.

"This says that after you read the Book of Mormon and desire to know if it's true, you can know for yourselves. You simply need to ask the Lord, and He will make it known to you. There are many ways the Holy Ghost does this, but usually it's by a warm, happy feeling inside. Mrs. Silva, how have you felt tonight as we've talked?"

"Good," Maria admitted.

Rae nodded. "We often feel the Holy Ghost testifying to the truthfulness as we teach, and you have probably felt that tonight." Rae reached down and removed a Book of Mormon from her shoulder bag on the floor by her feet and handed it to Tiago who was nearest her. "We want to give this to your family. We have marked some passages for you to read before we meet again. If you read and pray about this book, you will receive an answer. And once you know the Book of Mormon is true, you will know the rest of the things we've been telling you are true also."

Both Rae and Selena bore their testimonies of how they had tried the promise and how they knew the book was true. Rae briefly remembered what her father had said about bearing pure testimony and tried to put all her feelings in her words. She emphasized how important it was for the family to pray about the book, even if they didn't think they believed in God.

"Will you read the sections we've marked for you before we see you again?" Rae asked. She wanted to be sure the family was firmly committed to reading the Book of Mormon.

"I will," Tiago said, tracing the gold letters on the cover of the book with a fingertip.

"Sure, no problem," Marcela agreed with a shrug.

"I'm kind of busy at work, but I'll try." Maria's commitment wasn't as good as her children's, but it was the best Rae could get from her.

"Maria, will you offer our closing prayer following the steps of prayer that we talked about today? Thank you. Begin calling upon our Heavenly Father, thank Him for your blessings, ask Him for what you need—like to know if the Book of Mormon is true—and then close in the name of Jesus Christ. Let's all kneel." Rae, Selena, and Maria knelt but Tiago and Marcela refused. They did, however bow their heads out of courtesy for the missionaries.

After setting up another appointment the following Thursday, two days away, Rae and Selena said their goodbyes.

"Now remember," Rae said to Tiago and Marcela at the door. "It doesn't hurt to ask Heavenly Father about our message. It can't *hurt* anything, but you have so much to gain if He *does* exist and if our message *is* true."

As they left the Silva family, Rae was very quiet. She suddenly felt sad as it seemed so impossible that this little family would accept the gospel. In her experience thus far on her mission, she had seen many similar families listen, but ultimately refuse to become members. The fact that Tiago and Marcela didn't believe in God was a pretty good indication of probable failure. She sighed heavily. The discussion had sapped much of her strength.

Selena on the other hand was exuberant. "A whole family!" she exclaimed. "That was great! They're going to accept, I know it! And did you see Tiago's beautiful, big dark eyes? He is so good-looking—I could drown in those eyes!"

"Sister!" Rae was shocked. "What are you saying! Don't forget—we're missionaries!"

"That doesn't mean we're not people. They told me in the MTC I could look—I just had to remember that I was a representative of the Lord during my mission. Why even the president of the MTC told us he met his wife on his mission."

"Really?"

"Yeah. When he realized he had feelings for a sister missionary, he talked to his mission president who told him to put his feelings out of his mind for the rest of his mission, but that after his mission he should wrap his arms around her, give her a big kiss, and confess his love. Then the president transferred him to another city. When he got home he followed the president's advice and ended up marrying the girl. Isn't that romantic? Come on, 'fess up. You did notice Tiago's eyes, didn't you?"

Rae started to shake her head. She hadn't really noticed Tiago's eyes nor his good looks during the discussion. She was so intent on teaching the gospel that it hadn't occurred to her to see such things. But now as she thought about it, Tiago's face came unbidden to her mind.

"Yes, I guess he is a nice-looking guy." Then she added silently, *But I haven't much hope for his conversion.* That thought depressed her even more, as she suspected it was a lack of faith on her part. She glanced at the CTR ring Dave had given her, what seemed like so long ago, and felt somewhat comforted.

"Honestly." Selena gave a little skip. "How do you think it went?"

Rae shook her head and sighed. "I don't know." She didn't want to be discouraging, especially in the face of her excitement. Yet if the family actually read the Book of Mormon, put the promise to the test . . . well . . .

She smiled at Selena. "Let's pray for a miracle, okay?"

"I've got a head start on that," Selena answered. "I was praying the whole time you were speaking. I couldn't help much with the discussion—except for the Noah's ark thing—but I could at least pray."

"Then maybe we're on our way."

That night during companion and personal prayers, Rae prayed earnestly for Tiago and his family. *Please, Father. All we need is one little miracle.*

# Chapter Fifteen
## Pre-Earth Life

After Tiago left Rae in the garden, he went back to the Destination Building. His heart ached when he saw how much Rae was hurting inside about not being born in the States with the rest of the group. As he had walked with her and later caressed her golden hair, the color of the rays of the sun, he knew what he would do. He had never heard of it being done before, or even that it could be done, but he would at least try.

Arriving at the Destination Building, Tiago went up to the big glass desk where a counselor was sitting. In the long halls, many of Tiago's fellow spirits were laughing and talking excitedly about their coming births. Everyone seemed content. For the moment, there was no waiting at the desk.

"Yes? What can I help you with?" The man looked up as Tiago approached.

"I have a problem about my destination. That is, it's more my teaching partner's destination, and I wanted to know if there was any way I could . . ." Tiago paused. Even to himself his idea sounded ludicrous.

"Change places with her?" the councilor correctly finished Tiago's sentence without a trace of surprise in his voice. Tiago was surprised.

"Uh—I," he stammered. "I guess you get a lot of this, huh?"

"Actually, no. You're the first. But I was prepared. You must be Tiago."

"You were expecting me?"

"I'd say *advised* would be more accurate. I was advised that maybe you'd come to see me. By the way, I'm Zoram. Come this way, Tiago. Let's find a place where we can talk."

Tiago followed Zoram through the door behind him which opened onto a large, comfortable looking room. In a far corner of the room a group of spirits were talking excitedly, their faint voices reaching Tiago and Zoram.

"Isn't their excitement wonderful?" Zoram asked. "Oh, how well I remember my excitement when it was finally my turn. Of course, that was well over twenty-five hundred years ago—earth time, that is. Still, I remember that day like it was yesterday. That was why I asked if I could come and help out here in the Destination Building. It's all so exciting!"

"Have I messed up?" asked Tiago, hardly hearing what Zoram was saying. "I'm not questioning the Lord—I believe that His way is best—but I wondered if maybe things would still work out if I went down in Rae's place. She really wants to work with computers, you see, and she's terrified that she won't find the gospel."

"Well, maybe you'll go on a mission and baptize her, Tiago."

"I thought of that, but I haven't been foreordained to serve a mission. I've heard of people being foreordained to serve and then not serve, but can people serve if they haven't been foreordained?"

"It is possible," Zoram said.

"Well, I would give anything to be able to preach the gospel to Rae, but how can I be sure I'll be able to? What if I go astray? What if something happens to me? Either way, I can't let Rae down. I love her too much." Tiago's voice became even more passionate. "I'd give my life and my salvation for her, if necessary! I want her to go down to live with my member parents—I know they'll teach her right. Please, isn't it possible?"

Zoram smiled gently. "With God, all things are possible, Tiago. But is that really what you want? Are you willing to risk that you may not hear the gospel on earth? Are you willing to sacrifice that for Rae?"

"Yes, I am," Tiago answered without hesitation.

"Then be at the Birth Building tomorrow, before Rae's appointed time. I'll be waiting for you at the counter."

"Thank you, Zoram."

"Hey, I don't make the decisions around here." Zoram held up his hand to stop Tiago from saying more.

"I know, but thanks all the same."

\* \* \* \* \*

That evening Tiago went with Rae to say goodbye to some of their friends in their earth life class. They had fun talking excitedly about Rae's impending birth. Afterwards, they walked along the garden path and stopped in their favorite spot. Tiago knelt down on the grass before Rae and took her hand.

"What are you doing, Tiago?" Her laugh was self-conscious.

"I just wanted you to know how much I love you," Tiago said, looking up at her. "I wish I could promise that someday I'd be kneeling before you for real, asking you to marry me." There were tears in his eyes now. "I've given this a lot of thought. We have to believe that we'll find each other, no matter what the odds, no matter where we are born and what happens. I believe in you—I believe in us. We will make it!"

"We *will* make it," Rae repeated his words. Kneeling beside him, she shook her head sadly at the impossibility of their dream. She blinked rapidly in an attempt to control her tears. "I can't imagine life or eternity without you," she whispered.

"With God all things are possible." Tiago stared off into the distance for a moment. "I need you, too, Rae. More than you know. Find me, Rae, if you can. Help me."

Rae shook her head. "What are you saying? You're going to be fine. If anyone needs to be found it's probably me out there in that little country. I doubt I'll be in a position to help you there."

Tiago took her face between his hands, wishing he could tell her his plan. But she would never let him go through with it if he did. "I will need your help. You can do it. Don't forget that—ever."

"If I am ever in a position to help you, I'll do it with all my heart." Rae hugged him.

The next morning Tiago was with Rae as she said goodbye to the students in their family life class. Everyone had tears in their eyes, but the excitement could also be seen shining through. So many new experiences were in store for them! They hugged and hugged again, and finally it was time to go.

"We'll see you soon, Rae," Kira said in her quiet way as she left with the others. "You wait and see." Then the younger spirits were gone.

"You'll check in on them before you go down to earth, won't you?" Rae asked, staring after them long after they had disappeared.

"So much that they'll get sick of me," Tiago promised. He was trying to make her laugh, but knew that he failed. The moment was just too important for laughter.

"Well, let's go," Rae started for the path. "It's early yet, but we can stop off and talk to friends on the way."

"Uh—I'm going to have to go separately." Tiago carefully chose his words so that he wouldn't be lying. "I've got something I have to do first." Somehow he had to get to the Birth Building before her. He felt nervous, wondering if she could see right through him.

"Okay." Rae seemed puzzled but not upset. "I'll meet you later."

Tiago didn't reply. He simply stared for a long moment at her face, then turned and walked away.

When he arrived at the Birth Building well before Rae's appointed time, Zoram was waiting for him at the desk. "You're already cleared. Come with me." Zoram motioned, and Tiago followed him quickly. "You haven't changed your mind, have you? It's not too late."

"No, I'm sure about it. And I also know that the Father loves me, so if He's giving me His blessing to do this, things will work out for the best."

Zoram smiled. "You're right Tiago. He loves you very much. This is the way things were supposed to be."

"What? You mean—"

"Yes, Tiago, you were meant to go down to Portugal from the first."

"It was a test, wasn't it? Was it to prove my love for Rae?"

Zoram shrugged. "Could be. Perhaps it was to see how willing you were to make such a great sacrifice at all. Or maybe to see if Rae would accept the Father's will. Regardless, you both passed with flying colors. The Father is very pleased as He will no doubt tell you Himself." Zoram paused before an unassuming-looking door in the long corridor. "You're a very special spirit, Tiago. I look forward to seeing you when you get back."

"You mean *He's* waiting in there now?" Tiago motioned toward the door.

"Well, He never simply waits, but it's your turn for your departure interview."

"Goodbye, Zoram." Tiago reached out to open the door, his heart filled with gladness at the prospect of being with his Father.

"Not goodbye, Tiago. Until we meet again."

# Chapter Sixteen
## God Does Live

*T*he sister missionary's parting words penetrated deeply into Tiago's soul. "It doesn't hurt to ask Heavenly Father about our message," she had said. "It can't *hurt* anything, but you have so much to gain if He *does* exist and if our message *is* true."

Throughout the discussion he had been intrigued by the missionaries and their message. Their complete assurance—they called it their testimonies—that God lived and had restored His gospel to the earth had made him question his own conviction that God *didn't* live. That they were young and pretty and had wonderful American accents didn't hurt, either. Suddenly, Tiago wanted to know, one way or the other, if these missionaries could somehow be telling the truth.

Another factor weighed heavily in his decision to read the Book of Mormon. No, it wasn't his mother's hopeful expression, or Marcela's blatant curiosity. It was because his father had believed in God. Tiago had always considered his father a very intelligent man. *If my dad believed, maybe I'm wrong*, he thought.

Just maybe.

For the first time in four years there was a glimmer of hope in Tiago's heart.

After the missionaries were gone, Tiago took the Book of Mormon into his room and shut the door. As he turned each page, a happy, interested feeling pervaded his senses. He continued, completely absorbed, until he had finished the assignment. Afterward, he lay stretched on his bed pondering what he had read and what the missionaries had taught him. *Could they be right? Could my father have been right? Did God exist? Does He really love me?*

Tiago had been certain that his view of the world was the true one, but now all that certainty had dissolved with each piece of information the missionaries had taught. He *had* felt something with the missionaries and also when he had read the book. Yet, even as he questioned his beliefs, the pain and loss he'd felt at his father's death came back in a bitter, devastating rush. If God existed, why had his father died?

A knock sounded at the door. "Come in," he said, quickly blinking back the tears that threatened to fall.

"Excuse me, but I wanted to know if you'd read it yet." Marcela motioned to the Book of Mormon in his hands. You did? Well, what do you think?"

He shrugged. "I don't know—yet. But why did you give them so many problems during the discussion? You sounded like you were trying to fight with them or something."

Marcela sighed. "It's just that what they say is so new and sometimes . . . well, preposterous. Yet they have answers for all my questions, no matter how crazy, and it seems so logical."

"Well that boat question was stupid," Tiago said. "If you'd thought about it, you'd have remembered about the ark."

Marcela sighed again. "I know. I was getting desperate, trying to prove them wrong. They're so convincing."

"Yes, but is it true? That's the real question. The rest doesn't make much difference."

Marcela nodded. "Well, when you're finished with the book, I'd like to read it." She turned and left the room.

Tiago picked up the Book of Mormon again and began from

the first page. "I, Nephi, having been born of goodly parents . . ."

He read far into the night, struggling against his former beliefs and what his spirit recognized as truth. The next morning found him haggard, and at school he could barely concentrate. All that day the need to know grew. He couldn't eat or drink or focus on anything but the Book of Mormon and the missionaries' words. Something inside him thirsted for the truth—and to feel that truth deep inside where it really counted.

Finally, the struggle within his soul came to a climax. Despite the lack of food, his body felt strong, his mind clear and alert. With sudden enlightenment, he realized that the only way he could actually prove or disprove the Book of Mormon and the church it represented was to take Moroni's challenge: to pray. He needed to ask God, a Being he didn't even know existed, to confirm whether or not the book was true. If something happened, he would know for sure of its truthfulness. If nothing happened, he would know the missionaries themselves were deluded and that God truly didn't exist.

Praying was something he hadn't done for years, even before his father died. He hardly knew how to begin. Yet, with the clarity of his fast, he understood that a memorized prayer wouldn't do. He needed to use the steps the sisters had outlined.

Tiago locked his bedroom door and dropped to his knees by his bed. He read for a second time the pamphlet left by the missionaries which explained the discussion they had given, particularly the steps of prayer. He felt awkward at first but somehow the words came.

"Father in Heaven," he began, pausing for a few seconds to center himself on the words. "I have read the parts of the book the missionaries left us and more. I find myself intrigued by them and their message—and by this book. My father believed in You, and though I thought that You didn't exist, maybe I was wrong. If You do exist then tell me, is this book true? Do you exist?" Tiago searched earnestly with his heart open, waiting long minutes before the answer came.

At first the feeling was so gradual that Tiago didn't realize it had come. But it grew in force and with an intensity that shocked him. He recognized the feeling—happiness! It was also love, security, and every other good emotion, all rolled into one. Most especially, it was love. The feeling wrapped around him like a blanket. The tears came, slowly, then more rapidly.

Love from heaven continued to pour down upon Tiago. He felt a great relief as his heavy burden of pain and sadness lifted. *Oh, thank you!* he cried silently. *Thank you for these missionaries and for not giving up on me!* He didn't stop praying; there was so much that he hadn't said over the years, so much to make up for. He prayed until his legs grew numb, and then arose, his heart singing. *God does live! God loves me!*

\* \* \* \* \*

Thursday arrived quickly, and once more Rae and Selena were teaching the Silvas. Tiago was again attentive and listening, but there was something different about him. Throughout the discussion he asked various questions and seem satisfied with the answers. Marcela, on the other hand continued her some-times unusual questions, as if she was determined *not* to believe anything until it was proven to her. When they came to the baptismal challenge at the end of the discussion, Marcela was particularly disagreeable, and even Maria had objections. Only Tiago was silent.

After Rae taught each principle, both she and Selena bore pure testimony of it. *Dad was right*, Rae thought as she noticed that Marcela had no argumentative responses to their testimonies. *You can't argue with feelings, or at least when the Holy Ghost testifies of those feelings.*

In the end, she did get a commitment from the family to be baptized, but only on the condition that they meanwhile became sure the gospel was true—meaning, of course, that they weren't yet sure. Not exactly the enthusiastic response she'd prayed for, but it was a beginning. It was obvious to Rae that Maria and Marcela definitely needed to read and pray more. About Tiago, she was uncertain, and she was afraid to ask him directly how he was feeling.

When the discussion was over and more reading assigned, they invited the family to pray with them. Again Maria offered the prayer, but both missionaries were shocked when Tiago knelt with them on the floor, followed less readily by Marcela. Tears rolled down Maria's face as she saw her children kneel and bow their heads.

Things moved swiftly after that night. Both Tiago and Marcela read anything they were assigned and more. Rae and Selena offered each of them their own Book of Mormon so they could read without interference from one another. They also gave them the book *Gospel Principles*. Only Maria read little or nothing of the material.

Saturday evening the family heard the third discussion, and on Sunday morning they attended church where they were welcomed with open arms by the members. Sunday afternoon they also attended the baptismal meeting that brought members, missionaries, and investigators from many nearby branches who didn't have their own baptismal font.

The following Tuesday night, exactly a week after their first discussion, Rae and Selena met with the family to teach the fourth discussion. As they had became more involved with the Silvas and learned more about the deceased father, Rae and Selena had grown eager to teach them how families could be eternal.

"So at death our spirits separate from our bodies and go to the Spirit World. There they are greeted by loved ones and await the coming of those they left on earth. They also have the chance to accept the gospel . . ." Rae continued explaining about temples and the ordinances done in behalf of those already deceased. She stressed the temple sealing and how vital it was to their family.

"You mean that Papa is waiting at this place for us?" Marcela asked. "He's not really gone forever? We're all going to be resurrected and be together?" She was blinking furiously to hold back her tears. The questions were her first for the entire night. For once, she had found nothing to contest.

Rae nodded through her own tears. "Yes, you will be reunited with him again, if you live worthily. That's why Jesus Christ sacrificed His life. He loves us all so much!"

As Rae spoke, Maria, sitting next to Selena on the sofa, was trembling softly. Her love for her husband and her hope for their reunion was clear. But while she'd always had faith that Daniel had gone to heaven, Rae knew she finally understood that there were logical and specific reasons for her belief.

Selena laid a comforting hand on Maria's shoulder. Maria smiled, covering Selena's hand with her own. Gradually, her trembling lessened as she gained control of her emotions.

Tiago had been silent during the discussion. He had read all the materials Rae had given him, and she knew he must have surely read something about eternal families. Nevertheless, his eyes were filled with tears. Rae hoped he was prepared for her next question.

"Baptism into Christ's Church is the next step," she began quietly. "To be part of an eternal family we have to follow Jesus' example." She turned to Tiago, sitting expectantly in the chair across from her. "Tiago, do you want to be baptized?"

"I do," he said without hesitation.

"You do?" Maria asked in shock.

"Yes, I want to be baptized. I know it's true." Tiago's voice was firm, and Rae allowed herself to experience happiness from his words.

"What about you, Marcela?" Selena asked.

"I don't know yet," Marcela hedged. Unlike her mother, she didn't appear surprised at Tiago's decision. "I'll see."

"And how do you feel about it?" Rae asked Maria.

"No, no. I don't want to be baptized." Maria shook her head quickly. "But of course my children are adults and can choose for themselves." Even so, she didn't seem very happy about it. Rae knew she had wanted her children to find faith, but perhaps the fact that they might actually join a new church was something she had not given much consideration.

"How about this coming Sunday?" Rae asked and Tiago agreed. After setting up the remaining discussions for Thursday and Saturday, she and Selena went out into the cold winter night.

"He's going to be baptized!" Rae exclaimed. At that moment she was sure she was feeling the pure joy Alma had written about in the Book of Mormon. "It's a miracle! The others will follow, you know."

"I knew they were a special family!" Selena gave a little skip.

Rae was never more grateful for her companion's simple faith than she was at that moment.

\* \* \* \* \*

The following Sunday, Rae and Selena arrived at the church shortly after three. They had come early to the baptisms to make sure that Tiago had a baptismal interview with their district leader and had white clothes to wear. They were surprised to find their mission president at the church, making a special surprise visit. As the interviews were conducted and people gathered, the president talked to Rae and Selena about Tiago whom he had met and talked to at length before they arrived.

"Tiago is very special," he said. "He's one of those who is open to the Spirit. He didn't have to be convinced or taught for long, did he?" The girls shook their heads, and the president nodded. "I felt it. He's been blessed with the gift of belief. He's very lucky. Now, Sisters, do you have any other people to baptize this week?"

"Well, I'm sure Tiago's sister, Marcela, knows the Church is true, but she doesn't want to be baptized," Rae said. "I don't understand what the problem is. Do you think you could talk to her for a minute?"

"Sure thing. I'll be glad to. Where is she?" he asked. Rae pointed to Marcela who was leaning against the short concrete wall that lined the walkway to the meeting house talking to a few of the ward members. The president started in her direction, and Rae watched as he introduced himself and began talking.

Rae walked idly around the cobblestone walkways, keeping well away from the president and Marcela, and in sight of her companion. She adored the large, charming house that had been converted into a church. It was so different from the chapels back home. It seemed to speak of the essence of the Portuguese, and that made it special to her. Around the building were many flower beds, and she recalled in her mind how lush and beautiful they'd been in late summer. She could hardly wait for spring to see it all come alive again.

"Sister Love?"

Rae turned to see the mission president. She motioned to Selena to come and hear what he had to say.

"I've sent Marcela in with an Elder for her baptismal interview. She wants to know if you'll run back to her house and ask her mother to bring some underclothes—if she hasn't left yet. She's decided to be baptized!"

"But . . .what happened? Tell us!"

"Well, we discussed how she felt about the Book of Mormon and the experiences she had reading it," the president said. "She told me about a particular experience she had the very first week. I helped her realize that she actually had a testimony for herself.

Since she likes you sisters so much, she was afraid that she was simply believing in you two, instead of in the scriptures and the gospel."

Happiness burst through Rae. "Oh, thank you, President! That's wonderful!" She hugged Selena.

* * * * *

Tiago and Marcela were baptized together with their mother looking on. Tiago was grateful Marcela had also chosen to follow Christ, and prayed that his mother would soon follow. As he arose from the water, feelings of incredible freedom and rebirth spread throughout his entire body. *I'm new!* his soul sang silently. *Reborn! And this is the beginning! I'm a member of Christ's Church!* He couldn't stop smiling and laughing.

After the baptisms, a short testimony meeting was held for those who wanted to share their feelings. Unbidden, Tiago was first to the stand.

"Two weeks ago I thought I didn't believe in God," he began. "When my father died four years ago, I lost all interest in any God that could be so cruel. I decided that no such being existed. But that was before I knew He had a plan for us—that He loves us more than I ever imagined possible. When I learned this I knew I was wrong. God does live! I know this Church is true! I have read the whole Book of Mormon these last two weeks, and I testify to you all that it is the word of God. I hope I can share this message with my fellow countrymen. Thank you so much everyone, especially to Sister Catarina for caring about my family enough to send us those wonderful sisters!"

As Tiago closed his short testimony, his eyes fell on Sister Love, and he felt a strange pull towards her. He shrugged it away immediately.

After all, she was a missionary.

# Chapter Seventeen
## Challenges

*A* cool breeze blew in the open window in the sisters' room. In the kitchen they could hear the woman they rented their room from singing church hymns in her high voice, running up and down the scales as she exaggerated the melodies. Rae adored hearing her sing—a purely Portuguese mixture of the traditional music called Fado and the hymns of the Church the sister had grown to love. To Rae's delight, many of the woman in the ward sang that way. There was nothing like it anywhere else in the world.

She fingered the letters in her hand. Her mother wrote every week like clockwork, but her letters while she had been at Grandma's had been noticeably shorter. Of course, Holly had been busy helping Grandma around the house and also helping her raise money for her friend Carol's bone marrow transplant. Though the money was almost raised, the young mother's blood type was very rare, and a donor had not been found.

"I feel drawn to Carol," wrote Rae's mother. "You should see how cheerful she is. You know, I never understood how someone can be so close to death, and yet be influential in so many lives. Now I am seeing it up close. It's as if she can see beyond the veil—all the beauty and joy that awaits—and can share it with those around her. You'll have to come and meet her when you come home, though if a donor isn't found soon, she might not make it. There is another treatment doctors are trying—some breakthrough radiation—and we are hopeful for her recovery."

Andrew had also remembered to write, telling Rae about his impending marriage. He seemed very happy, and Rae felt a great weight—one she hadn't even known she was carrying—lift from her shoulders. She hadn't ruined his life by not marrying him. He had gone on and found happiness without her.

"Good news?" Selena asked without looking up. She was stretched out on her bed still in her pajamas since it was P-Day, propped up with pillows and writing furiously. Pages full of long-hand already surrounded her. Ten weeks of active missionary life had helped her loose fifteen pounds, firming her body. She was feeling good—spiritually and physically—and her happiness showed.

"Great news actually." Rae plopped herself on the bed by Selena, scattering her papers.

"Oh yeah?" Selena signed her name at the bottom of the paper and sighed. "All done." She picked up the scattered papers and folded them into a large envelope. "I'm going to have to pay extra postage for this one."

"Your mother will love it, though." Rae drew her legs up under her chin and lay her arms and head on top of them. "You know, I think at first when I found out that Andrew and Michelle were getting married, I was worried that Andrew had asked her because . . . well, because things didn't work out between us. But looking back I see that Michelle was in love with him almost from the first, and I think maybe he just finally woke up and realized what a wonderful person she is."

"Well, from what you tell me, I agree. They sound perfect for each other." Selena stretched her arms in front of her and lay back again on her pillows. "What about that other guy, Dave? He's Michelle's brother, isn't he? What does he think about them getting together?"

"Yes. Well, he says he was worried at first, too, but that they seem to be happy together. I trust his judgment."

"And what about you and him?"

Rae sighed. "I don't know. It's hard to tell. They say 'absence makes the heart grow fonder' and it's true. Sometimes I can't wait to see him again, and I imagine what we'll say and do when I finally get home. I find myself hoping that he doesn't find some-one else." Rae fingered the fat letter Selena had written, hoping to change the subject. "What did you write, anyway? You've only been in the mission field two and a half months and I think you've written enough today to last the rest of your mission."

"Just about how special our little family is, and especially how our 'children' are growing in the gospel."

Rae knew immediately that Selena was talking about Tiago and Marcela. They often referred to them as their children because they felt somewhat like parents, leading and guiding them to the gospel. "Did you tell her about Tiago baptizing his aunt and cousins?"

"Of course," Selena said. "He's grown so much—it's amazing."

"You know," Rae stared thoughtfully at the floor, "the more I learn, the more I realize that I don't know very much at all—that there's so much left to learn. I mean, I thought after the first discussion we had with them that there was no way Tiago and Marcela would accept the gospel. My other experiences here had shown me that those who don't believe in God are nearly impossible to convert. They don't believe in God, so they certainly aren't going to ask *Him* if the Book of Mormon is true."

"I see your point."

Rae raised her eyes to look at Selena. "But then here you come with your greeny excitement and you don't know they probably won't accept. Only they do accept—all but Maria whom I had thought would have been the easiest to convert—and now they've read so much about the gospel, and learned so quickly that yesterday at church Tiago taught *me* something during his

Sunday School lesson! It's incredible! Amazing!"

"He's going to be a strong leader in the Church, I think. And he's handsome, besides." Selena smiled gently. "You have noticed, haven't you?"

Rae pursed her lips. "Let's not go there." An emotion stirred in her heart, but before she could identify it Selena continued.

"You know, I feel I ought to tell you—since you are my companion and since you don't seem to know about it . . ." Selena's voice trailed off.

"About what? Tell me."

"Well, I think Tiago likes you—as more than a friend, I mean. Several of the members have noticed and have mentioned it to me. Can't you see how he looks at you?"

Rae opened her eyes wide in surprise. "That's ridiculous! I'm a missionary and that's that."

"But does he realize, do you think, that missionaries are off limits?"

All at once Rae felt confused. "Of course he understands."

"Yeah, you're right." Selena swung her feet off the bed and stood up. "But a mission doesn't last forever, and he knows that too."

Rae groaned and let her head fall back against the wall.

Selena gave a laugh. "It's not as bad as all that, is it?"

"I just don't want anything to hinder his growth in the Church," Rae explained. "And I certainly don't want to hurt him. I'll just have to distance myself as much as possible."

"What about Maria?" Selena pause as she reached for the top drawer in their dresser. "Are we giving up on her?"

"No." Rae shook her head almost violently. "Never. They need to be an eternal family, and we have a better chance than anyone to help her. I think we should go back over the discussions and basic gospel principles—maybe use the Book of Mormon more. The president keeps stressing how important that is. And maybe we could hold a special fast for her."

"Good idea. Just the two of us?"

"What do you think?"

Selena pulled out some underclothes and a T-shirt. "I think Tiago and Marcela have the right to fast for her as well."

Rae thought for a moment. "Okay. But I don't think we should tell Maria. We want her to feel the Spirit, and I bet she won't if she feels pressured."

Selena shut her drawer and headed toward the bathroom. "Let's think about it and see what Tiago and Marcela have to say tonight at family night." Nearly every Monday night for the past few months, they, along with other sets of missionaries in the ward, had a family night at the church for the new members and investigators. Doing so had strengthened those they worked with substantially.

"Perfect." But as Rae said it, she wondered how she would act around Tiago now that she suspected how he felt about her.

\* \* \* \* \*

Family night went smoothly. After a lesson given by Rae, the group played games and ate cookies. At times Rae felt Tiago's eyes resting on her, but when she returned his gaze, it seemed full of friendship. Was it only friendship? Rae couldn't tell, and she struggled to dismiss the thoughts.

Not until the evening was nearly over did Rae and Selena have the chance to talk to Tiago and Marcela privately. "We're thinking about having a fast between the four of us to help your mother gain a testimony," Rae explained in a low voice. She found herself looking deep into Tiago's eyes, and for a brief second in time she couldn't breath. She felt as if she were drowning in their depths.

"But the last time we tried something like that she became angry," Marcela told them. "She said if we didn't stop trying to make her believe, she wouldn't come to church with us anymore.

We stopped our fast because at least by coming to church she was feeling the Spirit."

Marcela's statement confirmed what Rae had felt earlier that day. "Okay, maybe we simply shouldn't tell your mother the purpose for our fast," she continued. "We don't want her to focus on us trying to make her believe, but rather on what she feels inside."

"Let's do it," Tiago agreed. "We want to help her anyway we can."

"When should we start?" Marcela asked.

"Right now," Selena said. "You did eat a good dinner before coming tonight, didn't you?"

Marcela nodded. "Cod fish and potatoes."

"Drizzled with olive oil. It was good—even for fish," Tiago added teasingly for Rae's benefit. Everyone knew she hadn't developed a taste for seafood, though she was making headway on olive oil.

"Good." Rae took a breath and then began in her best missionary voice. "Remember, fasting and prayer works—I know it does—but sometimes it doesn't work overnight."

"But at times it *does* work overnight," Tiago countered lightly. Rae felt herself color, remembering when he had shared with them the experience he'd had while reading the Book of Mormon and fasting. For him, it *had* worked overnight. He smiled at her, as though to apologize for his impudence. "Don't worry, Sister. We know the Lord has His own timetable, and we'll have faith in Him. Right, Marcela?"

"Right." Marcela exchanged a glance with Tiago. Rae saw admiration for Tiago in Marcela's eyes, and, remembering what Maria had told her about the siblings rarely spending time together before they were baptized, she was glad the gospel had helped their relationship.

"Then let's go somewhere to begin the fast." Rae took a step toward the door. "Tomorrow we'll have to end it separately since we won't be seeing you." She led the group out of the main room and up the polished wooden staircase to a small classroom where the young women of the ward met on Sundays. Together they knelt on the carpet and took turns praying aloud to begin their fast.

After the prayer, they walked back down the stairs and out onto the church's large porch. Rae glanced at her watch. "We have to leave right now or we'll be late for curfew."

"Tell your mother we'll stop by the store tomorrow and arrange another appointment," Selena added.

Before taking their leave, they shook Tiago's hand, exchanged *beijinhos* with Marcela and some of the single sisters who had come out to support the activity, and waved to the elders and their investigators. Rae forced herself not to look back over her shoulder. For the first time since she had begun her mission, she wished she could take a week off.

\* \* \* \* \*

As Tiago watched the sisters disappear through the gate at the end of the church walkway he smiled. She *had* felt something tonight when she looked at him earlier, that missionary with hair the color of the rays of the sun—something other than her usual feelings toward him. That meant that he had at least a chance with her, as impossible as it might seem. For the first time since he had become aware of his feelings for her two or three weeks after his baptism, Tiago felt that maybe there could eventually be something more than friendship between them.

Just maybe.

Of course, he would have to wait until she finished her mission and fulfilled her obligation to the Lord. Only then would she be free to discover how she might feel about him . . . if there was any chance for them at all. But he knew he was more than willing to wait to find out.

* * * * *

Late Monday evening, Maria sat on her bed to remove her shoes. She heard her children in the next room talking quietly and occasionally laughing. Apparently, they had enjoyed themselves at the church together. She couldn't believe how much they had changed. Tiago was no longer sullen. Though he had moments of quietness and deep thought, his face clearly showed the hope that now lived in his heart. She no longer worried about him taking his own life. He also treated Marcela better, addressing her without the scorn that had begun to lace his voice before the missionaries had come. And Marcela, well, she thought about others instead of herself all the time. Twice, she'd helped Maria at the store in the past week. Yes, Maria was content with the changes in her children—even though it resulted from joining another church.

"No way!" Maria heard Marcela protest in the other room. "It was me who beat you last time we played."

"Oh yeah? Prove it!"

"Okay, but you'll see." The friendly voices faded as the two moved down the corridor to the living room.

Maria sighed and stretched out on the bed, still thinking about her children and the new church that had come into their lives. Though she still resisted baptism, she had attended church every Sunday since hearing the first discussion. She felt an irresistible pull to the gospel, which went beyond what she had ever expected. She enjoyed hearing about the Lord and making new friends, but most of all she loved spending meaningful time with her children. Since their baptism, there was music in the house, much laughter, and plans for the future—things she had once believed had died forever with her Daniel.

Most recently, Tiago had found a job and doubled up on his classes at school. Maria couldn't have asked for more.

*Maybe there is something to this gospel,* she thought to herself, sitting up abruptly. She picked up the Book of Mormon on her night stand. *Maybe I should read this book, after all. Yes, I'll begin right now. I want to know for myself if it is true.*

# Chapter Eighteen
## Realizations

On a Saturday morning, nearly two weeks after the fast for Maria, Rae awoke knowing something was dreadfully wrong. She couldn't explain it even to herself, though she had some idea. It had something to do with Tiago's eyes, and the fact that they matched so well the ones in her dreams. She felt guilty about her growing feelings for him and also upset with her companion. Selena was the one who had first noticed Tiago's eyes and his attractiveness—and had kept bringing them to her attention. Still, deep down, Rae knew that she had no one to blame but herself.

Over the weeks since Tiago's baptism, Rae had honestly grown to love the Silvas, including Tiago. At first, the love was the same she'd experienced for the many others she had taught and helped convert to the Church—love mixed with friendship, pride, fear, and responsibility. In all, it was a feeling parents would have for their growing children. But ever since that P-day when Selena had suggested Tiago had feelings for her, Rae's own erratic feelings came more and more often to the surface, though the change had been so gradual that she wasn't sure exactly when it began. The feelings were romantic, intense, and quite unlike any she had ever felt.

Now every time she saw Tiago, she was painfully aware of her emotions, though she was careful not to allow them to show. She remained distant and sometimes spoke maybe a little too sharply.

But what else could she do? She found the best way to forget her predicament was to throw herself into missionary work . . . so she did, focusing on it with unparalleled zeal.

As part of that effort, they'd met several times with Maria, who had still not committed to baptism. But at least she was finally reading the Book of Mormon. Today they had another appointment with her. They would read and pray together, hoping the Spirit would touch her. Rae was determined never to give up. So was her companion.

After a morning contacting people near the flea market with the other missionaries in their zone, Rae and Selena, rang the outer doorbell to the six-story apartment building where the Silvas lived. They were buzzed in promptly and walked up several flights of stairs where Tiago was waiting for them in the open doorway. Rae's emotions raced and collided inside her. Swallowing hard, she squelched the feelings.

She wasn't surprised to see Tiago. He nearly always made sure to be at the house when they planned to visit. Even though he usually spent much of his free time doing missionary work with his friends and relatives or going on divisions with the elders, he made it a point to be there for his mother. Rae was pleased with his loyalty, though she wished she didn't have to face him so often.

"Come in, Sisters." He shook their hands enthusiastically, and Rae noticed he seemed especially happy today. "I've got great news," he said. "It's about Mom, but I'll let her tell you herself. Suffice it to say that I think we'll need some white clothing for her tomorrow!"

Rae flashed him a smile, careful not to gaze too long into his eyes. "What happened? Where is she?"

"In the TV room."

Rae and Selena hurried down the short corridor to the small sitting room where Maria sat serenely in one of the comfortable chairs. A dark blue book with a gold angel on the cover—the Book of Mormon—was in her lap, cradled gently by both hands.

"What happened?" Rae asked, her heart pumping excitement.

"Sit down, please." Maria indicated the cushion next to her. Selena sat down on it, but Rae went up to Maria and crouched down near her chair. Tiago had also come into the room and sat in the other chair opposite his mother.

"I've been reading the Book of Mormon," Maria said softly, somewhat bemused. "I didn't believe it was true, though I probably would have been baptized because of my children." She glanced up at Tiago, and Rae recognized the love in her expression. Then Maria looked back at Rae. "It happened a couple of hours ago. I was sitting here reading, relaxing from a long week of work, and then it happened. Suddenly, I just had to know if it was true, and I sat here and prayed—I didn't kneel because Tiago was in the kitchen, bound to come back at any moment—and suddenly I felt warm all over. And, well, it's hard to describe, really—I just know this book is true." Maria shook her head in wonder, holding the book up with slightly shaking hands.

"Oh, Maria!" Tears had come to Rae's eyes as Maria spoke. Now she leaned forward and hugged the woman who also began to cry with joy. After a time of hugging and rejoicing, Rae finally had to ask the missionary Big Question.

"Are you ready to be baptized now, Maria?" At her nod, Rae continued, "How about tomorrow? It'd be perfect because it's not only Fast Sunday, it's also Easter when we celebrate the resurrection."

More happy tears slid down Maria's smooth cheeks. "Yes. Oh, yes! I will."

"And you'll baptize her, Tiago?" Rae turned to look at him, who had come to stand behind her. His eyes were also wet.

"Yes." His voice was choked as he glanced at his mother and

back at Rae. "How can we ever thank you two for coming into our lives?" he added.

"You thank us?" Rae shook her head. "No, thank *you* for letting us teach you and be a part of the Lord's work."

Tiago gazed at her strangely for a minute, then nodded. He looked as if he wanted to say something, and he opened his mouth, only to clamp it shut again.

"What's going on in there?" Marcela's voice came from the corridor. "You guys are making so much noise that you didn't even hear me come in."

"Your mother's going to be baptized!" Selena jumped up from her seat to explain.

"What? Oh, Mom, is it true?" Marcela crossed from the doorway to her mother and wrapped her arms around her. "Now we can someday go to the temple and be an eternal family with Papa! I'm so happy!" Marcela smiled at the Sisters. "Thank you so much!"

Rae and Selena had to leave soon after Marcela came home, having much more work ahead of them that afternoon and evening, but they promised to break their fast with the family after church the next day and go to the baptisms together. As they walked down the cobblestone sidewalk away from the apartment, they turned to wave to Tiago and Marcela who were watching them from their balcony.

\* \* \* \* \*

"It's so strange the way I feel when he looks at me," Rae confided to Selena as they were getting ready for bed that evening.

"It's about time you've noticed," Selena said dryly.

"I didn't say the way he looks at me is different, I said the way I feel when he looks at me is strange." Rae sat down on her bed and dropped her head in her hands.

"Sister?" Selena came to sit next to Rae and put an arm around her in a motherly way. "Are you saying what I think you're saying?"

Rae looked up at her, feeling suddenly very weary. "I don't know anything. I need time to think, but I can't think—not about that stuff anyway. I'm a missionary!"

"Yes, you are, but that doesn't mean you stop being a person, does it?"

"I've tried to put this out of my mind—sometimes I go to sleep praying about it." Rae let her head drop back into her hands.

"I've noticed that," Selena said, rubbing her hand along Rae's back. "And you're having trouble sleeping. I didn't know it was because of Tiago."

"I feel like I'm doing something wrong. But I'm trying so hard to do it right!" Tears welled in Rae's eyes.

"And you have been. Look! We've baptized five people in just the last two weeks. The Lord wouldn't bless us like this if you were doing something wrong, would He?"

Rae felt marginally better. "You know," she said, "after receiving my mission call, I prayed every night before I went into the MTC that I wouldn't meet Mister Right before going on my mission." She gave a short, mirthless laugh. "I'd heard of that happening and since I'd decided to go on a mission, I didn't want any interference. But now here I am, a successful missionary, and I feel more attracted to this man than I can ever remember feeling for any of my other boyfriends. What happened?"

"I don't know." Shrugging, Selena smoothed Rae's hair. "But if you take it literally, this is not *before* your mission."

"What?"

"You said you prayed not to meet anyone *before* your mission. I guess you should have prayed not to meet anyone until *after* your mission."

"But that's what I thought I *was* doing!" Rae wailed. "Oh,

how did I get myself into this!" She flopped onto her back and pulled her legs and feet onto the bed

"Well, Sister, he is an attractive man." Selena stood up and started changing into her pajamas. "Who knows, maybe he's right for you and someday—after your mission, of course—you'll get together."

"But that's crazy! Sisters don't *ever* marry people they meet on their missions."

"Oh, I see. It's only okay for elders to meet and baptize future spouses? Really, it must happen to sisters here and there as well."

"It's not okay for elders *or* sisters!"

Selena shrugged. "I don't think it'll feel like such a big deal after your mission is over." She laid down on her own bed.

"Well," Rae said, sitting up again. "Let's say for a moment that what I'm feeling isn't a figment of my imagination and that I do care for him." Rae didn't say Tiago's name but Selena, of course, knew who "him" meant.

"How could I possibly look up to someone that, well, hasn't been on a mission?" Rae paused. "I guess that what I'm trying to say is that I want a man who will be a strong leader in my home, one who will serve diligently in the church and guide our family with sureness. Someone I can go to with my problems, and who can . . . Oh, I don't know." She wanted someone like David.

"Tiago will be twenty-five before he could go on a mission," Selena said. "Sometimes they won't even let them go that late. Is that what you're worried about—that they won't let him go?" Rae knew Selena was thinking about Paulo in the ward who had put his papers in twice and each time had been told that his next mission in life was to find a wife and get married, not to go on a mission.

"I think Paulo is older than twenty-five," Rae said. The room was silent for a minute. They could hear the sound of the primitive-looking washing machine in the kitchen and their landlady talking on the phone in the next room.

Rae sighed. "Even if my feelings *are* true, *and* he returned them, *and* if they did let him go on a mission, I don't know if I could wait two years to start a family. I mean, I used to worry about having a family because maybe I wouldn't be able to achieve other professional goals that I have. But since working here in the mission field, I've completely lost that fear. Having a family is the most important goal in my life now. It's what matters eternally. I want to be married more than anything. How could I wait like three more years just to see if things might work out?"

"You've got a point," Selena agreed. "So what are you going to do?"

"First things first," Rae replied, coming to a decision in that instant. "I'm going to ask the president for a transfer. I can't hinder the work with my feelings. It's too important to me. Once my mission is over, I don't want to regret anything, or feel I didn't do my best."

Selena frowned. "I wish you wouldn't. I don't want to lose you as a companion."

"I know. Me either." Rae came over and sat on the end of her bed. "I just don't know what else to do."

Now it was Selena's turn to sigh. "Well, I guess a transfer is best under the circumstances. But then what?"

"I don't know." Rae really didn't know; there were too many "ifs" involved. The best thing to do would be to forget it all. "I guess only time will tell."

Rae arose and turned out the light. Before slipping into bed, she knelt to pray. She hadn't meant to ask about Tiago, but the words came anyway. *Is he important to the rest of my life?* she asked. *Could he be . . . the one?* For a long time she felt nothing, but just as she was about to end her prayer, the answer came with unexpected clarity. Not a voice she heard with human ears, but a communication directly to her soul: "That's not for you to know now."

Rae was a little disappointed with the answer, but also relieved. At least she knew her decision to ask for a transfer had been a good one.

* * * * *

The next day Maria was baptized along with many others. The ward was growing at a tremendous rate—a result of how exceptionally open and believing the people were in Portugal. Rae knew they had been especially prepared by the Lord, and she felt lucky to play a part in bringing so many of her fellow brothers and sisters to the gospel. A mission wasn't easy, by any means, but she knew that having success made the trials far easier to bear.

She looked at everything in a new light now, knowing that she would likely be transferred the next week. Each person seemed more special than they had before, and Rae studied their faces so she could remember them forever. Most she would never meet again in this life. Seeing the spring flowers beginning to bud in the garden at the church was especially difficult as she knew that she would never see all the flowers bloom.

Maybe someday.

Rae tore her thoughts away from the future; they had no place in her present. She wrote the letter to the president asking for the transfer. She didn't go into detail, except to explain that her feelings for the people in the area were becoming a hindrance to her missionary work. If the president wanted to know more, he would call, she was sure. Besides, she didn't really know what else to say. She didn't even know for certain if her feelings for Tiago were real.

Writing the letter was the hardest thing she had ever done. A tear rolled down her cheek as she folded it into the envelope. As she wiped away the tear, she noticed the small silver CTR ring on her hand and remembered her family and friends at home. Everything would be all right—somehow.

The next week was difficult, but bearable. Her feelings of sadness at leaving those she considered her children—the many people she had taught and baptized—was compounded by her awareness of Tiago. Each time she saw him might be the very last.

The night before her transfer, Catarina, the sister in the ward who had introduced her to the Silvas, invited the sisters to her house for a farewell dinner. There they found the Silva family, along with many other dear and familiar faces. After a delicious dinner of turkey steak, rice, fried potatoes, and salad with onion and tomatoes—topped with olive oil, vinegar, and salt—the friends sat around the large table and began giving small presents to Rae, remembrances that she would treasure for the rest of her life.

"Thank you so much," Rae said as she opened the last present— a silver chain with a heart pendant from the Silvas.

"Tiago and Marcela picked it out for you," Maria told her.

"It's to remind you that you will always be in our hearts even though you're not with us." Tiago was smiling, but there seemed to be a sadness in his face as well. Rae wasn't sure.

"And you will always be in mine as well," Rae responded, making sure she used the plural form of the word "you" so as to include the whole family. She tried to keep a happy face, though she felt despondent. "And maybe next year after my mission is over, I can come back and visit." She didn't know where that came from, but she meant every word.

As the conversation moved to other topics, Rae sat quietly on her wooden chair. She stared out the sliding glass door behind the table which opened onto a small yard. Catarina and her family lived on the bottom floor and so had the advantage of having a bit of earth, unlike most apartment owners. Outside, Rae could see short rows of garden the family had planted, making her realize how much the members in Portugal were much like the members back home in the States.

"Did you mean it when you said you'll come visit?" Tiago sat down on the chair next to her, recently vacated by their hostess who had gone to the kitchen for the dessert.

"Yes, I meant it. I love Portugal." Then she added, almost to herself, "I never knew I could grow to love it so much."

"We would like you to stay with us when you come back," Tiago said. "Especially me."

Rae looked up in surprise. Her gaze shifted toward her companion across the table but she seemed deeply involved in a conversation with one of their investigators who had also come to the dinner.

"I would love to come," Rae admitted. "I'm going to miss your family."

"We're going to miss you, too" Tiago spoke in a low voice. There was more he wanted to say; she could see it in his eyes. But he didn't need to say it—not really. She knew. She knew because she felt the same way.

He left her and went to talk once more with the others.

Rae blinked twice and shook her head. Her heart ached within her chest. The last thing she wanted to do was to leave. But there was no way she could stay.

\* \* \* \* \*

After her transfer, Rae missed the Silva family and Selena more than she could remember missing her own family back in America. At first this worried her, but she gave up trying to figure things out and concentrated even more devoutly on her mission and the real reason she had come to Portugal—to bring people to a knowledge of the truth.

During the rest of her mission, she served in three additional areas, trained two more new missionaries, and touched many lives. She loved her companions—even the two difficult ones—and felt pride watching them turn into powerful missionaries. None, however, were ever so close to her as Selena had been. They kept in touch with phone calls and letters.

Rae also wrote to the Silva family as she did to many of the people she had taught, even those who had not been baptized. She made sure to always address the letters to Maria or to the family in general. Maria would always write back and tell her the news of the family and the ward. One time she wrote that Tiago had decided to serve a mission, and his decision brought peace to Rae's heart, as though the Lord had taken him out of her reach. She sincerely believed that once back home and involved in her life, she would forget the feelings she harbored for him.

The month before she finished her mission, Selena, now a senior companion and training a greeny herself, was transferred into Rae's district. Rae was delighted.

"Will you come to see me after you get home?" Rae said to her one day after their weekly district meeting. It was mid-December and this month's transfers would be the week after Christmas. Rae was going home. She wouldn't be making it in time for Christmas as Lisa had hoped, but certainly for the new year.

"Of course I'll come," Selena agreed immediately. Then she sighed. "At least, I will if I survive the next four months." She was having a difficult time in her new area with her greeny and was feeling discouraged. "Anyway, I've been planning to go to BYU."

Rae leaned back in her chair and thought for a moment. "You know, since the first time we met, I was impressed by you—your practicality, your motherliness, your spirit and dedication. I know you can make it, and make it big in your last few months." Rae paused and twisted Dave's CTR on her finger. She moved to a chair closer to Selena, sliding off the ring and holding it up for her to see.

"Do you remember my friend, Dave? Well, he gave me this ring before my mission. His sister had given it to him before he left on his own mission, telling him that if he ever needed comfort or assurance that he was to look at the ring and remember her. He gave the ring to me for the same reason. It has helped me so often on my mission that I can't even count the times. Now that I'm going home, I want you to have it so you can always know that someone, somewhere, loves you and is praying for you." Rae grabbed Selena's hand and pushed the ring onto her finger.

Selena blinked to hold back the tears. "Thanks. I could use it about now."

"Then it's settled." Rae sat back in her seat. "After your mission, go see your mom and do what you have to do, then come and see me. Hey, maybe we could even share an apartment. I've still got one more year left at school. How about it?"

"I'd love to—if you're not married before I get off my mission." Selena twisted the silver CTR ring on her finger.

"I guess that could happen," Rae admitted, glad that she had not mentioned Tiago. "But it's not too likely."

"Will you write me?"

"Of course."

\* \* \* \* \*

The Silvas came to see Rae at the baptisms in her ward the Sunday before she left Portugal.

"Why don't you come to visit me?" Rae asked Tiago with practiced nonchalance.

"Maybe I will," he said with a smile.

"He's already been to the U.S. Embassy to get papers for our visas," Marcela put in excitedly. "We have to go back this week to see if we pass their requirements. You wouldn't believe all the things they want to know!"

Rae felt her heart jump as she looked at Tiago in surprise, but he simply smiled and winked.

# Part Four

# Chapter Nineteen
## Welcome Home

*H*ome. Though everything was pretty much the same, it also seemed foreign to Rae. The roads were wide and houses—not apartments—were uncrowded. She particularly noticed the mountains the next morning, as the sun came up—she was still operating on Portuguese time—and only then did she realize how much she had missed them. Of course, it would still be a few months before she could go camping, picnicking, and hiking in the mountains, but it was enough to know they were there.

"Glad you're home, Rae." Chad hugged her as he came into the kitchen that same morning. She was sitting with a cup of hot chocolate and was surprised to see him up so early on a day with no school. She also couldn't get over how much he'd grown in the past year and a half since she had been gone. He'd turned twelve just before she left and in another six months he'd be fourteen.

"Since when do you get up early?" she asked him.

He smiled. "Well, let's put it this way. I've got shopping to do at the mall."

"More like girl watching," Bria said, coming down the stairs. "Don't you remember hanging out at the mall at his age?" Rae did. In fact, it seemed as if it were only yesterday.

"Well, Jimmy's mom is probably outside ready to take us now." Chad picked up his jacket and headed for the door, stopping for a moment to spray a jet of breath freshener into his mouth. His sisters watched him, smiling, but waited until he was gone before bursting into laughter.

"And where are you off to?" Rae studied her younger sister. Of everyone, Bria had probably changed the most, suddenly maturing into a beautiful young woman, both physically and emotionally. The braces were gone, and she was driving now—dating too. The seven-and-a-half-year age gap between them was considerably shortened.

"I'm going to the store. I promised Mom to decorate for your homecoming/New Year's Eve party tonight. We told your friends that they'd have to wait until tonight to see you. We wanted you all to ourselves at the airport."

"I was tired anyway," Rae yawned. "You all picking me up last night seems almost like a dream. And because of the time difference I'm still lagging. I couldn't sleep past four this morning—too close to lunch time in Portugal. I bet in a couple hours, I'll be ready to sleep again."

"Well rest up because we'll all be staying up late tonight."

"Staying up late won't be a problem," Rae said. "Not sleeping through lunch and dinner might be." They laughed and looked at each other a bit shyly. Rae figure it would take some getting used to, this new relationship of theirs.

After Bria left, Rae's parents and Taylor made their appearances. Her parents were unchanged, but Taylor, nearly eighteen, was graduating from high school this year and had grown taller than both Jon and her father. He was working part-time after school and was planning for his own mission when he turned nineteen.

"Will Jon and Lenna be here tonight?" Rae asked. Her older brother and his wife hadn't been at the airport the night before, and she was looking forward to seeing them and her nephews.

"Lenna wasn't feeling well so they didn't come last night," her mother said as if reading her mind. "They'll be here tonight, though, even if she's not feeling better. She can always lie down here." Suddenly Rae knew the rest of what her mother wasn't telling her. Strong Lenna had never been sick unless—

"They're going to have another baby!" Rae exclaimed. "Why didn't they tell me?"

"You blew it, Mom." Taylor helped himself to some hot chocolate.

"Rats! They wanted to surprise you." Their mother made a face. "Oh well. At least I won't tell you when it's due."

"Rae," her father sat down at the table next to her, "why don't you call the stake president to get released today? Officially you're still a missionary, you know. He left his work number for you to call and arrange an appointment before the party tonight."

"I guess that's a good idea." Rae took the paper from her father. Something inside ached at the idea of being released but she knew it was time to move on with her life. The Portugal part of it was over now.

Tears came to her eyes, and she bit her lower lip hard and looked down at the countertop. *Oh Tiago!* Noticing the suddenly silence and curious stares from her parents, she excused herself to take a shower. As she climbed slowly up the back stairs, she could hear her parents talking, though they had lowered their voices considerably. She caught only a whisper of her name and little more—just enough to know they were worried about her adjusting to normal life again.

Rae wondered if she would ever feel the same as she had before her mission. She didn't even want to. She had been so close to the Spirit, to the Lord, in Portugal, and she didn't want to lose that—ever. And then there was Tiago and her feelings for him. She didn't want to forget him, either. Even now as she paused in the hall and shut her eyes, she could see his face.

*It's over*, she thought. *Over before it ever began.* Her heart felt as if it were breaking.

Rae went into the upstairs bathroom and shut the door. She stepped into the shower, letting the water wash away her tears. Afterward, she felt much better. Ready to face reality. "I'll forget him," she whispered to herself. "The whole thing is too crazy."

A short while later after she dressed and went downstairs again, she found her mother sorting the mail. "That's funny," she said. "There's already a letter for you from Portugal." She handed Rae the letter. "How about us going shopping? I thought we could get you a few outfits."

"That'd be great." Rae was about to say more when she read the return address on the letter.

"Tiago," she whispered. Her heartbeat quickened.

"Who?"

"A man we baptized in Almada. The one I wrote to you about where the mother, Maria, received a testimony after finally reading the Book of Mormon."

Her mother frowned with concentration. "Oh, yeah. I think I know the one. He has a sister, right? A sister about your age? I remember thinking it was strange they both still lived at home."

"It's because housing's so expensive there. Most children do live at home until they marry—usually until their late twenties."

"That's right. I remember you writing that. Well, aren't you going to open it?" Her mother ripped open a letter of her own.

Rae nodded and awkwardly opened the envelope, her hands suddenly seeming to have more thumbs than fingers.

*My Dear Rae,*

*By the time you receive this letter you will be home with your family, your mission behind you. Now I can finally say that I love you! You are like a ray of sun in the dark of my previous life.*

*We have been such good friends, and I can't wait to get to know you better. I'm coming to see you! My first request for a visa was denied last week, but before you leave Portugal, I'll have new papers to add. I am coming! It will be wonderful to see you again. I'll call you as soon as I find out about the visa.*

*Yours, Tiago*

Rae felt her heart beat heavily in her chest. A glad smile spread across her lips. Could it be true? She almost didn't dare hope.

"He's coming to visit, Mom," Rae said. "Is that okay?"

"Just him or the whole family?" Her mother looked closely at her.

Rae knew her face was flushed, but didn't care. "He and his sister, Marcela—I think." Rae read Tiago's words again, glad for the opportunity her lowered lashes provided to hide her emotions.

"Is he important to you, Rae?" Her mother wanted to know. Her voice sounded as though she feared the answer.

Rae met her mother's gaze and recognized the concern, but underneath she also sensed understanding. She smiled softly and said, "I think I might love him."

\* \* \* \* \*

"Lisa!" Rae shouted as she opened the door to see her friend. In her arms was a small, blanket-wrapped bundle, and the two girls hugged as best they could. Rae turned to hug Mark while Lisa began unwrapping her daughter.

"Oh, she's beautiful!" Rae reached for the infant. "May I?"

"Sure." Lisa gently laid the baby in Rae's arms. Rae sat down on the sofa in the front room and removed the blanket to reveal a miniature Lisa with a mess of dark hair shooting in every direction.

"What a gorgeous baby!" Rae cooed and kissed the soft cheeks. "Kimberly Rae Thompson, you are beautiful! But that's probably because you were named for your exceptionally stunning aunt."

"Who, by the way, is a lot skinnier than she should be," commented Lisa, looking down a bit ruefully at her own figure which had not quite returned to her pre-baby size.

"Well, a mission's hard work," Rae teased. "I haven't had time to sit home watching soap operas and eating chocolate." They all laughed. "Oh, you guys, it's so good to be home. It makes missing Portugal and everyone there so much easier. I—" The doorbell rang again. Rae gave the baby back to Lisa and went to open it.

"Jon, Lenna come in." Rae hugged her brother tightly and then hugged Lenna. "So out with it, when's the baby due?"

Lenna laughed. "Oh, they told you!"

"No, I guessed. You're never sick unless you're pregnant."

"Well, it'll be here in a month." She opened her long, heavy coat to show her big stomach.

"How exciting—now you'll have three!" Then Rae bent down to talk to Shane and Jonny. "That means I must be getting old. Maybe I'm going to need help blowing out my birthday candles. Will I have any helpers?"

The children smiled and nodded but were too shy to speak. Rae sighed. She knew it would take a few hours for them to warm up to her since she had been gone so long.

"How about we all go into the family room and start this party?" Jon held aloft two videos in his hands. But Lenna had gone over to see Lisa and baby Kimberly, and they were already deep into a conversation about babies.

Mark sighed. "Let's go. There's no tearing them apart now." Everyone else nodded in agreement and headed toward the family room, with Lisa and Lenna bringing up the rear, talking full swing.

Soon the large family room was full of people. Andrew and Michelle had also arrived with the happy news that they were expecting their first baby together! Little Hope, now nearly six, was quiet at first but after a while raced off to run loudly through the house with Shane and Jonny. Michelle quickly joined Lisa and Lenna to add her own expertise to their mothering conversation, leaving Rae alone with Andrew. They smiled at each somewhat awkwardly.

"It's good to see you, Rae," Andrew said finally.

"And you too. You look happy."

Andrew nodded. "Happier than I ever thought I could be after you turned me down. But you were right. We weren't supposed to get married. It was Michelle all along. I owe you a lot for following the Spirit. I could have made us both end up miserable."

Rae laughed. "I doubt that. First and foremost, we were always friends. But I'm glad you and Michelle are happy."

"Thanks. And I hope you find the man you're waiting for."

Rae bit her lip. "So do I."

"Hey, Daddy, come help us play this game." Hope reappeared at his side. In her hands she carried a card game. "I can't read all of the words yet. Will you help me?"

"Of course, honey." Andrew laughed and let himself be pulled to where the other children sat waiting. Rae smiled. It seemed Andrew was in his element.

Despite the growing crowd, Rae felt lonely. Each of Rae's brothers and sister had a date, or in Chad's case a friend, and though Rae was happy to be with those she loved, she couldn't help feeling a little left out. A short time ago she had led an important life as a missionary in a country where she had stood out, not only because she was a missionary, but because of her height and blonde hair. She had grown used to being the center of attention. But here life had gone on quite well without her; she was now one among many. Her thoughts turned to Tiago, and her longing for the country she had left returned in force.

"Rae, Love," came a voice behind her. Rae whirled to find Dave staring at her. "No one answered the door," he said, "so I let myself in. There must be too much noise in here."

"Oh, Dave!" He looked so handsome and happy to see her that Rae threw herself into his arms for a hug.

"Still Dave, I see," Dave said, his blue eyes sparkling. He hugged her tightly for a minute and asked, "Uh, this is okay, isn't it?"

Rae chuckled. "Oh, yes. I was released a couple of hours ago. The stake president simply shook my hand and handed me the release letter from my president, the same one I carried home on the plane in a sealed envelope, and that was that."

"How well I remember!" Dave loosened his hold on Rae and both looked at each other a little self-consciously. "You look the same except that your hair's longer."

"Well, I've got a few wrinkles from the stress, not to mention more muscles," added Rae. "But *you've* changed a bit." And he had. His slender figure of before had been replaced by a bulkier one, and his hair was obviously thinning in front. The effect made him seem older, more manly—and just as charming as before.

"Yeah, you know us lawyer types. We spend too much time sitting at our desks preparing our cases—eating with one hand and pulling our hair out with the other." He cast her a stunning grin and Rae smiled back. Her heart skipped a beat.

"How are you adjusting?" Dave asked.

"Well, it all seems very strange. For instance, today my mom and I went out shopping and none of the stores closed for lunch. In Portugal, the whole country just about shuts down between one and three!"

"That's not what I meant. I was talking emotionally and spiritually. I remember when I first got home I was amazed at how wicked everyone seemed—even people I had looked up to before. Suddenly, I realized they were human, or something. I don't know."

Rae smiled at him. "I guess I haven't been home long enough

to notice that. But I'll be okay. Come on, let's join the others." She motioned with a hand.

"That reminds me," Dave said looking at her hand. "Do you still have the CTR ring?"

Rae shook her head. "That ring helped me out so many times Dave—as you well know from my letters—and I wanted that tradition to go on. So before I left I gave it to my old companion. As *you* suggested in one of your letters, I might add. She's been having a rough time of it, lately." She punched Dave playfully on the arm. "If you want it back, you'll have to see her when she comes home in four months."

"Well, maybe I will!"

For some unfathomable reason, Rae felt a stab of jealousy.

* * * * *

"And there we were walking down the street during the first day of Carnival and some young guy threw an egg at us." Nearly a month after her homecoming party, Rae lay slumped on the family room sofa talking with Lisa and looking at her mission photo album. Everything seemed almost the same as before her mission except that now baby Kimberly was with them—and Rae was still living at home with her parents.

"Now," she continued, "the Carnival celebration isn't as wild in Portugal as it is in Brazil. There I hear they don't even let the missionaries out of their apartments the whole week. It's like for that week the whole country goes crazy. Anyway, in Portugal it's not that bad. We were only warned to watch for flying eggs and such."

"So did he hit you?" Lisa wanted to know.

"No, he was too far away. But it made me a little upset. Here I had this new greeny and I wanted to impress her, so I yelled at him and told him to come and talk with us. I was going to start giving him the Church pamphlets and stuff—that usually stops them dead. But this guy shakes his head and runs further down the street. After a while he stops and moons us!"

"He didn't!" Lisa squealed.

"Yes, he did. Of course, he was far enough away by that time that all we saw was a pink blur. But I can tell you, I sure kept my mouth shut during the rest of Carnival. We had to dodge a few more eggs, but I wasn't risking that again!"

Laughing, Lisa turned the page. "Who are these guys?"

Rae's smile faltered. "That's the Silva family. I'm sure I wrote you about them."

"You wrote about so many. Remind me."

Rae quickly outlined how she and her companion had met and helped convert the family, and how special they were.

"Why, Rae," Lisa said when she was through. "I think you really like this guy, Tiago. Don't you?"

Rae grimaced at Lisa. "Oh, yeah. I more than like him."

"No way, you're kidding!" Lisa's eyes grew wide. "But that's wonderful!"

"It was a little difficult, at the time." Rae shook her head. "You're not on a mission to meet people to date."

"Well, what about now? You're off your mission. Does he feel the same about you?"

"I think so."

Baby Kimberly let out a tiny peep, and Lisa put a pacifier in her mouth. "I can't believe you didn't tell me! Why am I always the last one to know anything these days?"

Rae frowned down at the picture, but despite herself she began to trace the lines of his face with her finger tip. "I guess I should have told you," she said. The truth was it had been too personal to share with anyone, though in the past weeks she had shared her feelings with her mother.

"How old is he?"

"Twenty-five. His sister there beside him is a couple years younger."

Lisa bent forward and studied the picture. "I swear he seems familiar somehow. I don't know. It's something about his face—I know, it's those eyes! Where have I seen them before?"

Rae laughed. "You haven't. But I suppose you will soon. I think he's coming to visit."

"That's too cool!"

Rae sighed. "But it all seems so impossible. I mean, I'm not even sure how I feel. I don't really *know* him, you know? Besides, there's a little matter about him wanting to go on a mission." She looked over at the baby in Lisa's arms. "I want one of these—I don't want to wait to start my family. Remember our old stake president and his talk about ladders? Well, I'll be twenty-four soon. I'm ready to move up to the next step now."

Lisa nodded and smiled. "That's exactly how I was right before I met Mark."

"I remember."

"You know, Mark has two older brothers who didn't go on missions." Lisa shifted the baby so her head rested on her shoulder. "They were too old when they were converted—one was engaged at the time. They're two of the most spiritual men I've ever met. And since they did study out and research the gospel, I *know* they're really converted. Maybe you should give Tiago a chance. It's not his fault he wasn't born into the gospel like we were."

"It's different. I was the missionary who taught him."

Lisa wasn't convinced. "But shouldn't the real issue be if you love him and if Heavenly Father approves of your relationship?"

"I guess so."

"What about Dave?" Lisa asked. "I hear he's been calling a lot."

Rae shook her head. "I don't know. I mean, all this time, I did somewhat hope in the back of my mind that everything would change and that when I came home, he'd sweep me off my feet. But, I think I'm too hung up on Tiago to give Dave and me another try. It's not fair to him."

Lisa was quiet for a moment as she rocked her baby. "What you probably don't know is that Dave's been going through a spiritual crisis lately. I'm really worried about him. I think a lot of it has to do with watching his friends get married and go on with their lives while he's still alone. He's sort of turned into a recluse. He still goes to church, but his heart is aching. I was hoping that you could help me with him."

"Dave, having problems?" Rae blinked. "I can hardly believe that. He was always so strong. Of course, I'll help—anything you ask." Maybe she could use some of the things she had learned on her mission.

The phone's shrill ringing cut through the silence, making both girls jump. Rae picked up the phone. "Hello?"

There was static and a short delay and then, "Olá? Rae?" said a familiar deep voice.

"Tiago!"

"Yes, it's me. How are you?"

"Good. How are you? And your family?" Rae couldn't believe how wonderful it was to speak and to hear Portuguese! It seemed so long since she had done either.

"Good. We're all good. Did you get my letter?" Tiago asked.

"Yes, I . . ." Rae's voice trailed off. How could she explain how she felt reading his words? Or how much she wanted him to come for a visit?

"Well, I got the visa! And Marcela too. Do you *want* me to come?" Though he didn't spell it out, Rae knew what he was asking. Was there a chance for him? A chance for them?

Her heart pounded furiously. "Oh, yes! I *do* want you to come." In case she had been too exuberant, she added, "You will love America."

"Do you have a pen?"

Rae opened the drawer of the end table and fumbled for a pen. She only found one of her nephew's crayons. "Yes. Go ahead." Rae wrote down the flight information in the margin of the phone book. Her excitement mounted when she realized that he would arrive on a Tuesday evening, only five days away. "How long can you stay?"

"A month, if that's okay."

"It's wonderful!" A month sounded like an eternity at the moment, especially since it had been almost that long since she had seen him. "My parents say it's okay. You'll sleep in one of my brothers' rooms and Marcela will stay in mine with me. I'm in school a couple of hours in the morning but after that I'll be able to show you around. I haven't had the heart to get a real job yet, so I have plenty of free time. Hey, what about your school?"

"I got the time off. I only have a couple of tests to take before I finish anyway. I can take them anytime I'm ready. Our schools are much different than yours."

"Great. I'll be at the airport to pick you up." Rae knew the call was costing him a lot of money—more than it would have costed her to call him.

"Well, I'll see you there," Tiago said. Then after a short pause. "Rae, I . . ." He added something, very low, but Rae couldn't make it out. Could it have been, *I love you?*

"Goodbye!" she yelled loudly into the phone, hoping he could still hear. "See you soon!" She set the phone gently into the cradle.

Looking up, she saw Lisa smirking at her. "Hmm," she said. "I was wrong. I don't think you like him at all. No, I think you are completely and totally gone on him—nuts."

Rae smiled. "Well, he'll be here in five days. So I guess I'm about to find out if this feeling I have is real or if I truly am crazy."

# Chapter Twenty
## The Crescent Moon

*R*ae stood outside gate eight at the airport, waiting nervously. She was alone. Her mother, Bria, and Lisa had all wanted to tag along, but she had wanted to savor the pleasure of being with her Portuguese friends without worry about translating. It had been so long since they had spent any time together!

*And I'm not a missionary anymore.* Her heart seemed to skip a beat at the thought. What would she feel seeing Tiago on more even footing . . . on civilian footing . . .

Passengers poured from the secured area outside of which Rae and others waited. Gradually, the flood of people subsided. Around her people were hugging and kissing their loved ones, but Tiago and Marcela were nowhere to be seen.

*Could they have missed their plane?* Rae thought. She waited anxiously as a few more people straggled in. At last she caught sight of them and waved. Tiago was one step ahead of his sister, and he quickened his pace when he saw her. In a fluid motion, he set down their carry-on luggage and pulled Rae into a bear hug that left her breathless.

She was in his arms! They felt strong and sure around her, as though she was meant to be there.

All too soon, he held her back to look at her intently before gently placing the customary Portuguese kisses on each cheek. How strange and exhilarating to exchange *beijinhos* with Tiago!

Since he'd been traveling for nearly twenty-four hours, Rae felt the stubble of his beard scrape against her cheeks, and she loved the feeling. She could smell his aftershave, too, and she spied the most adorable tiny mole on his left earlobe. After the kisses, he hugged her tightly again. Oh, how she'd dreamed of this day!

"Come on, it's my turn," Marcela grumbled. Laughing, Rae disengaged herself from Tiago and turned to exchange hugs and *beijinhos* with Marcela.

"It's so great to see you," Rae said.

"And you," Marcela returned, "although one of us seems to be more excited at seeing you than the other."

Tiago grinned, making Rae's heart jump. "What about your mother?" she asked quickly.

"She sends her love and about a million presents," Tiago answered. "She would have liked to have come, but she couldn't get away from the store." He leaned over to pick up both carry-ons with one hand. "I brought a present for you, too," he added.

"I can't wait to see what it is." Rae hooked her arm through his. "Let's go get your suitcases."

Rae hadn't known exactly what to expect, but being with Tiago and Marcela was better than old times. She had worried that she might not fit in with them, or that because of her role of bringing them into the church, she might seem more like a parent than a friend. But that was obviously not the case. They spent the long drive home regaling her with all the news from home and how the ward was doing since Rae had left the area. Many of their stories were spiritual and Rae was impressed at the progress they had made.

When they arrived home it was nearly midnight. Rae's father had gone to bed because he had to get up early for work, but the rest of the family was waiting up for the visitors.

"Family, this is Tiago," Rae announced. "And this is Marcela." She introduced the family members one by one.

"It is very nice to meet you," Tiago said in faltering, accented English. He had never taken English—only French—in school, but Rae knew he had been practicing with tapes.

"Welcome to our house," Rae's mother said somewhat formally. She spoke slowly and precisely so both Tiago and Marcela could understand.

After exchanging more pleasantries and presenting the various small presents that their custom demanded they offer to Rae's family, it was time to go to bed.

Rae said good night to Tiago at the door to Taylor's room. Once again he kissed her on both cheeks, and once again Rae could smell his aftershave. Her pulse quickened.

"I told you I'd come," he said softly in Portuguese.

"Well," she teased, "maybe we'll see if we do have unfinished business between us."

"Oh, we do," he assured her, "and I'm going to prove it to you."

Rae could hardly stop herself from dancing with joy. But, "Maybe," was all she said.

As she went down the hall, Rae heard her mother showing Marcela around in her room. Rae headed toward the sound of their voices—only to be waylaid by Bria.

"He's so dang good-looking!" she exclaimed. "And tall, too. But I thought you said all the Portuguese were short! Is he in love with you? I think he is. It's the way he looks at you with those gorgeous eyes! Oo!" She gave a little squeal. "And you stare right back at him, you know—are you in love?"

Rae laughed at her sister's excitement. "It's so good to be back at home, Bria. Did I ever tell you how much I missed you?" She hugged her. "As for your questions, I think I'm going to have to wait to see what happens. But you can sure help me show them around Utah while I'm figuring things out."

"Great. But I still can't believe it! You go on a mission and bring back the best-looking guy in the country! Where can I sign up?"

At that moment Chad came running up the stairs. "Mom, Mom!" he shouted. "Come quick!"

"Whoa!" Rae grabbed him as he headed for their parents' room. "She's in my room. What's the hurry?"

"It's Lenna!" he panted. "She's at the hospital having the baby! They want us there. They've got a neighbor home with the boys. I'll wake up Dad." Everyone scurried around to find shoes and coats. It took two cars to get the whole family plus the visitors—who also wanted to go—to the hospital where Lenna had not waited for them to have the baby.

After a short time they were all allowed inside to see the new member of the family. Lenna even insisted that Tiago and Marcela come into the room briefly, wanting to meet them and show off her new little girl. When it was Rae's turn to hold the tiny baby, a feeling of awe came over her.

"You just came from Heavenly Father, little Allie," she whispered to the baby. "How are things up there—can you tell us?" The baby opened one eye briefly as if to say, "I could, but I'm too tired. I've been through a lot," then drifted off to sleep.

Much later, back at the house, Rae once again said good night to Tiago, this time at her bedroom door.

"You looked like you know how to handle babies," Tiago said softly.

Rae smiled. "Well, I hope so, I want a lot of them." She returned his intense gaze, wondering what he might say to that. The Portuguese didn't usually have big families, though there were members who did.

"My relatives have a saying," he said. "'Many children make poor parents.' But the gospel has taught me that children are important. Besides, I'm not afraid of being poor."

Before Rae could respond, he leaned over and kissed her once, quickly, on the lips. It was a brief kiss and so unexpected, already over just as Rae began to feel the gentle pressure of his lips. Then he was walking down the hall.

She wished it had lasted a little longer, that he had wrapped his arms around her and proclaimed his love. But fear also arose within her heart. What if she was building herself up for another broken relationship? She brought a hand up to her mouth, tracing her lips with a finger. Almost, she could feel his kiss again. Sighing, she went into her room and shut the door.

\* \* \* \* \*

The next week was spent in a family-wide effort to show the visitors the various nearby sights in Utah. One of the first places they visited was Temple Square in Salt Lake. Of the two Portuguese, Marcela knew more English, and Rae didn't worry when she and Tiago became separated from Marcela and the rest of the family on the temple grounds. As they walked through the many displays, hand in hand, Rae was surprised that Tiago knew as much as she did about the various gospel concepts, some of which she had always taken for granted.

Soon they were staring up at the lighted temple, huddled together against the cold January air. "You know," Tiago said softly in Portuguese, "ever since you taught my family about the temple I have longed to see one, to go inside one, to seal my family forever. Today at least part of my dream has come true."

Rae did a rapid calculation in her head. "Let's see, you have only six more weeks until you can take out your endowments. Oh, Tiago! That means you'd have to go back to Portugal two weeks before you could go through!" She was dismayed that he had come so far, only to miss going to the temple by two weeks.

Tiago laughed. "Yes. I already figured that out."

"But why didn't you wait two weeks to come? Then both you and Marcela could have gone through the temple here."

Tiago turned to her, holding both her hands in his. "The

temple means a lot to me," he began softy. "But two more weeks without seeing you would be an eternity."

Rae felt her mouth round to an *O*.

He smiled. "Besides, Marcela and I will take our mother through in Switzerland or Spain after we go home. It won't be long."

Rae turned her head away sharply. "What is it?" Tiago asked, clutching her hands more tightly.

She turned to him again, hoping he wouldn't misunderstand the tears in her eyes. "I just wish I could be there with you and your family when you go."

He pulled her to him and stroked her hair almost hesitantly. "I know. I feel the same."

Rae rested her head against his bulky jacket, feeling comforted. He had only been in America a week and already he was a big part of her life. She marveled at how wonderful he seemed to her. During their tour of Temple Square, her worries about him not being strong spiritually vanished as he shared his feelings about the gospel.

The next day Rae and her family took Tiago and Marcela out for juicy hamburgers, which they had never eaten before. Marcela took one big bite and sighed in contentment. "Now this is real food," she said.

Tiago shook his head at her. "The next thing you will say is that you like this red stuff too," he said in hesitant English, motioning to the ketchup.

"But you *have* to eat fries with ketchup," Chad said, dipping three fries into the "red stuff" for emphasis. "They're just not good without ketchup."

"Right!" Marcela also stuck a fry into the ketchup and into her mouth, then wrinkled her nose slightly at the taste. "It's good," she said finally, not very convincingly.

Tiago also dipped a fry and ate it. "It'll take time to get used to this," he said, laughing. Everyone laughed with him. Rae noticed that neither he or Marcela used ketchup with the remainder of their French fries.

When they arrived home, Chad tumbled out onto the snow-filled lawn before his father could stop the car, marring the perfect expanse of white that had fallen earlier that day. He quickly packed a few snowballs and threw one at Rae and Tiago as they climbed from her car, and the other snowball sped through the open garage door at his father, who had driven the rest of the family to the restaurant.

"Oh, yeah?" shouted Rae. She dropped her keys into her pocket and bounded into the snow. In seconds she had a ball and threw it at Chad. Tiago and Marcela were right behind her and the rest of Rae's family as well. From all sides Chad was pummeled with soft-packed snow balls.

"Teams!" he screamed. "Teams! Let's divide up."

Snowballs stopped flying. "Okay," Rae said. "Tiago, Marcela, Chad, and me against Mom, Dad, Bria, and Taylor."

"With five minutes to make ammunition," Chad added. Everyone went furiously to work. Soon the balls were flying again. Rae's hands grew red and numb as she had forgotten her gloves. Everyone else was in the same predicament and finally Rae's father pleaded a truce. The family and visitors dropped to the snow, exhausted and panting.

Tiago looked over at Rae and laughed. "So it has some uses after all, this snow. I was beginning to wonder if it was only beautiful to look at."

Rae had never seen snow as being beautiful before. She looked around at it now, glistening in the moonlight and saw that he was right. Snow did have its own austere beauty, especially in the pure, untouched areas. Rae shook her head. She had wanted to show Tiago her world, instead he was showing her the beauty she had long taken for granted.

Another week rolled by. Aside from her morning classes, Rae spent all her time with Tiago. Marcela often went out with Bria or Taylor and their friends, leaving Tiago and Rae alone. Rae adored those times. They spent hours discussing—in Portuguese—everything from politics to car repair in great detail, often disagreeing, but rarely getting angry. They also studied the scriptures with the family daily, which confirmed Rae's confidence in his spirituality. She felt contentment as she had never known before. She tried hard not to think about the day when his visa would expire and he would have to go home.

During the time Tiago had been with her, Rae had not seen much of her friends. But Lisa was persistent, and she called halfway through his visit. "I've got it all planned," she informed Rae. "We're taking them ice-skating. All of us will be there. We want to meet this guy you're dating. Especially Dave."

"I don't know why he'd care," Rae said. "But I'm game. When?"

"Friday night."

"We'll be there."

Just about everyone close to them was at the skating rink that Friday night—Andrew and Michelle, Lisa and Mark, Dave, and Rae's family, including Jon, Lenna and the kids. Lenna with her brand new baby didn't skate but sat watching from the sidelines with the pregnant Michelle, who held Lisa's baby so that she could skate.

Lisa and Jon were experts at ice-skating and quickly went about teaching Tiago and Marcela as Rae stood nearby, watching. Rae herself had only been ice-skating twice and had trouble making it around the rink without falling or bumping into something or someone, usually one of her younger brothers who raced around her teasingly. To her surprise, Dave appeared at her elbow and began to guide her over the ice.

"I'm that bad, huh?" Rae asked.

Dave flashed her his handsome grin. "I'm afraid so."

They were quiet for a few moments and Rae couldn't help but turn her head to see how Tiago was faring under her brother's tutelage. He seemed to be doing better than she was.

"Haven't seen much of you since you got back from Portugal," Dave commented, noting the direction of her stare.

She turned her head toward him. "Yeah, I've been busy."

"With *him*?" Dave's voice sounded odd, but Rae couldn't pinpoint the emotion.

"Yes . . . and with school." Her gaze went again to Tiago who saw her and waved.

"Do you love him?" Dave persisted.

Rae stopped sharply, almost falling in the process. Dave grabbed her arms to steady her. "I'm not sure," Rae said. Unbidden tears pricked her eyes.

Dave looked grim, but Rae didn't understand why her possible love for Tiago could upset him. Hadn't they already put their relationship behind them? "When does he go home?" Dave asked.

"Two weeks." Rae couldn't keep the sadness from her voice.

"Well, I'll call you again then. Maybe we can have some fun. Like old times."

"Yeah. Sure, Dave."

Tiago was coming towards them, his face triumphant. "It's not so hard," he said in English. But instead of stopping, he barreled into Rae, knocking them both to the ground in a flurry of arms and legs.

"Are you okay?" Tiago asked.

Rae could feel the cold of the ice through her pants, but other than that she was all right. "I think so. What about you?"

"Well, I guess I've fallen for you!" They both laughed and began to disentangle themselves. When Rae looked around, Dave was nowhere to be seen.

After an hour, both Rae and Tiago were tired of ice-skating. Marcela was still going strong so they left her at the rink with the rest of the family. Soon they found themselves at home in the family room.

Tiago was suddenly very quiet, and Rae wondered if he was thinking of how little time they had left together. She certainly was. She led him to the couch, but Tiago reached out and grabbed her hand before she could sit. "Only two more weeks," he said in a near whisper.

"I wish you could stay." Rae found she meant every word. Their time was running out.

Suddenly they were in each other's arms. Tiago's face lowered toward hers. *What if I don't feel anything?* Rae thought fleetingly. But as their lips met, seemingly in slow motion, she felt love pour over her in a way she had only dreamed about. She never wanted their kiss to end.

"I love you so much," Tiago whispered after a while, his voice heavy with emotion.

"I think I love you too." Rae could hardly breathe because Tiago was holding her so tightly, but she didn't want him to let go.

"Will you marry me?" Tiago held his breath for the answer.

"Yes." At that moment Rae didn't think about any of the obstacles facing them. What were thousands of miles and a vast ocean anyway? She only knew that she loved Tiago.

"I've been waiting so long to hear you say that." Tiago loosened his hold and brought a small box out of his jacket pocket. Inside, Rae discovered a thin gold band of diamond cut gold—a band that was custom among Tiago's peers to give to a fiancée.

"I love it!" Rae exclaimed. "I wanted one of these—I almost bought one for myself!" She let Tiago slip the ring onto her finger.

"Well, you can pick out your own wedding ring later on—I'm learning that's important for you American women." His smile showed he didn't mind. He kissed her again, setting Rae's heart to thumping.

"Do you know when I first knew that I wanted to marry you?" he asked, smiling tenderly.

"No, when?"

"It was at one of those family nights, the ones you used to have at the church for new members and investigators. It was the Monday night after my cousin was baptized. I think I had been a member about three weeks. After your lesson you led the group in that silly game where the people who don't know how to play ask the ones who do various questions in order to find out the secret—only the secret was that you answer the question asked to the person sitting next to you instead of the question directed to you. Do you remember that night?"

"Yes, I do." Rae smiled fondly at the memory. She sank down to sit on the couch, pulling Tiago with her. "I don't think I ever played that game again the rest of my mission."

"That was the night I knew I loved you." Tiago cradled her in his arms. "You were sitting up there in the front, and I had figured out the secret but I didn't want to say because I was enjoying watching you so much. You looked so adorable and, well, it's hard to explain. You were so vivacious and alive, and suddenly I knew that I wanted to be with you for eternity. It didn't matter that I'd have to wait so long to be with you, to hold you in my arms, to kiss you." At that he placed a tender kiss on her temple. "That night when I prayed I knew for sure it was right."

"I never knew," Rae said. "A couple of weeks before your mother was baptized, my companion said you liked me, but it wasn't something I had even noticed before then. After that I realized I was attracted to you and I felt guilty. I asked to be transferred, and I was, though I probably would have been anyway since I'd been in the area for so long."

"I hated seeing you go." Tiago traced her hand on her leg with his finger, as if making a crayon drawing of a hand for a child. His other arm was around Rae. "I didn't know you'd asked for a transfer. Still, I thought it would be easier with you in another area."

"And was it?" Rae asked.

He grimaced. "Not at all. I missed you so much. You always lit up any room you were in, and after you were gone, it was like a light was missing from my life."

"I missed you too." But Rae was beginning to suspect he'd had the worst end of the deal. She at least had been able to throw herself into missionary work. During those times she had been focused and able to put aside her feelings.

"But here we are."

"It's all so unbelievable." Rae snuggled her head close to Tiago's shoulder. She felt so loved and wanted and beautiful here with Tiago. Somehow their love had changed her, had made her beautiful. "So what now?"

"I've been giving it some thought—I've had a lot of time to think—and when we get married we'll have to live in America."

"Why?" she asked, lifting her head up to look at him. But even as she said it she felt relieved. As much as she loved Portugal, Rae didn't want to give up her country and her family.

"Because of you. I don't want to leave my country, but I don't feel I can ask that of you, either."

Rae opened her mouth to say that she was willing—she loved Portugal and its people—but then she started thinking about her mother, her sister, and her brothers. Lisa, Andrew and Michelle. Her nephews and new little niece. Leaving them in a more permanent way would be hard. But too hard?

Tiago went on, "I can work in computers anywhere, and my English is coming along well. I'll be able to find a job easily, I think."

Rae felt guilty at her relief. "What will your mother say?"

Tiago frowned. "She gave me her blessing before I left Portugal. She wants me to be happy."

Rae hugged him then, her heart full of all he was willing to do for her. Of what Maria and Marcela were willing to give up for her. Tiago took a deep breath, and she pulled back to see tears in his eyes. "What is it?"

He buried his face in her neck. "Oh Rae, I was so afraid you'd turn me down," he whispered.

That surprised her. He seemed so confident. "But I didn't."

"I know." He smoothed her hair with his hand, making her shiver with goose bumps. She had the strange feeling of déjà vu, that sometime, somewhere, he had touched her this way before. The feeling was gone before she could examine it closely, replaced by another, more confusing thought.

"What about your mission?" Rae was fearful of his answer, but she couldn't decide if she was more afraid that he still wanted to go or that maybe he had changed his mind.

Tiago lifted his head. "I want to go, if they'll let me."

At his words Rae felt a mixture of pride and sadness. But the joy she'd felt suddenly dimmed. Could their love wait, untarnished, for two whole years? Could she wait when her arms ached to hold him and their future babies? She didn't have the answer.

\* \* \* \* \*

When Rae's family arrived home that night they all noticed the new ring on her hand right away. It was as if they had been waiting for it all along.

"Oh, Rae, I'm so happy for you!" Bria gushed. "How romantic! I'm going to be a bridesmaid!"

"What is bridesmaid?" asked Marcela. Bria laughed and hurried to explain.

"Not for a while," Rae added. "We haven't set the date."

Rae couldn't help but notice that behind the smiles, concern lurked in her parents' eyes. Still, there was nothing she could do about that; she loved Tiago and somehow things would work out for the best. At least she hoped so.

Tiago and Rae took a short walk that night before they went to bed. Though the night was calm and beautiful, it was also very cold. But it was certainly worth braving the frigid air to be alone. The moon and stars shone brightly in the cloudless sky, illuminating the cement sidewalk.

Tiago stopped. "You see that?" He pointed to the crescent moon. Rae nodded and he continued. "It's ours. Wherever we are we can both look at the moon and know that the other will see the same moon—then we won't be that far away. And one day, when we're finally together, the moon will be ours."

"Our moon," whispered Rae, looking up into the night sky and gripping Tiago's hand tightly. It was indescribably beautiful.

And so very far away.

Before Rae slipped into bed that night she prayed about Tiago. Afterwards, she still felt right about marrying him. She shoved all thoughts of his mission and their prolonged separation away from her. Surely it was what the Lord wanted. She must accept it. Somehow she would make it through.

The next two weeks passed even more quickly, as if time was purposely working against them. Rae held onto every minute she could with Tiago, knowing it was almost her last. She saw very little of her friends in those weeks, wanting to spend all her time with him. The few times she did see Lisa, her feelings became even more bittersweet as there was always Lisa's tiny daughter, representing the baby Rae couldn't yet have.

Tiago tried to extend his visa, but the request was denied. So on the appointed day, Rae and her mother drove Tiago and

Marcela to the airport. She hugged and kissed Marcela and then turned to Tiago.

"I love you," he said. Tears stood out in his eyes, and Rae could see herself reflected in them. She blinked hard, refusing to let her own tears fall.

"I love you, too." She threw herself into his arms.

Tiago's face was a mask of misery as he turned and strode down the corridor toward the security check. He didn't look back. Maybe it was easier that way.

"Should we go?" Her mother asked.

Rae shook her head. "Let's wait for the plane to take off. In case something goes wrong at the last minute and the flight is delayed."

So they waited until the plane took off—without problems. When at last they turned to leave, Rae's tears finally came. Her mother put an awkward arm around Rae, apparently uncertain how to comfort her.

Rae accepted her mother's embrace, sobbing into her shoulder. The tears eventually subsided, but she felt no better. *I guess*, she thought, *some things can't be hugged away.*

# Chapter Twenty-One
## Long Distance Romance

Rae lived for Tiago's phone calls and letters—and for cloudless nights when she could look at the moon—but it wasn't the same as being with him. Tiago's many letters were full of the most romantic things she had ever read. He called her "my darling" and "my life," told her his most inner thoughts, and talked of their future together. "I miss you," he wrote once. "You are my life. The emptiness I feel without you is so very great, greater than I ever imagined possible. Only you can fill that void. I find it hard to concentrate on anything other than my eternal love for you, my beautiful fiancée." Rae echoed his feeling completely. She felt almost lost without his constant presence.

Though his calls and letters did make her feel temporarily better, they brought fear as well. She kept waiting for the one that would tell of his mission call and confirm the two more years they would have to wait until they could obtain their moon. She found herself silently grateful when his paperwork was delayed because of his dental work.

At first she didn't think she could live without him, but after a few weeks, she put together some semblance of her old life. To do so, she had thrown herself into her schooling with a vengeance, and had taken a low-paying job at a marketing firm. The days went by faster after that.

At least once each evening, she would feel connected to him as she stared up at the glowing moon.

* * * * *

Tiago missed Rae more than he had ever thought possible. It was much worse than when she had been transferred away during her mission. This time he could remember the feel of her lips on his and how wonderful it was to hold her. He felt utterly alone and miserable, a feeling he hadn't experienced since becoming a member of the Church. It was hard to continue to work, go to school, and to fulfill his calling as the first counselor in the Elder's Quorum Presidency. Each day he dragged through the motions, but the prospect of two more years until he could be with Rae loomed, seemingly without end, before him. He felt torn. He would be a great missionary; the fire of the gospel was in his soul. He had already had much success on his divisions with the elders. But as much as he loved the work, he had to admit that he loved Rae more—oh, so much more! Could he live two more years apart from her? And if so, could he take the risk that a mission might mean an eternity without her?

He had seen how popular she was when he had visited her, especially how her friend Dave had looked at her longingly. Tiago understood only too well. She was so easy to love—how could others not love her? And he had heard the loneliness in her voice over the phone. She was ready to move on with her life. Did he have the right to ask her to wait? Would she be able to? Could he leave her for two years? And would she even marry him if he didn't go on a mission? He knew she had been proud of his decision.

Tiago yearned to serve a mission to try and repay the great debt he felt he owed to the Lord for sending him the gospel and Rae. He also longed to marry Rae and start a family with her. He didn't sleep until late most nights as he lay in the dark going over the alternatives. He also studied the scriptures diligently, seeking an answer. His mother and sister had urged him to ask

Rae to marry him now. They didn't think it was wise to wait.

In late March, Tiago went through the temple in Spain with his mother and sister. With them was a member of another ward who had just proposed to Marcela. As Tiago watched the two together in the temple, and seeing Marcela's obvious happiness, he was filled with a longing to be in that sacred place with Rae. But there was still so much time until that day would come!

They stayed a week in Spain doing temple work. On one hand Tiago was learning and experiencing things he had only dreamed of and found contentment, but back at their hotel, he felt a part of him missing. He wrote Rae a dozen letters during this time, but didn't mail any of them because they said things like, "I'm applying for another visa the minute I get home. I have to be with you. Is it so important for me to serve a mission? I've been doing missionary work every day since my baptism. I cannot exist another moment without you."

Each day this fury of thought was overridden by the calm spirit of the temple. In that sacred place, Tiago felt a communion with his Savior. He promised the Lord to serve him—no matter what the future might bring.

Upon arriving in Portugal, he called Rae, waking her up in America. "It was wonderful," he said of the temple experience, "but I wish you could have been there."

"I do, too." Her voice sounded choked.

He could envision her in the kitchen or in the family room, long hair in becoming disarray. So far away. He could see the moon above and felt a bitterness knowing he was closer to attaining that silver disk itself than he was to marrying Rae.

They talked further, but neither could seem to bridge the distance between them. When Tiago hung up, he had the distinct feeling Rae was slipping from his grasp.

\* \* \* \* \*

Rae was happy for Tiago's visit to the temple, but she found herself weeping after she hung up the phone. Trying to hold back her emotions, she ran up the stairs.

Bria followed her to her room. "Maybe you should just go to Portugal," she said. "I can't stand to see you this way."

Rae tried to smile through the tears. "Oh, Bria, the worst thing is that sometimes I wonder if . . . well, maybe I imagined my feelings for him. Maybe he's not the one for me."

"But I thought you prayed about it."

"I did. But . . ." Rae stopped. Dave had been calling and while so far she had avoided going out with him, her loneliness was growing. She wanted—needed—to be with other people. She felt torn.

"Is it Dave?" Bria asked. "He called again while you were working yesterday."

Rae shook her head, then nodded. "I don't know," she admitted. "I just wish Tiago were here now. I don't feel uncertain when he's with me."

Bria sat on the bed with her. "Romance stinks!"

Rae had to agreed.

Another month dragged by. Rae finished her school finals with high grades. After a promotion at work, she started thinking about moving out on her own again. After one more semester, she'd be finished with school permanently. So the last Wednesday in April, Lisa went with her to look at apartments near campus. "I like this one," Lisa said as they left the second place. "It's cheap and it reminds me of our apartment together. Remember that?"

"Huh?" Rae looked at her blankly.

"Aren't you listening?"

"Yeah, sure. Well, no, not really. I was thinking . . ."

"About him." Lisa put an arm around her. "Oh, Rae, I'm so sorry."

Rae shrugged with feigned indifference. "It's okay. We'd better get back to your house. Kimberly's probably hungry. There's only so much your mother can do for her."

"She'll be okay. What I'm worried about now is you. What can I do to help?"

Rae's facade crumble. "It hasn't even been two months without him, and I feel like I'm dying. How can I wait two more years? He hasn't even left yet!"

Lisa shook her head. "I don't know . . . unless . . ."

"Unless what?"

Lisa had the crazy look in her eyes that Rae recognized so well from all their years of friendship. "So, go visit."

"Visit?"

"Yes, instead of getting an apartment, use the money to go see him. At least you'll be together a few weeks before he goes."

Bria had suggested the same thing last month, but Rae hadn't really considered it. Doing so now made her feel better. "I could stay with someone else," she said, her mind racing ahead as her excitement grew. "I could at least see him part of the day. Oh, thank you, Lisa. Thank you!" She hugged her friend.

Rae soon discovered that Lisa and Bria were the only ones who supported her plan. Her parents didn't think it was a good idea, and when she went to talk to her bishop, he also discouraged her from going.

"It would be different if you were going to marry him," he said. "But just going to see him for a few weeks . . ." He shook his head. "I can see how much you care about him, and I remember myself how strong the feelings of attraction can be at the beginning of a relationship. You have to keep in mind that Satan will be working overtime to destroy your plans of a temple marriage. I would really think twice about going. Either he stays home from his mission and you go see him to get married, or he goes on a mission and you stay home. That's my advice."

Rae prayed and pondered over what she should do. She wanted

so much to see Tiago! One look in his eyes and she would be all right. But would it be enough to hold her for two years?

\* \* \* \* \*

At last Tiago had all his paperwork ready to go. His dental work had taken an extra month, but he was finally ready for his interview with the bishop. He left work early to make the appointment.

"Come on in," the bishop greeted him later that afternoon. "How're you doing?" They sat down in his office and began to chat about things in general. Tiago wondered if the bishop could feel the turmoil in his heart.

Finally, the bishop said, "So you have those papers finished, do you?"

Tiago swallowed hard. "Yeah."

"I wondered if you changed you mind."

"I had to get some dental work done," Tiago said. "Stuff I let go way too long."

The bishop sat back in his chair. "I wondered if it was because of your fiancée."

Tiago looked down at his hands. "No," he whispered. His heart ached.

"Your mother and sister tell me you're engaged. I remember Sister Love from when she served in our ward. Very good missionary."

"She was."

"And how does she feel about you serving?"

"She's proud of me, I think." Tiago frowned. "But I worry . . . I mean . . ." Before he knew it, he was pouring out his conflicting desire to serve a mission and to be with Rae.

The bishop listened intently, a sympathetic expression on his face. "Well, Tiago, it's not easy to give a man advice about something that could affect the rest of his life." He leaned forward slightly to rest his arms on the desk. "But I can tell you from my experience working with many missionaries over the years, that girls rarely wait for their missionary. They usually end up marrying someone else. And probably not because they didn't love the missionary, but because they met another man they loved just as well, someone who was immediately available. That's the reality.

"I'm not saying it couldn't happen, only that the odds are almost completely against you. Even more so in your situation because Rae's already a returned missionary and ready for the next step in her life. Now, I know you want to serve a mission, and I'm sure you'd be a welcome addition. But you're twenty-five and quite a bit older than the regular missionary. Should you be going on a mission or starting a family? I've made that decision for some of the men in our ward because they were really too old, but there is some leeway with you. I think the decision must be yours."

"I always knew it was." Tiago hung his head. "And I also know that I would be ungrateful if I didn't serve the Lord. He has given me back my life and my father."

"Then you have your decision."

Tiago knew then that he'd been half-expecting the bishop to deny his request. Heart thundering in his ears, he slid the papers across the desk.

The bishop looked them over. "Everything looks in order. I just need to ask you a few questions and then next week you'll visit with the stake president. Afterward, he'll send the papers to Salt Lake."

A short while later, the bishop walked Tiago to the door. "I admire your commitment," he said. "You'll be a great missionary."

"Thank you." Tiago could hardly breathe. He had promised to sacrifice everything to the Lord. He believed strongly in the teaching that if a church could not require such sacrifice, then it would not have the power to be the Church of God.

But was he sacrificing eternity with Rae?

*No!* Surely not. Tiago would have to maintain his faith. Somehow things would work out for the best.

\* \* \* \* \*

Tiago called the day after Rae had seen her bishop about going to see him. She wanted to ask his opinion in the matter, but he began first. "I submitted my papers." His voice sounded strained, but she couldn't tell if it was from nervousness or excitement. "I had an interview with the bishop and next week I'll see the stake president. I should know in a month or so where I'll be serving."

Rae shut her eyes, struggling to be supportive when all her dreams of being in his arms were shattered. She'd knew suddenly that there was no way she would be able to go see him and then say goodbye for two years. She would end up begging him not to leave. She would have to stay home.

"That's great, Tiago," she managed. "I'm happy for you."

"You don't sound very happy."

"I just miss you."

He was silent a long time. "There'll be a moon tonight," his voice was like a tender caress. "Try to find it."

"Okay."

"I love you, Rae. I'll always love you." His words seemed somehow familiar, and she shivered.

"I love you, too." Tears slid down her cheeks.

That night, she looked for the moon, but clouds filled the sky.

\* \* \* \* \*

Loneliness and despair flooded through Rae. She moved through the next two days in a miserable haze. Early Saturday evening, Grandma Jill called. Rae welcomed the distraction.

"Hi, honey," her voice was warm and sympathetic. "How are you holding up?"

"I'm okay, Grandma. I'll live—I think." They talked for a few minutes about different things, purposely steering clear of her engagement. Rae felt herself relax.

"Is your mother home?" Grandma asked at last.

"No, or she probably would have wrestled the phone away from me by now."

"Well, could you give her a message?" Grandma's voice was suddenly serious.

"Sure."

"Well, my friend, Carol, is sick again. They've decided they have to do the bone marrow transplant as soon as possible. The other radiation and stuff they've been doing isn't working anymore. Six months ago they thought they had arrested the cancer, but it's back. I don't understand the whole of it, but it seems it's a miracle she's lived this long. Anyway, they've finally found a donor—not a perfect match, but hopefully close enough to work. Of course, she realizes she may not make it. She's asking for your mother—they've become good friends during her visits." Grandma sighed. "I'm so tired. Things have been crazy here. We started another fundraising project a month ago because Carols bills keep mounting and . . ."

Grandma's voice trailed off, and Rae knew she was crying.

"I'm sure she'll come right away. She tells me all the time what a great person Carol is. I'll have her call you."

"Thank you, honey," Grandma said. "I'll expect to hear from her. I love you. And give my love to the family."

"We love you too, Grandma. Goodbye."

As Rae hung up the phone, she began to think about Carol, the young widow who was fighting for her life. It amazed Rae that she could be an inspiration to anyone after losing her husband in an automobile crash months before she herself was diagnosed with leukemia. How could she keep from becoming bitter? And how, in the face of her courage, could Rae feel such depression about her own relatively unimportant problem with Tiago? Suddenly, Rae knew she had to meet this woman.

"Mom," she said, when her mother walked in the door later. "Grandma called and said that Carol's asking for you. She's going in to get a bone marrow transplant soon. I guess they've found a donor. She wants to see you. And Grandma said something about a project they were working on to raise more money."

"Oh, I hope this is good news." Rae's mother looked worried. "Carol seemed much better than the last time we were down there. I thought she was doing better. Your dad went through the accounts of all the donations and such, and she had nearly enough to cover the bone marrow transplant if she could find a donor."

"What kind of project is it?"

"Well, they're fixing up a house to sell that a member donated. But anyway, Carol was hoping after these last treatments that she wouldn't need the money, that they could give it away to someone else who needed it."

Her mother sat on the couch beside Rae and put her head between her hands. "Poor Carol. She has no family, you know. She was an only child, and adopted, which has been one of the reasons why it's been so hard to find a donor. Her adoptive parents are deceased. Her husband, who died in that car accident also had no one. He grew up in a series of foster homes. No one knows what happened to his birth mother—they think she's dead." She stopped talking and stood abruptly. "There's no use in sitting here thinking about it. I'm going to Arizona, and that's that. You kids can get along without me for a while. Of course I'll have to put a few things in order first. Pick up the dry cleaning, reschedule my dentist appointment and our family picture . . ."

An idea was slowly working its way into Rae's mind. "Mom," she said. She had to repeat the word several times to get her mother's attention. "I want to go with you."

Her mother blinked in surprise. "What about work?"

"I can get off. I think." She shrugged. "If not, I'll quit. I need a better job anyway."

"I'm sure your grandmother would be pleased to see you. And I know for a fact that they need people to work on the house."

"Great." Rae jumped up from the couch. "When do we leave?"

"How about Monday, bright and early."

"Deal. I'll go pack."

Her mother reached for the phone. "I'll call Grandma to let her know we're coming."

Rae had only packed a few items when she heard the doorbell downstairs ringing. In a few minutes Chad appeared at her door. "Dave's here," he announced. "He's waiting in the family room."

"Thanks." Rae dropped a stack of clothes into her suitcase and hurried downstairs.

Dave had a bouquet of flowers for her. Rae grinned, remembering their first weeks together when he had brought her flowers so often. "Mmm, they smell beautiful," she said.

"Not as beautiful as you look, Rae, Love," Dave said.

Rae felt her face flush. "Thank you. Well, I'd better go put these into water."

"What's going on around here, anyway?" Dave asked, following her into the kitchen. "Your mother was in here a minute ago talking to herself. I don't think she even saw me."

Rae laughed. "That's because we're getting ready to leave for Arizona." She updated him on her grandmother's friend and the house project. "So while Mom's with Carol and Grandma, I'll be swinging a hammer . . . or a paintbrush maybe."

"Sounds like fun," he said.

Rae shrugged. "It'll be time away. I need that."

Dave studied her for a moment. "I wish you could be happy, Rae. You deserve it. I wish I could help you be happy."

"I wish that too," Rae said in a small voice. Truth was, it felt wonderful being here with Dave. He was real and solid, whereas Tiago was so far away.

"Well, how about a video?" Dave pulled out *Somewhere in Time* from his jacket pocket. "I know it's your favorite."

Rae blinked back tears. "Oh, it is. Thank you. Look, you put it in and I'll make some popcorn."

Dave took her hand between his, his dark blue eyes fixed on her face. "Everything's going to be all right. You'll see."

Rae tried to believe him.

# Chapter Twenty-Two
## Mesa, Arizona

On Monday morning as Rae as stumbled out to the car for the drive to Arizona, she was surprised to see Dave and two other men sitting in his car outside her house. Rae put her purse in her mother's car and went down the driveway. Dave jumped from his car and met her halfway.

"What are you doing here?" she asked.

"Seeing you off, of course."

"What. At this hour? Are you insane?"

"I might be."

Despite herself, Rae was pleased. "Do you always bring friends along when you see girls off?"

Dave grinned. "Only when they own hammers and paint-brushes."

"What? You're not making sense."

"We're going with you. Uh, well, not exactly with you. More like behind you . . . going in the same direction."

"You're going to Arizona?"

"Yeah. I've never been, but my buddy's family lives there. So when you told me how they needed help with the house so they could raise money for your grandmother's friend . . ."

"You're just taking off work to help on the house?" Rae shook her head. "You can't do that. You can't just drop everything."

He lifted his chin. "You did."

"Yeah, but you have a real job."

"For which I'm owed a lot of vacation."

"At such short notice?"

He shrugged. "Don't worry about it. My boss is a real do-gooder. He supports about a dozen charities. When I told him about your grandmother's friend, he even offered to buy me a plane ticket."

Rae's eyes slid past him to the two men in the car. "And your friends?"

"One's the buddy whose family lives there. He just finished school and was going home anyway. The other one is my boss's son. He's getting ready to go on a mission soon." Grinning, Dave reached out a hand and touched her chin. "Uh, you should shut your mouth, Rae. Flies are getting in."

Rae snapped her jaw shut. "Fine, come."

"Don't you want me to?" His voice was suddenly serious.

She thought about it and sighed. "Actually, yes. I'm glad you're coming. It'll be nice to spend some time together." She started back up the driveway. "But don't expect me to be holding any ladders. I'm the one who's going to be doing the climbing."

\* \* \* \* \*

Rae stretched lazily in the king-sized bed as she glanced around the familiar room. This was the room she always used when she visited Grandma. It was a room made for children, with clowns and balloons on the wallpaper and a toy box in the corner. Grandma enjoyed having her grandchildren around and there was always plenty of space for them in the great bed or in the bunk beds that stood against the far wall.

Rae sat up quickly and looked more intently at the bunk beds. To her surprise she saw they were occupied. But not, she noticed, with any of her Arizona cousins, who were all as blonde as Rae herself. These two little heads peeping from the blankets were a dark brown.

Rae arose quietly and tiptoed across the room to stare at the sleeping children. They looked as peaceful and serene as miniature angels. But who were they?

"Hi," said the child on the top bunk, opening eyes that were as deep and blue as the ocean.

"I'm Rae. My grandmother lives here."

The little girl nodded. "Oh, yeah, she told us you were coming. I tried to wait up for you but I was too tired."

"It's no wonder. We got in kind of late. We stopped for lunch and for dinner on the way. But who are you?"

"I'm Katherine. Katie for short. And my sister down there," the child pointed with a small finger, "is Micaila. We call her Mickey."

"How old are you, Katie?"

"I'm five."

"And how do you know my grandmother?"

Kathy's face fell and tears prevented her from speaking.

"She's our friend." The voice came from the lower bed, and Rae looked below to see what appeared to be the same child. "We almost always come to Grandma Jill's house when Mommy goes to the hospital."

"Your mommy must be Carol." Rae looked from one child to the other. "But I didn't know you were twins."

"We are," the girls chimed.

Rae dipped her head. "Well, I'm happy to meet you both. I hope we'll have a fun time together while I'm here."

At that moment her grandmother bustled into the room. Everywhere Grandma Jill went, she always bustled purposely, as though juggling a million things to do. "I see you three have met. I forgot to tell you about them when you came, Rae. I was half asleep myself. We've spent a lot of time at the hospital in the past few days."

Rae grinned. "I didn't even notice them until now. I dressed in the bathroom last night, and I didn't even turn on the light in here. How come I never heard that Carol's children were twins?"

"You didn't know?" Grandma Jill shrugged. "Well, here they are, Mickey and Katie. After breakfast we'll go down to the hospital to see Carol. Come along." She bustled out the door.

Rae found it easy to forget herself with Mickey and Katie. They were full of energy and curiosity about everything, including Rae's family and Tiago. During breakfast and the short trip to the hospital, the twins and Rae talked so much that they felt like old friends.

"Mommy! Mommy!" Once at the hospital, the girls ran to their mother's bedside.

"Hi, girls! I'm glad you're here. What's up?" Carol reached to give her daughters a hug. Afterwards, she lay back exhausted from the effort. Her skin was very pale, made even more so by the tufts of short black hair on her head. She seemed impossibly thin, as if a breath might blow her away. But her smile was alive and her eyes, the same deep blue as her children's, sparkled.

"Mommy, we have a new friend. She's Aunt Holly's daughter. Her name's Rae."

Rae couldn't tell which twin was speaking. She had gotten them mixed up on the way up to the room, and she didn't know them well enough to tell them apart yet, especially since they were wearing identical outfits.

"Yeah, and she went on a mission to some place that begins with a P, and has a boyfriend there. They're getting married some day, only he's going on a mission first." Rae thought it was Mickey, but couldn't be sure.

"That's wonderful, Katie," Carol said with her eyes twinkling. "I'm sure they'll be very happy together."

"Mommy, why don't they get married now?" Mickey asked. "Rae's so sad to be without him."

Rae was embarrassed by the question and hoped they would change the subject.

"Well, I suppose she knows what she's doing." Carol looked at the twins with an indulgent smile. "Now if you two will look in that drawer over there, I think you'll find a treat I've been saving for you. And your coloring books are there, too. Do you think you could color a picture for me and maybe one for Rae as well?" The girls agreed enthusiastically and ran to the drawer, leaving the women with a sudden gap in the conversation.

Rae was glad when her mother approached the bed and reached for Carol's hand. "Well, as you've heard, this is my oldest daughter, Rae."

"It's nice to finally meet you," Carol said to Rae. "I've heard a great deal about you."

Rae smiled. "I'm glad to meet you, too. And your kids are adorable."

"Thanks." Carol glanced wistfully toward the girls who had made themselves at home on the floor and were coloring madly. "They've been spending too much time in hospitals. I'm very thankful to your grandmother for giving them a home away from home every time I have to come back."

"I enjoy having them around," Grandma Jill said.

"So it seems you'll be getting a bone marrow transplant after all." Rae's mother gently rubbed Carol's arm. "When?"

"It's been moved up to this afternoon."

"Why did they wait so long?" Rae asked.

Carol shifted her position, grimacing at the pain. "Well, a transplant's what should have been done in the first place, but when there wasn't a donor, and the radiation treatments seemed to be going so well, they figured that I might stay in remission. But now a transplant is my only hope." Her voice lowered. "My chances aren't too good even with the transplant." She waved away their attempts to encourage her and looked at Rae's mother.

"That's why I called you here, Holly. I need to talk to you about the girls." Carol glanced at her daughters again, this time with a look of fierce love.

"I know there's always a chance I'll beat this—and don't for a minute think that I'm giving up hope—but there's also a chance I won't make it. I have to be prepared in case it's my turn to go home."

Rae wanted to look away to avoid Carol's gaze. She felt like an outsider witnessing something personal that didn't have anything to do with her. Only Rae couldn't leave *or* look away. There was a fascination about the moment, something that somehow involve Rae and her whole family.

"Last Christmas, after meeting your wonderful husband and the rest of your children," Carol continued, "I asked my lawyer to write up some papers giving you two custody of the girls in case I don't make it." Her voice was calm and assured but Rae's mother started crying.

"Carol, I . . ."

The sick woman put a hand on Holly's to stop the words. "I couldn't let the state pick someone out for them. I had to know they would have a good family who holds the same beliefs my husband and I had—have. I talked to Jill about this, and she was sure you would agree, but I need to hear it from you. Would you be willing?" Carol's eyes finally had tears in them as she waited for an answer. She looked even more exhausted than before.

"With all my heart," Rae heard her mother whisper through her tears. "I've longed to have more children—I told you that once, didn't I? But, still, I can't bear the thought that I would get my dream through your . . ." She couldn't complete the sentence.

"Of course we're not giving up hope," Grandma Jill said. "Carol simply wants some piece of mind. And knowing her children would have both a mother and a father as good as you and Rich, just in case, gives her that. She's not giving up."

"We're done, Mommy!" The girls came running over with their papers. To Rae's relief, the tense feeling in the room seeped away. Like the others, her eyes were drawn to the energetic twins. They appeared much different to Rae than they had a few minutes ago. Now they looked like family.

\* \* \* \* \*

Rae and her mother were still at the hospital when the bishop of Grandma's ward and a young man Rae didn't recognize paused outside the open door.

"Knock, knock," the bishop called. "Can we come in?"

"Sure, Bishop," Grandma said. "Come on in."

He did so with a wide smile. "Hello, Carol, how are you today?"

"A little nervous. Did you come to give me a blessing?"

"We did at that," he said as he looked around the room at the others. "Holly, it's good to see you again. And Rae, it's been so long. I hear you've been on a mission since I saw you last."

Rae shook hands with the bishop. "I'm surprised you remember my name." She couldn't remember his.

"I'm pretty good with names." He turned to the twins. "Hello, Mickey. Hello Katie." He shook their hands solemnly as Rae wondered how he could tell them apart. He turned to his young companion, a good-looking man of medium height with dark blonde hair.

"This here's my new next door neighbor, Brett Lambert. He and his wife bought that place next to mine about three or four months ago. He also happens to be a member of our church, as well as a former missionary himself. He's in charge of the house we're fixing up to sell to pay for some of Carol's transplant."

"I'd like to help with that," Rae said.

"Great." The bishop's eyes gleamed. "That will help us get out more of our single guys to work, eh, Brett?"

Brett smiled. "Most certainly."

"Oh, but haven't you heard?" Grandma asked. "Rae's, engaged to be married."

"That's great! When's the happy day?" At the bishop's question, Rae's smile vanished.

"Uh, I don't know yet. We haven't set the date."

"Well, make it soon. It's hard to wait at your age. Now why don't we give this lovely lady here a blessing?"

Rae stayed for the blessing, but afterwards she and the twins left Grandma Jill and Rae's mother at the hospital. Rae agreed to be back before dinner to pick them up. Before she left, she also promised the bishop that she and the girls would help paint the house that was being refurbished. "I'll bring a few friends," she added.

"Wonderful. We need as much help as anyone is willing to give to make our deadline."

First Rae drove back to her grandmother's house where she wrote a letter to Tiago, telling him what had happened since her arrival. She'd called from home yesterday to let him know where she was, and he'd promised to call her on Sunday. Regardless of the expense, they talked on the phone at least twice weekly.

"Rae, why are you so sad?" A small voice penetrated her thoughts.

"Just missing my fiancé," said Rae, stumbling over the word, slightly.

"Well, let's go mail this letter to him, so he can get it faster," suggested one twin.

"And then go to Project House," the other added, cocking her head back to look at Rae.

"Project House?" questioned Rae. "Oh, you mean the house the ward is fixing up."

"Yep. It's going to pay for Mom's hospital bills. Brother Lambert always lets us help him."

"Okay, let's go." Rae held up a hand to stifle the screams of excitement emitting from the girls. "But first, one of you have to either change shirts or teach me a way to tell you apart. It's going to take a little while for me to be able to do it on my own."

"We like dressing the same," one of them said with a trace of stubbornness. "And besides, these are our working clothes. You know, to work on the house in."

"Yes, but you can tell us apart because I have a mole right here by my ear." The other twin drew back her thick, shoulder-length hair to show Rae.

"A lot of good it does there," Rae said. "It's covered by your hair." Then she had an idea. "Okay, I've got it. Which one are you?" she asked the girl with the mole.

"I'm Katie."

"Okay, Katie. Have you ever heard of a French braid?"

"Yes, I—" began Katie.

"—Oh, do mine too!" Mickey interrupted enthusiastically.

"This is the plan." Rae held up her hand again for silence. "I'll braid both your hair, so that I can see Katie's mole and know who's who." Of course, she knew it would be even easier to braid only one of the twins' hair, but she didn't have the heart to disappoint either of them.

A short time later they arrived at the Project House. Rae had no trouble finding it, though the area had changed a great deal since her last visit. To her surprise, the house was alive with many ward members, who must have taken off work to be there. There were also several young children, and the twins deserted her almost immediately to join them, leaving Rae feeling suddenly alone.

"Can you believe it? Many of these people have taken their vacation time to work on the house." said a familiar voice behind her.

"Dave!" Rae stifled an urge to hug him when she spied fresh paint on his T-shirt.

He grinned. "What took you? We've been here since dawn."

"I was at the hospital. And I had to stop by the post office."

A shadow passed over his face and then vanished. "Well, I'm glad you're here now," he said lightly. "I need your help holding the ladder."

"Ha!"

"Come on," Dave said, taking her hand. "I'll show you around."

He showed her through the house, pointing out improvements that had been added and introducing her to the working members, some of whom Rae recognized from her previous visits to her grandmother's ward.

"Mostly, you can see they have the texturing and painting inside the house left to do," Dave said.

"When does it need to be finished?"

"Monday morning. That leaves today, Wednesday, Thursday, Friday, and Saturday, to finish up here. The guy in charge says they already have a buyer."

"So where's a brush?" Rae asked. "I'm here to help."

"Uh, what about your clothes?" Dave eyed her short-sleeved sweater.

Rae grimaced. "These are the oldest clothes I brought with me I'm afraid. Somehow the stack of painting clothes didn't get in my suitcase. Must have left them on the bed. But I don't mind. I still want to help."

Dave motioned her out the door and over to his car. "I've got an old blue sweatshirt in here somewhere. You can use that over your sweater, at least. And I have a special knack for getting paint out of jeans, if you need it. Ah-hah! Here it is." He brought it from underneath the seat.

"Thanks." Rae slipped it on over her sweater. "I'd better check on the girls before I start. I hope they don't wreck anything."

"Don't worry about it. They have some grandmas in the backyard watching the kids. It's so funny. The old ladies are actually out there knitting and crocheting. They've set up relish plates, chips, and cookies, too."

Rae began working with enthusiasm, and soon began to sweat. She decided to go to the bathroom to remove her sweater under Dave's sweatshirt. She felt slightly awkward doing so, as if it were almost too personal, but she waved those feelings aside. A sweatshirt was a sweatshirt, no matter whose it was, and besides, there was nothing she could do about it.

She spent the rest of the morning and afternoon working side by side with Dave, his friends, and the ward members, stopping only once to eat the pizza Brother Lambert brought for them. The twins were remarkably well-behaved, and Rae was surprised at how Brother Lambert actually let them paint strips of molding. The time flew by, and before she knew it, she was late to pick up her mother and grandmother at the hospital.

"I have to go," she told Dave. "I'll bring your shirt back later."

He shrugged. "Use it for as long as you like. I like to see you wearing it."

Rae blushed and pushed back a strand of gold that had escaped from the barrette she had fastened in her hair earlier. "Are you flirting with me?" she asked.

"Maybe." Dave laughed. He kept his eyes fastened on hers, and added more seriously, "That would depend."

"On what?" Rae couldn't stop herself from asking.

"On if you wanted me to." He looked meaningfully at her and Rae was suddenly aware of how close he was.

"Uh, well, I have to go now." Rae stepped back, looking at her watch but not really seeing the time. "I'm late. We'll see you tonight." She turned and hurried out the door, calling the twins as she went.

# Chapter Twenty-Three
## Pre-Earth Life

*L*ittle Kira said goodbye to Rae and Tiago, but she didn't go directly to her next class with fellow spirits. Jenny, Michael, and the others were so excited about being teachers for a change, and discussing who their teachings partners might be, that they didn't even notice when Kira turned off down the path leading to the Counsel Building.

"Hello. May I help you?" One of the women at the desk welcomed Kira warmly as she approached.

"Yes, I would like to see a counselor, if I could, please." Kira pushed her hair back with her small hand.

"I'm available," said the woman. "My name is Sarah. Come this way." Kira followed her to one of the many doors that flanked the long corridor.

"What can I do for you?" Sarah said as soon as they were comfortably seated on a plush sofa.

"Well, I want to ask the Father a question, if I could," Kira said.

"Of course, you can see the Father, any time you need to, but do you think that maybe I could help you? I am His representative here."

"Yes, I guess." But Kira looked sad. "I just thought if I could tell him myself that . . ."

"That He'd hear you better?" Sarah smiled gently. "You know, Kira, the Father knows everything. He has heard your earnest prayers and knows your innermost desire."

"He already knows how much I want Rae and Tiago to meet and become our parents on earth?" Kira asked. "Oh, they do so belong together!"

"Well, they'll have agency on earth like everyone else, but I can tell you that they will meet and that the Father will see to it that they have some very good friends and counselors when they need them the most. Still, the final decision is up to them."

Kira's expression brightened. "Oh, thank you!" she said. "I know that'll be enough. Everything will be all right. With Father's help, they'll make it." She stood and walked to the door, mumbling quietly to herself, "Oh, they just have to make it!" With a wave over her shoulder, she hurried down the hall and out the entrance, heading to class where the others were surely waiting.

# Chapter Twenty-Four
## Carol's Wisdom

*R*ae settled into a regular routine over the next few days in Arizona. In the mornings she would take the twins to see their mother for a two hour visit, then they would go to Project House where they worked until dinnertime. For dinner, they would pick up something to eat on the way to the hospital where they would visit Carol for a couple more hours, and afterwards return to the house to work until bedtime. Occasionally, Rae's mother and grandmother also worked at the house, taking turns so that Carol was rarely alone. The transplant hadn't gone well, and the doctors were trying everything they could to help Carol's body accept the new marrow. Only time would tell what the outcome would be.

At night after the twins had gone to sleep, Rae would finally be alone, with plenty of time to stare at the moon and think about Tiago. During these times instead of feeling comforted, she felt totally and completely alone. It was almost more than she could bear. She would read and reread Tiago's old letters, waiting for any new ones that Bria had promised to send from Utah. Even when they did arrive, the news was already a week old—it took that long for his letters to reach the U.S.—and they made her miss him even more.

On Saturday morning Rae and the girls arrived at the hospital for their usual visit. This time they were alone because her mother and grandmother had been running late. As usual, Carol greeted her children joyfully. The girls snuggled up to either side of their mother and sighed contentedly as she stroked their hair.

"How's the house coming along?" Carol asked after a while.

"Great. We're almost finished, aren't we girls?" Rae pulled a chair close to the bedside.

"Yeah, it looks real pretty, Mom." Mickey tilted her head back to look at her mother's face. After spending so much time with the girls, Rae no longer needed Katie's mole to tell them apart.

"Let's draw her a picture of it." Katie suggested. Mickey agreed and soon the girls were sprawled out on the floor coloring.

"You look tired, Rae," Carol said, studying Rae's face. "Are you working too hard on the house?"

Rae smiled wistfully. "I wish that was all it was." She sighed.

"Tell me. Maybe I can help." Carol looked at her earnestly, and Rae suddenly felt the urge to confide in someone. They had become pretty good friends during the long visits each day. Maybe Carol, so close to the other side, could actually give her some insight.

"Well, it's Tiago. You see, he's been a member over a year now, and he's just given his bishop his papers so that he can serve a mission. I'm so proud of him for wanting to go and I know he should go, and yet . . . I'm so lonely." Rae bit her lower lip to stop from crying.

"I see everyone around me starting their families and living their lives," She continued. "I'm ready to move on with my life too. I don't want to tell Tiago not to go on a mission, but I feel like I'm going nowhere. How can I wait two more years? I've always wanted a large family, and I'm not getting any younger. I mean, many of my old high school friends are expecting their third children already. At this rate I'll be twenty-five before I get married—and likely twenty-six before I have my first baby."

"So you don't really want him to go on a mission, yet you worry that it's his duty to go?" Carol asked.

Rae nodded. "And that he'd regret not going. My brother still regrets not serving a mission after all these years. He has three kids now. I don't want Tiago to ever regret that he didn't go."

"But from what your mother tells me, that was a completely different situation, wasn't it? I mean, not going because of transgression is one thing, but not going because you weren't a member is something entirely different."

"I guess so, but I still don't want to stand in his way." Rae heaved a sigh.

"But that's not all, is it, Rae?" Carol asked perceptively.

Rae sighed. "Well, like I said, I've been feeling pretty lonely, and while I've been working on the house with Dave, we've become really close—like we were before my mission. He's fun to be with, he makes me feel pretty and admired, and I know he would like our relationship to go further." Now Rae looked at the floor instead of Carol. Aloud, her motives sounded so selfish.

"And how do you feel about that?"

"I think I might want it to go further, too," Rae said softly. "But perhaps not exactly because I think I love him—though I think I could grow to love him—but because I'm lonely. And that makes me feel guilty. How can I wait faithfully for Tiago for two years when right now I'm thinking about a relationship with Dave? If that's already happening now, what will happen after Tiago and I have been separated a year or more, and the feelings I have for him are not so tangible?"

"You're afraid you won't wait for him."

Rae nodded. "And I know right this minute that Tiago and I are meant for each other." She twisted the small band around her finger. "What if I blow that simply because I'm lonely? I don't want to miss out on the life we could have together. What if I regret losing him for eternity?"

Carol looked thoughtful. "You know, when my husband and I were first engaged, he took a high-paying job in Alaska for two months so that we could get a good financial start in our marriage. The first month was okay, but then the loneliness hit. I kept imagining him meeting other girls and wondered if he still loved me. I also kept getting invited to parties and such by my friends, many of them guys. I wanted so badly to accept, because I was lonely. One day my husband called me to tell me they wanted him to extend and I started to cry. We talked and decided that the risk of losing each other wasn't worth the money, and he came home."

"What are you saying?"

"Just that the feelings you're having are completely normal. That's why married people need to spend time together and shouldn't be consistently alone with a person of the opposite sex—someone they're not married to. You need to be together to make marriage work."

"But we're not married."

"But it's a similar situation because you're supposed to be faithful those two years, but you have no support from your mate. That's not fair to you. It's not as if you're a young high school girl waiting for a missionary. You need to move on."

"That's how I feel," Rae admitted. "But when I consider that we might not get married, it tears me to bits inside. I want to be with him so badly."

"Well, now we're back where we started." Carol patted her hand. "If you ask me, I don't think you can commit to wait. Either you marry him or you go on with your life. If you happen to be single when he gets back, that's a different story. Either way, you both have to make up your minds. You get married *or* he goes on a mission. It's very unlikely that both can happen."

Rae nodded. "Maybe you're right, Carol. I guess I've got some thinking to do."

That afternoon Rae worked alone, finishing up a wall in one of the rooms at Project House. Her hair was once again pinned up out of the way, with stray locks falling randomly around her face and neck. She still wore Dave's sweat shirt, now speckled with paint, but her jeans had been replaced by Grandma's old sweat bottoms.

"How's it going?" said a voice behind her.

"Bishop! Good to see you. Did you come to help?" Rae jumped down from the stool she was standing on and put down her roller.

"Yes, that's why I've got on the old painting clothes." He smiled and reached for Rae's roller. "Why don't you take a rest while I finish this wall? The others have everything else under control for now."

"Thanks. I *am* pretty exhausted." She watched him put paint on the roller and start to work. Rae sat down on the plastic-covered carpet and drew her legs up to rest her chin on them.

"By the way," the bishop said after he'd been working for a few minutes. "I went to see Carol a little while ago at the hospital. She mentioned you were having a tough time with something and asked me to talk with you, if you were willing."

Rae smiled. "Dear, sweet Carol. She lies in that bed fighting for her life, and she's concerned about me."

"Yeah, she's really something. Well, what about it? Do you want to talk?"

"I guess I could use a man's point of view, as well as a bishop's. But stop pretending to paint that wall for a minute and come and sit down over here."

The bishop laughed and stepped down from the stool. He tossed the roller carefully into the rolling pan, half-filled with paint, and sat down by Rae. His smile was warm and inviting, and soon Rae found herself repeating what she had told Carol.

"Well," he said when she was done. "I see you've got a little problem. And I tend to agree with what Carol told you about separations. I was once separated from my wife when I was in the army a couple of years before we were baptized. We were apart one long miserable year and we nearly got a divorce because of it. I think you both have to decide what is most important in this case. But I would like to add, Rae, that while a mission is very important, it is not a saving ordinance like eternal marriage. Keep in my that your fiancé probably would have already served a mission if he had heard the gospel earlier. It's not his fault he didn't go."

"That's what my friend, Lisa, told me," Rae said softly. "Only that was when I was more concerned about whether he'd be strong enough spiritually without a mission. I did finally realize that he could be, and was, strong enough. But I still felt he was supposed to go and that it was my duty to support him."

"A family is very important too. Maybe *you* have to decide what you want, Rae."

"But what if he regrets it forever? What if he regrets . . ."

The bishop held a hand up to her mouth to stop the words. "But what if he loses you and regrets *that* for eternity? If you were both younger, I'd urge you to focus on missions, but that's not the case, is it? Think of it this way, you can always serve a mission together later, but he can't marry you if you're already married to someone else." There was a sudden silence in the room as Rae thought about what he had said.

"But that's an argument any young couple just out of high school could use," she protested.

The bishop shook his head. "It's not the same. You're a mature woman who's already been on a mission and is ready for a family, and he's a man who's finished college and is working at a real job, not a nineteen-year-old boy. That's the difference."

Rae nodded, but she still wasn't convinced. How could she tell this to Tiago? What would he think of her? If the situation were reversed, she suspected that he would be able to wait for her. Did that mean she didn't love him as much as he loved her?

"Thanks, I appreciate your advice." Rae jumped up from the floor and reached for the roller. "Well, are we going to finish this wall or not?"

"Uh, excuse me, Bishop," a woman from the ward was at the door. "You've got a phone call from your wife. She needs to talk to you right away."

"Thanks, Helen."

"Ah, saved by the bell," Rae said.

He smiled. "Let me know what happens. And if you ever want to talk, I'm here."

"Thanks. You've helped me a lot already." Rae turned back to her painting.

Half an hour later she had finished the wall and was pouring the rest of the paint back into the container when Dave came up behind her and tickled her sides, causing her to shriek with laughter.

"Dave! Stop! What are you doing? You're going to make me spill the paint!" She set down the paint and glared at him in mock anger. He began to laugh.

"What's so funny?" Rae asked, smiling.

"It's you. You see how speckled that sweatshirt is? Well, your face is just about as bad. And you've even got it in your hair!"

He walked closer to Rae and began pointing out the little white spots that freckled her face with his finger. "There, and there, and . . ."

He stopped and bent his head abruptly to kiss her lips.

"Dave!" Rae pushed her hands against his chest, but not soon enough to completely avoid the kiss.

"I'm sorry." Dave's lower lip jutted in a pout. "I couldn't help myself. You look so beautiful in spots."

Rae grinned. "Oh, Dave. You've been so patient with me. And this week—it's been so fun."

"It has been, hasn't it? All of it. I've enjoyed being down here.

I've been struggling, but I think I'm on track now. Service really has a way of helping you look outside yourself."

"I'm glad."

"So . . ." He trailed off. "What about us?"

She shook her head. "I guess I have some decisions to make."

"And those are?"

"Well, either I'm marrying Tiago or going on with my life. When I figure it out, you'll be the first to know."

"That sounds fair." But he frowned.

"What wrong?" she asked.

"That look in your eyes. Sort of dreamy. I guess it might be too much to hope for, that you're thinking of me."

Rae had no answer he would appreciate. She *wasn't* thinking of him. She was thinking of the call Tiago would make to her on Sunday night just as his moon was fading from the early morning sky. The moon in Arizona would just be appearing, and if everything went as planned, they would see their moon at the same time.

But what would come of the call, she didn't yet know.

# Chapter Twenty-Five
## Tiago's Truth

*T*iago was glad the stake president set up their appointment for Saturday. He didn't like traveling long distances by bus on Sunday. His heart was heavy as he walked up to the church that also serve as the stake center. He had come to a decision during this difficult week. No matter how painful it was, he had to give Rae her freedom. He couldn't expect her to delay her life anymore than he could give up the opportunity to serve a mission.

*Would she marry Dave?* The thought cut to his core. Dave was a nice guy. A good guy. Tiago felt that. And if he couldn't be with Rae, maybe being with Dave would be the next best thing for her.

Before entering, Tiago shut his eyes and lifted his face toward heaven. *Thy will be done,* he prayed.

The stake president met him in the hall. "Tiago Silva, isn't it?"

Tiago nodded.

"Well, come on in. I've been looking forward to talking to you. Your bishop has no end of good things to say about you."

"Thank you." Tiago barely managed to squeeze out the words. He followed the stake president into his office and sat in one of the chairs by the desk.

"I know you've been looking forward to a mission," the stake president said. "Unfortunately, there seems to be a slight problem."

\* \* \* \* \*

On Sunday morning, Rae took the twins to visit their mother at the hospital. They were all dressed for church, with both girls sporting freshly French-braided hair. When they arrived in Carol's room, she was leaning back on the bed as usual, but the minute Rae stepped into the room, she felt there was something different about her.

"Hi," Carol greeted Rae after her customary hugs to her children.

"How are you?" Rae asked. She'd meant to thank Carol for sending over the bishop the day before, but she had to know what had happened first. "What's up? There's something different about you."

"Can I confide in you?" Carol asked. "It's something I haven't even told Jill."

"Sure, what is it?"

"Well, last December when your family visited, I dreamed that my husband came to me and told me I needed to make sure the kids were taken care of. At first I was frightened, but he was so loving and positive, that I agreed. I knew then I probably wasn't going to make it."

Rae shook her head. "But you've fought so hard. You're still fighting."

"Yes. As hard as I can, and at times I feel like everything's going well." Carol paused and glanced at the girls who were once again in their customary place on the floor, scribbling with crayons. "Then last week I dreamed he came to ask me again if I had taken care of the girls. That was why I wanted your mother here so I could ask her. I had to be sure of what she would do."

Rae didn't know what to say, but a response didn't seem necessary to Carol. Her voice grew even softer and her bright eyes stood out in her thin face. "Last night he came to me again and told me he was waiting, that I had to let go. I started crying because of the girls and suddenly I saw them!" Carol's face shone with an unexplained light as she continued. "I saw them at different times in their lives—special times with your family, laughing together at a swimming pool, and dancing with some boys. I saw them again in the temple, and then even later with their own families." Carol reached out to hold Rae's hand. "I can't tell you what it means to me to know that they will be happy and safe. And very well loved."

Tears inched down Rae's face as she clutched Carol's hand almost afraid that her grasp was the only thing keeping her in the mortal world.

"Oh Rae, this isn't a sad time. I'm going to be with my husband again. I've missed him so badly. I'm going home!"

Later that afternoon, while Rae and the twins were having lunch, Carol died. She slipped away quietly with Rae's mother and grandmother at her side. The girls, who had been well-prepared by their mother, nonetheless cried heartbreakingly, turning to the older women for comfort.

Rae watched their grief helplessly. She knew that as time passed, their pain would dull, and felt grateful for that last conversation with Carol. One day she would share with the twins the story of how their mother had seen them growing up, and how they would be with her again.

The rest of the day was full, as they received visitors and began preparations for a funeral. The twins were very fragile, but Rae managed to coax a few smiles from them. Her mother and grandmother didn't leave them alone for a minute. Rae knew that already Carol's vision was coming to pass—her daughters were loved and cared for.

When at last the girls fell asleep, Rae realized Tiago had not called at the appointed hour. It was already midnight now. *What happened?* she wondered, experiencing a sense of dread.

She went out to her grandmother's backyard. Overhead the moon was rising higher and higher in the sky. Their moon, their dream. Was it closer tonight?

Rae turned back into the house. She wasn't waiting around any longer. If that was her moon out there, she had to start climbing toward it. By memory, she dialed the international area codes, followed by Tiago's phone number. It would be just after seven there. Likely no moon, but there was enough filling her sky for the both of them.

"Hello?"

She recognized Marcela's voice. "Hi, it's me, Rae. Is Tiago there?"

"No, he got up really early."

"Is something wrong? He was supposed to call."

"Not that I know of." Marcela paused. "He was very quiet yesterday, though. Truthfully, I didn't see him much. I was at my fiancé's parents' house most of the day."

"Well, tell him to call, as soon as he gets home, okay?"

Rae hung up, feeling very discouraged. She took a blanket to the backyard and sat in a lawn chair where she could see the moon, the portable phone in her hand. After what seemed like a long time, her eyes finally shut.

A ringing called her back to consciousness. She fumbled with the phone. "Hello?" Overhead the moon was heading toward the horizon, signaling that much of the night had passed.

"Hi."

She recognized Tiago's voice immediately, though it sounded more gruff than usual. "You're late. Did something happen?" She tried to steel herself for the response. Could he have met someone else? No, that couldn't be possible. She knew how he felt about her. She *knew*.

All at once there was more she knew. A lot more. They belonged together.

"No," he said. "But I had to go to the U.S. Embassy."

"The Embassy?"

"Yes. I applied for another visa. But there's something you have to do on your end if I'm to come. You'll need to request a fiancé visa."

Rae held her breath. "What do you mean?"

"They won't let me go on a mission, Rae. The stake president heard about us. He told me my next mission in life was to get married."

Rae wasn't sure, but she thought she heard him sob. "I'm sorry, Tiago. We can cancel the engagement. Then they'll let you go." She was crying as she spoke. Though it had been her plan to set him free so that he could serve the Lord with all his heart, her very being seemed to fight against the idea.

"No!" His voice was agonized. "I want to marry you. But, Rae, will you still have me? I know you wanted me to go—I wanted to go—but I don't think it was meant to be. Will you still marry me?"

Tears fell onto the phone in Rae's hand. "Oh yes, Tiago. I will, I will."

The moon hanging in the sky filled up Rae's entire view now, made larger by the tears blurring her vision.

"Then let's go and get our moon!" Tiago almost shouted.

They both laughed with joy.

# EPILOGUE

Rae sat on the couch in the living room of the apartment cradling a tiny figure. The curtains were open and fingers of quickly fading light touched the room. Tiago was in the kitchen dishing up the homemade fried chicken, potatoes, and green salad that Dave and Selena—Rae's old mission companion—had brought less than fifteen minutes before.

Rae smiled. Funny how well the two of them had hit it off when Selena had come to Utah for Rae's wedding. Dave had asked her out that same day, and now it looked as though they would be following Rae and Tiago to the altar.

Tiago brought a filled plate to Rae. "Here you go," he said, trading her for the infant. She smiled her thanks as he sank onto the couch beside her.

"Aren't you going to eat?" Rae asked.

"In a minute." His eyed fixed on the miracle in his arms.

Rae stared, too. The baby's hair was dark and her eyes an exotic grey-brown. She was so perfect, so delicate, so completely heavenly. Every time Rae looked at her, it was as if the veil grew very thin.

"You're ours for eternity, you know," Tiago crooned in Portuguese. In the year since their marriage in the Provo temple, Tiago had become fluent in English, but he was determined to teach their children his native language.

The baby opened her eyes and stared at her father. Soon her attention drifted toward the tendrils of light still coming through the window.

"She always looks for the light," Rae said.

"I wonder what she's looking for?"

Rae shrugged. "Something we can't see? Something beyond the veil?"

Tiago waved a hand in front of the baby's face. "What about it, Kira? What do you see?"

But Kira wasn't telling. She drifted off to sleep, a content expression on her face.

## About the Author

Rachel Ann Nunes (pronounced noon-esh) learned to read when she was four, beginning a lifetime fascination with the written word. She avidly devoured books then, and still reads everything she can lay hands on, from children's stories to science articles. She began writing in the seventh grade and is now the author of nineteen published books, including the popular *Ariana* series and the picture book *Daughter of a King*, voted best children's book of the year in 2003 by the Association of Independent LDS Booksellers. All her books have been bestsellers in the LDS market.

Rachel enjoys camping, spending time with her family, reading, and visiting far off places. While growing up, she lived in France for six months when her father was teaching French at BYU, and later she served an LDS mission to Portugal. She and her husband, TJ, and their six children live in Utah Valley. She believes that raising her family is the most important thing she will ever do.

As a stay-at-home mother, it isn't easy to find time to write, but Rachel will trade washing dishes or weeding the garden for an hour at the computer any day! Her only rule about writing is to never eat chocolate at the computer. "Since I love chocolate and writing," she jokes, "my family might never see me again." For more information on other books by Rachel Nunes, or to join her e-mailing list, visit http://www.rachelannnunes.com. You can also write to her at P.O. Box 353, American Fork, Utah 84003-353.